The Cowboy's Unexpected Christmas Miracle

STAND-ALONE NOVEL

A Western Historical Romance Book

by

Sally M. Ross

Disclaimer & Copyright

This is a work of fiction. Names, characters, places and incidents either are products of the author's imagination or are used fictitiously. Any resemblance to actual events or locales or persons, living or dead, is entirely coincidental.

Table of Contents.

Letter from Sally M. Ross

"There are two kinds of people in the world those with guns and those that dig."

This iconic sentence from the *"Good the Bad and the Ugly"* was meant to change my life once and for all. I chose to be the one to hold the gun and, in my case…the pen!

I started writing as soon as I learned the alphabet. At first, it was some little fairytales, but I knew that this undimmed passion was my life's purpose.

I share the same love with my husband for the classic western movies, and we moved together to Texas to leave the dream on our little farm with Daisy, our lovely lab.

I'm a literary junkie reading everything that comes into my hands, with a bit of weakness on heartwarming romances and poetry.

If you choose to follow me on this journey, I can guarantee you characters that you would love to befriend, romances that will make your heart beat faster, and wholesome, genuine stories that will make you dream again!

Until next time,

Sally M. Ross

Prologue

Wolfspell, Montana

Late November, 1860

Eliza O'Connor shivered and tightened the shawl draped around her shoulders, but no matter how tightly she hugged herself, nothing could stave off the bitter winter chill. Reports had been swirling for weeks, and everyone in town was preparing for the biggest storm Wolfspell, Montana, had seen in years. The last time Eliza remembered feeling a cold like this—one so relentless and harsh people feared simply standing in it for more than a few minutes would lead to severed limbs...

No. Now was not the time to surrender to melancholy thoughts. She ground her teeth and pushed the memory away, venturing further into the warmth of the barn. Another unforgiving breeze ripped through the barn door, and Eliza's teeth chattered as it ruffled the hems of her cream dress with forest green accents.

It slammed closed with a loud, metallic bang.

"Oh!" Eliza yelped, glaring daggers at the door when a final gust of wind whipped her coppery red hair into her face, making it stick to her cold, pale cheeks.

"Pah! Plah!" After flinging the loose strands from her face with her frostbitten fingers, she scowled and tried in vain to pull her multilayered skirts further down. Even in her thickest stockings, goosebumps rose along her legs.

"This would be so much easier if I could wear trousers," she muttered.

Not only were they simpler to move in, but they were leaps and bounds warmer than this infernal piece of useless drapery – no matter how extravagant it may look.

Sunbeam, a beautiful Palomino with white stockings on all four hooves and a sun emblem between her eyes – hence her name – whinnied loudly. Eliza smiled and shook her head as she moved to undo the latch on the horse's stall. "At least someone agrees with me." She glanced around to make sure no one would see, quickly shed her skirts and petticoat, and switched them for a pair of trousers she always kept hidden in her tack trunk. Just because her stepbrother had practically forbidden her desire to wear manly clothes didn't mean that had to impede her ability to do her work. Especially since, between the two of them, she was the one who helped their foreman on the ranch. It was a ridiculous notion when she thought about it, considering it was her stepbrother who officially owned it. But no matter how much her father had tried to instill the sense of ranch hand pride in him that seemed to run as naturally as blood through the O'Connor's veins. He showed little interest and care for the place and even less after their father passed away.

Fredrick O'Connor had always wanted a son. Despite how hard Elisa tried to be the perfect ranch woman, fixing the fences, breaking in the horses, and roping the bulls with skills that could rival any other ranch workers, he always found something that Russel did better.

Sunbeam huffed, nudging her shoulder with its soft wet nose and breaking Eliza from her melancholy memories. She stepped closer and gave her a pat on her muzzle; the horse leaned into her touch and shuddered.

Eliza bit her lip and frowned. "I'm sorry, old girl. If I'm cold, you must be freezing."

As if to prove her point, the Palomino shook her mane. Eliza snickered and hurried out of the stall to the left corner of the barn where they'd been keeping extra supplies. She selected the largest, warmest blanket they had and draped it over the mare's back. "There you go. Is that better?"

The horse whinnied and nuzzled her cheek.

Eliza grinned. "I'm glad. Now, let's see how that little one of yours is doing." She rounded the other side of the animal and carefully inspected her protruding belly. Sunbeam had been a gift from her father on her fifteenth birthday – the last gift she would receive from him, as it turned out, since he died only a few weeks later. Eliza had always loved horses, but ever since that day, she cared for Sunbeam as if she were the third member of their small, broken family. And in many ways, she was. Russel hadn't cared a bit when they'd found out Sunbeam was carrying a foul eleven months ago. He went so far as to suggest they put Sunbeam out to pasture as, in his eyes, she would no longer be seen as a valuable asset if she was too weak to run.

Eliza's world had turned a fiery red at such a preposterous, ridiculous declaration.

She'd marched forward and stood nose-to-nose with him, giving him her most intimidating death glare. Despite him being nearly six inches taller than her, with a burly frame and unkempt black hair that stuck out at every angle but only extenuated the defiant fire that lay so often behind his cruel, ice-blue eyes and pale, freckled skin, Eliza tried not to be intimidated. She ground her teeth before she finally made words come out in anything more than a glass-shattering shriek. "And what would you know? You wouldn't know the value if it walked up and bit you in the nose."

Russel had smirked, and she shrunk a little as he crossed his arms and puffed out his chest, pushing himself up to his full height and towering over her. "I know more than you. You addle-headed   girl. Shouldn't you be off tryna rustle up suitors?"

Eliza's temper boiled, and she glowered at him. "Why you–" Her nostrils flared, and she felt as if steam was coming out of her ears, but as hard as she tried, she couldn't think of a better comeback.

Russel smirked triumphantly and snickered into his palm. "Not like you'd get any, anyway; you'd make a freight train take a dirt road with that charm of yours. And you don't know more about owning a ranch than a hog knows about riding sidesaddle." He burst out laughing at his insult. As much as Eliza wanted to punch his lights out because, by this point, her whole body had begun trembling from anger, she did her best to inhale and exhale through her nose. When words finally managed to escape her quaking lips, they were low, steady, and deliberate. "Now listen here, you boneheaded scallywag of a man. You may be older than me, but this ranch is my home. I've been through the mill, and I know every lock, shock, and barrel in this place. Insult my appearance all you want, but don't you tell me I don't know what it takes to run it."

Russel had arched an eyebrow and cocked his head to the side, his single left dimple peeking out around his infuriatingly impish grin. "Oh yeah?" He chewed twice more on the blade of grass stuck between his teeth before plucking it out between two fingers and blowing on the tip like it was a cigar. "Then why did your father leave everything to me?"

Much to her dismay, Eliza didn't have a comeback for that one. Mostly because it was the only thing he ever said to her that got under her skin. Three years ago, when she was fifteen and Russel was eighteen, their father had gone out for a ride in the storm, much like the one rumored to be on the way. She tried to keep him from going alone, to wait until the storm passed, or at least until Perry, the ranch foreman, arrived. But he'd insisted.

"Don't get your knickers in a twist. I just need to check on the hen house at the other end of the property. I'll be back before you know it."

Even now, Eliza remembered how her stomach had dropped at those words. It was as if something inside her knew, deep in her soul, that this was a horrible idea, but she would never be able to say exactly how or why.

"Please," she'd begged. "Don't go."

But he didn't listen. And the image of him riding away, smiling indulgently over his shoulder as he waved until he rode out of sight, was the last Eliza had of him.

When the storm passed a few hours later, one of the ranch hands rode out to find him, only to discover his horse without a rider. Her father's body lay nearby. Something had spooked the stallion, and he'd bucked his rider. According to the doctor, her father had hit his head on impact and died instantly.

Eliza, Russel, Perry, and everyone on the ranch had been devastated. Still, it hit Eliza the hardest when it was discovered via her father's will that, despite Russel not being Fredrick O'Connor's biological son, he'd inherited everything. The ranch, her father's life savings, and, to his and Eliza's chagrin, her guardianship. Now that she was technically an adult, she could do whatever she wished. If only she knew what that was.

In truth, she didn't have any other place to go. The O'Connell ranch was her home. It had always been and always would be... provided her stepbrother didn't waste away his inheritance on his gambling habit and dig the place an early grave.

"You all right there, shaver?"

Eliza's hand flew to her heart, and she whirled, once again startled from her thoughts. But as soothing and paternal as the male voice was, she didn't fully place it until his features came into focus in the dusty hue of the early morning light filtering through the barn windows. A tall, somewhat unkempt but well-built man in his mid-thirties with a crop of unruly blond curls that almost always poked out around his hat smiled at her. He had a well-trimmed, thick beard and matching mustache. His kind brown eyes watched her curiously, and she ducked her head.

"Oh, Perry! It's you!"

The older man laughed and ran a hand down the back of his neck. "Didn't mean to scare you or anything." He smiled sheepishly and removed his hat with a shrug. "I was just headed to the loft to count the hay bales we have left. Didn't think anyone would be up this early." He chuckled to himself and winked indulgently. "Guess I should've known better. It's not like your lazy lay-about of a stepbrother should be helping with these preparations." His voice dripped with disappointment, and Eliza couldn't help but roll her eyes as she brushed a piece of hair behind her ear.

"Well, you know you've always got me."

Perry smiled, crinkling the lines around his eyes. "That I do."

A long but amicable silence stretched between them. Perry made his way to the tack room while Eliza did her routine check-up on Sunbeam and inspected the birthing area. She had set her up in one of the empty stalls. It contained blankets, a basin for warm water when the time came, scissors to cut the cord, and any other medical equipment she thought they might need in an emergency. After all, they

11

never knew what could happen during the birth of a foul and the upcoming storm.

"How's she looking?"

Eliza turned away from organizing supplies as Perry strode back into the main area of the barn. "Mother is happy and healthy. Sunbeam is a real trooper, being this pregnant this far into winter. I don't know if I could do it."

Perry laughed and walked over to scratch the horse between her ears. "Of course she is. And I have no doubt you could do it if you really wanted to."

Eliza shuddered slightly at the thought. It wasn't that she didn't want kids. "One day. But not yet. And especially not given my most recent marriage prospects."

Perry pressed his lips together in a thin line and eyed her. "Oh? Why is that? And don't give me that hogwash about no one tryna to scoop you up yet. I've heard the rumors in town, and I know it ain't true."

Eliza froze, halfway bent down, trying to keep herself occupied by emptying and refilling a spare medical bag she had found in the storage room earlier in the day. Her stomach dropped, and her heart jumped into her throat.

She straightened, and very slowly, timing it almost purposely with her pulse hammering in her ears, she turned to face the foreman more fully. "Even if he were the last man on earth, Hell would have to freeze over before I ever even considered marrying such a wretched skin gamer as Benjamin Boyle," she seethed, nearly spitting the words as her cheeks flamed.

Russel had met Bennie 'Bullettooth' Boyle during one of his seemingly endless jaunts at the local saloon. Ever since their father died, it seemed to Eliza that Russel spent more time at that seedy, dilapidated bar than at his ranch. Rather than accept that they were on their own now, Russel dove head-first into his worst indulgences after their father's funeral; he liked to call himself a "sportsman" when defending his not-so-secret addiction to gambling. Still, Eliza knew better–he was a rooster, a speeler, and no one could convince her otherwise. Too often, he came home in the wee hours of the morning reeking of bottom-of-the-barrel liquor.

The night he met Bennie, it had only taken a couple of shots before the chiseling, flannel-mouthed nibbler had Russel wrapped around his sticky fingers tighter than a noose. From the moment they met, Eliza knew he was nothing but a no-good hustler and begged her brother to kick him as far away from the ranch as possible, but Russel refused.

Perry swallowed so hard she saw his Adam's apple bob. He stumbled a few steps backward until the latch of Sunbeam's stall dug into his skin. "Heavens, no! That rat would have to strike me dead before I ever let him say one rousing word to you!"

Despite the seriousness of the situation, Eliza couldn't keep the corners of her mouth from curling up, and she managed a dry, hoarse laugh. "Little late for that," he mumbled.

Perry's brows furrowed. "What do you mean?"

Eliza looked away and traced her fingers over the splintered wood on top of one of the stall doors. "He proposed three months ago." She peeked at Perry through her hair. His features had gone slack, and his eyes bulged. "Russel tried every honey-tongued trick in the book to get me to agree so they could solidify their 'business partnership,' but I refused. Russel may be my guardian, but nothing he can do would make me marry into a life of crime."

Perry's shoulders relaxed as he exhaled, but his posture stayed tense, and his features remained rigid. "I'm gonna kill that lazy, no-good –" He marched toward the barn doors, but Eliza blocked his exit.

"I appreciate that. Really, but this is exactly why I didn't tell you."

Perry blinked. "What on earth are you talking about, Eliza?"

She smiled warmly. "Perry, you've been like a father to me since the day he died. I knew you'd react like this if you ever found out Bennie tried to have his way with me, and there's no need for you to lose your job on my account. I can handle myself."

Perry frowned, then pursed his lips and crossed his arms. "I have no doubt that you can, but mark my words, if that lowlife scoundrel so much as looks at you funny the next time I'm around, he's going to find himself stuck with a whole lot more than a black eye."

Eliza shook her head and squeezed his shoulder. "Thank you for caring so much, Perry."

The foreman smiled and took her free hand. "Of course. Your father would roll over in his grave if he didn't think he left this place in the hands of someone that could look after you."

Eliza said nothing. She doubted the truthfulness of that statement with every fiber of her being, but at least, if nothing else, she had Perry in her corner.

***

It was past two in the afternoon when Russel finally emerged from his room, and he barely muttered a good morning before he put on a fresh set of clothes and headed for the door. He was a large, well-built man, but cared little for his physique as he always bore a heavy belly—no doubt a result of his countless nights at the saloon—along with an unkempt beard and a raggedy mop of brown hair which was forever falling into his eyes.

"And where do you think you're going?" Now back in her usual attire, Eliza placed her hands on her hips and glared at him from the living room. "Didn't you hear? A terrible winter storm is coming, and it could be here any day now. We have preparations to do!"

Russel snorted and rolled his eyes. "Ain't that what the foreman's for?" A thick southern drawl accentuated his words.

Eliza glowered. "Perry and I have been working our tails off since four in the morning. You're the one who owns this ranch. When are you going to do something to keep it up?"

His sneer turned mocking. "Says the little daddy's girl who never even got a cent of his money," he teased. "Why don't you stick to keeping house and making tea? Leave the work to the real men."

"A real man would help his family, not waste all his father's hard-earned money at a bar every night."

Russel snarled, and his upper lip curled back. He stomped closer to the door and rested his hand on the handle. "Shows how much you know. Bennie and I are working on a business proposition that will make us richer than your pathetic father ever was."

Eliza curled her hands into fists. "You mean a robbery," she spat. "Your mother always said you were a troublemaker, but I bet she'd give you a heck of a Jessy if she saw you now."

Russel paled a bit, and his hand tightened around the doorknob. "What would you know? You barely even knew her."

Eliza shrugged. "Maybe. But I knew Papa. What would he say if he found out you'd gotten yourself mixed up with a wanted bandit?"

Russell's features scrunched, and he opened his mouth, but nothing came out.

Eliza's gaze turned serious. "You know, I heard from some of the tongue-waggers in town that Bennie is so ruthless he'll even rob children. Is that really the kind of man you think Papa would want you hanging out with?"

Some of Russell's bravado returned as he barked out a laugh and yanked open the door. A biting breeze knocked them both backward. "Not everything you hear from the rumor mill is true, little sister," he jeered as he stepped out onto the windy, snowy front porch. "Don't wait up."

Before she could reply, the door slammed closed, plunging the house into an eerie but blissful silence. Eliza slid a hand down her face. "Okay, fine. Guess I'll just have to finish the storm preparations on my own." Someone had to make sure this place didn't go to heck in a handbasket. It might as well be her.

Chapter One

"I think we need a few more over here." Eliza clucked her tongue and gently kicked her gray horse, Natalie, in the flanks, rounding the fencing of the cattle paddock. She nodded at Perry, who trailed a few feet behind her on his painted mount carrying saddlebags of extra lanterns. When she pointed to a post over her head, Perry nodded and rode to it. Eliza proceeded to the other side of the fence while he hung the lamps.

Thankfully, the impending winter storm, hadn't hit Wolfspell as quickly as anyone thought it would. That led to endless jabs and teasing for Russel whenever Eliza mentioned their preparations over the last three and a half weeks. But unlike him, she and Perry weren't giving up. It was always better to be safe than sorry, especially in the middle of an unpredictable Montana winter. But judging by the way the temperature dropped by multiple degrees every day, and the wind and scatterings of snow they had received, Eliza wasn't quite ready to call out the predictions as a falsehood.

She shivered as another gust of wind rippled through her riding clothes—once again, she'd foregone tradition and disobeyed her stepbrother in favor of functionality. At least for now, since he wouldn't be up for six more hours and would be none the wiser to her current wardrobe choice: the warmest coat she owned over a white riding vest and black dock skin pantaloons, covered by a heavy pair of boots.

Russel would be appalled to find her in such gentlemanly, 'senseless' attire, but a lifetime on the ranch had taught her to be pragmatic, and she would much rather receive a tongue lashing than lose her balance as the stirrups swayed in the gale.

She finished mounting the lantern and rocked back on her heels, guiding her body down until she was safely seated in the saddle. She clapped her gloved hands together and blew into her palms, her breath puffing in a crystalized cloud that lingered in the air after she exhaled.

"All right," she breathed. "I think I'm done here; how are you doing?"

Perry met her eyes and said something, but it was swallowed by the roar of the breeze nipping at their noses and frosting their skin. She cocked her head and squinted, turning up her palms. His eyes crinkled in the misty morning light, and his lips twitched. She couldn't hear, to be sure, but it almost looked like he was laughing. He just nudged a hand toward the barn, and Eliza couldn't help but giggle at this impromptu game of charades.

She guessed he was telling her to go ahead and warm up, so she obeyed, sinking her heels into her horse's sides and tugging the reins until Natalie obediently spun around. But instead of heading back toward the horse barn, she swiveled in the opposite direction and took off toward the bull pen. A little cold wasn't going to keep her from working. Well, not completely, anyway.

She fed Natalie some extra treats after she let her into one of the few empty stalls and looked through the saddlebags she always kept tied to her horse's right hip. Eliza fetched a spare blanket and saddle pad and replaced the heavy leather saddle on Natalie's back. The horse let out a sigh of relieved contentment when she unfastened the last latch and hung the saddle over the stall door.

"There, is that better?" Eliza gave her neck a few gentle pets and the horse nickered. "Rest up for a while, girl. I'm gonna go check on the cattle."

Every fall, and a couple of other times throughout the year, like when there was a big storm, or during calving season, ranchers took extra care to watch for the health and fitness of their animals. For the bulls and cows, splitting them into groups relied on their body type and chances of surviving the winter. Work like this was one of the many things her brother found tedious about keeping up the O'Conner ranch, and while Eliza would never say she enjoyed it, she knew it was necessary.

She smiled and searched for the bundle of parchment they kept in the back room. When she found it and a fresh quill dipped in ink, she went down the lines of animal count one by one, carefully marking scores right after writing the date at the top.

December 18, 1860.

Eliza blinked, her lips parting slightly as the last flourish of her quill completed the zero. Christmas was only seven days away. The Thanksgiving holiday had gone by so fast, and with such little celebration, she barely had time to register it has passed at all . Year after year, she tried to convince her stepbrother that they should do something to get into the spirit of the holidays. If nothing else, Eliza felt they at least owed the ranch hands a grand meal as a thank-you for everything they had done to help them keep this place together over the last three years since they had become orphans.

But year after year, his answer was always the same.

"You can do something if you want," he would drawl, words half-slurred and clipped from the ever-present bottle of whiskey dangling from his left hand as he slumped on the couch.

Like many businesses, most of the saloons were closed for Thanksgiving, so he was left to his own devices when it came to numbing himself to the world. "But don't expect me to pitch in. Men don't waste their time flitting about in the kitchen." He always spat the last word like poison, and it took every ounce of decorum Eliza had to hold her tongue.

Russell's birth mother had run away with a traveling salesman only two years after marrying Eliza's father when Eliza was eight and Russel eleven. To Eliza's knowledge, he had never had a proper motherly figure to look up to, and since her father died not long after that, he barely had a father figure. She supposed that explained his reckless and apathetic behavior, but in no way would it ever excuse it. So many times over the past three years, she had wanted to slog some sense into him – tell him that nothing about his sorry, miserable life would get any better unless he got off his butt and did the work.

But she couldn't.

Society, and more importantly, the law, deemed it improper for a lady to ever speak to her guardian in such an impertinent manner. They'd gotten into plenty of squabbles over the years, but Eliza always stopped herself from inching away from the territory of bickering frustrated stepsiblings and into complete defamation or insubordination. Irritating and insufferable as Russel Rivers could be, the last thing she needed was to be kicked out and homeless in the dead of winter.

So, she kept her thoughts and desires to herself – just as she had for most of her life.

The first year after her father died, she had tried to put together the fanciful feast she had always fantasized about, but as she should've expected, most of the ranch hands already had plans and families of their own to attend to. As such, Thanksgiving and Christmas for the last three years had been silent, lonely affairs, free from joyous carols echoing through the house and that special spark of excitement that only happened on Christmas morning when she would scamper down the stairs to inspect the pile of presents once left beside the fireplace.

With the storm preparation taking up all of her time this year, she hadn't even mustered the energy to mount a Christmas tree.

Yet another holiday season without any real reason.

The barn door cracked open once again, and she sighed, shaking herself free of the dark gray thundercloud that seemed to have overtaken her mind lately. Perry pushed the door aside and stepped inside as quickly as possible before shoving it shut behind him. A whisk of wind whistled through the open space, and Eliza gasped as it skittered beneath her trousers again.

"How's it going in here?" His gloved hands were nearly white from the cold as he rubbed them on either side of the opposite arm in an attempt to warm himself.

Eliza looked up, then winced when his expression turned inquisitive. She tried to mask her emotions behind an expression of indifference but wasn't quite fast enough.

Perry raised an eyebrow. "Penny for your thoughts?"

Shrugging, Eliza looked down at the notebook again and tried to appear nonchalant. "Oh, nothing. I was just checking the herd's body score numbers before the storm and..." she tapped her quill against the parchment, the date seeming to mock her. "I guess this month got away for me. I didn't realize Christmas was so close. I haven't done any decorating, let alone gotten a present for Russel." Not that she expected him to reciprocate the gesture.

Perry laughed a hoarse laugh as he walked over and took the notes from her. "You know he'll be painting his nose before the sun even fully rises in the sky," he said, a hint of melancholy dancing behind his teasing words. "At the rate he goes, he wouldn't know a golden nugget from a pile of horse dung."

Despite the increasingly gloomy feeling taking shape within her, Eliza shook her head and gave a small chuckle. She dropped her eyes to the barn door and kicked at a loose pebble with the toe of her boot. She didn't want to admit it, but it seemed highly unlikely that Russel would change his swindling, frivolous ways. Until he did that, their so-called family would be nothing more than names written on a piece of paper. Whether or not she remembered to give him a gift wasn't likely to make any difference.

One of the bulls snorted, and Eliza returned to the present moment. "Do you have any Christmas plans?" She clasped the papers in front of her and looked at the foreman.

A wide genuine smile broke out on his face. "I do. My son and daughter-in-law are coming to stay with me this year. I'm going to meet my grandson for the first time."

Eliza's heart swelled, and she hugged him. "You're a grandfather! That's wonderful! Congratulations! I didn't even know they were pregnant."

Perry shifted his weight. "She just had the baby in October. They weren't really telling people until they knew everything was going the way it should first."

Eliza's smile widened. "I bet you'll be over the moon to meet him."

Perry nodded. "I only hope they get here before the snow does." He craned his neck and peered nervously out the window. It was growing darker and drearier with each passing day.

Eliza placed a reassuring hand on his shoulder. "Don't worry." She squeezed it gently. "I'm sure everything will be fine."

He turned around, inhaling deeply and running a hand through his motley curls that dropped outside the brim of his hat. "Yes. I'm sure you're right." He paused, but his exuberant brown eyes brightened as if a lantern had just been lit above his head. "You can join us if you like. I'm sure they would love to meet you."

Eliza's heart jumped in her chest, and she barely kept herself from bouncing on the balls of her feet at the invitation, but she fought to keep her decorum as she cut her hand through the air. "Oh, no! I couldn't impose on your family's Christmas!"

"Nonsense!" He draped an arm around her shoulder and gave her a side hug. "You were the closest thing I had to a daughter before my son married, and I can't stand the thought of you spending another Christmas in that dreary old house alone while your stepbrother drinks himself into oblivion. Please, say you'll come."

Eliza's cheeks warmed, and she dipped her head. "All right. If you insist."

He pulled her in for another hug. "Then it's settled."

***

That afternoon, when Perry insisted they take a break for a hot meal, Eliza had an extra bounce in her step as she meandered toward the house, trudging through the snow, which was now nearly up to her calves. It had started coming down not twenty minutes after she had received his invitation and had no sign of stopping. She only hoped it wouldn't delay their newly made plans.

As she mounted the stairs to their father's estate, a two-story home mostly made of brick with a small wraparound porch, she fingered the soft tufts of pine needles that made up the wreath decorated with pinecones, cranberries, and popcorn that she had managed to hang on the front door. It was the only glimmer of Christmas anywhere around their property, and she often forgot she even had done it. The front door came open with a soft click, welcoming her into the dark entryway of the otherwise empty house. She didn't bother lighting a lantern and instead stripped herself of her boots, gloves, hat, and coat to avoid trekking snow across the newly gleaming house that had taken two full days to clean. Russel would dirty it again soon, anyway. Since they barely entertained any company, he often wondered why she cared so much for having a clean home, especially since the task of keeping it up fell upon her shoulders.

If she were honest, she truly wasn't sure why it mattered so much. Especially when she had already worked herself from dawn till dusk trying to keep this place afloat, she supposed it was just one of those things ingrained in her from an early age. Her father never cared what kind of rancher she would be. She only received any sort of praise when she stuck to her traditionally womanly duties. A part of her knew it was ridiculous to continue to try to keep up such a façade when nothing and no one could bring him back. Still, every time she completed the task, she half expected to see his hulking silhouette lingering in the doorway, inspecting every nook and cranny of her work before finally rewarding her with a half-smile or a single kind word.

She changed into a dress to avoid a tongue-lashing from her stepbrother, then cut through the living room on the way to the kitchen. It was silent and pitch black, made all the

THE COWBOY'S UNEXPECTED CHRISTMAS MIRACLE

more obvious by the few beat-up pieces of furniture scattered about. Shadows adorned the walls where picture frames full of cherished memories and display shelves had once been. Now they held only cobwebs, dust, and chipping paint. Most of their furniture had been pawned off by her stepbrother only because Eliza had tried to find a way to fund his addictions rather than draining his entire inheritance. But then, she hadn't considered the consequences. The once immaculate living room now housed a lonely torn-up couch and two dust-riddled armchairs.

A heavy sigh escaped her lips, and her shoulders slumped as she ventured into the kitchen. The washing basin nearly overflowed with dishes, bread lay forgotten on the counter, and strips of fatty, fried overland trout sat in a frying pan, which looked as though it had spewed grease all over the stove.

So, Russel was awake after all.

Her hands curled into fists as she spun on her heel and stomped through the house. "Russel!" She peered into his bedroom, which was as much of a pigsty as always, but empty nonetheless.

"Russel Rivers! Come out and take care of this mess you left. Just because I live here does not mean I'm your maid."

She braved the outdoors again to peer into the cellar but still found no sign of her stepbrother.

"Twenty-one years old, and yet still he refuses to clean up after himself," she grumbled. Resigned to her fate, she returned inside and made quick work of restoring the kitchen to a workable environment. Just as she quickly opened the pantry door to return the bread to its proper place and hunt for some ingredients for a filling and warm afternoon meal, the creak of the back door made her ears prick.

"Russ, I'm telling you. One swipe, and that'll be the easiest job we've ever done."

The bread slipped from her hand, and a gasp escaped as Bennie's "Bullettooth" Boyle's maniacal laughter ricocheted through the rafters, rattling her bones and sending shivers down her spine.

"I...don't know." Russel's already prominent southern drawl was thicker than usual, the way it only got when he was more nervous than a cat in a room full of rockers. "Seems a bit risky, what with the weather reports, don't ya think? Mayhap we ought to wait till spring."

Eliza's heart pounded in her ears, and it was an effort to steady her breathing as she bent down to pick up the bread. She maneuvered back into the main kitchen and left it on the counter, slinking as quietly as possible down the hall toward her brother's study. The doors stood ajar, and sure enough, two stalky silhouettes stood in the streaming light from the dusty windows just behind her stepbrother.

Though his profile faced away from her, she saw how his posture twitched, his hands clasped purposely behind his back as he fought to maintain eye contact with Bennie.

The bandit scoffed, and Eliza swallowed thickly as she watched her stepbrother through bleary, bloodshot eyes. "You've been with me long enough to know the risk is just part of the game, at least if you want to reap the reward. If you're still only interested in slumming it here at this crusty ol' ranch and wasting away on Daddy's money," he chuckled as he shrugged, and Eliza's lips pressed into a thin line, "I ain't gonna stop ya, but I ain't gonna bring you in for any more of the cuts either."

The scar over his left eye gleamed in his tanned complexion, and Russel gaped before his features twisted.

"What? But that ain't fair. You said as long as you and your crew could use this place as a base, I would get a cut o' the booty."

Bennie picked at his nails with a knife he pulled from his back pocket. "I told you last week that ain't how we work no more. You were just three sheets to the wind."

Russel scowled. "All I'm saying is, why can't we wait till spring? There won't be as many bobtail guards out, and the predators will be out of hibernation, so we can pawn off suspicion."

Bennie barked a laugh, but his scowl turned menacing. "You've come up with just about every excuse in the book to weasel your way out of this." He flung the knife in the air and pointed the sharp end right at Russel's Adam's Apple. "Maybe Danny was right about you, and you really are nothing more than a lily-livered, yellow-bellied coward."

Russel held up his hands and laughed uneasily, stumbling a few steps back until he was literally backed into a corner.

Eliza swallowed a shriek, curling her toes and forcing her feet to stay rooted to the carpet in spite of every instinct telling her otherwise. As much as she disdained her stepbrother, she had no desire to see him maimed before her eyes. Though the same age as her stepbrother, Bennie "Bullettooth" Boyle stood a whole head taller than Russel. His eyes were so dark they were almost black. They looked extra menacing in the golden hue of the midday light. His biceps bulged beneath his long, tailored jacket, which he had no doubt stolen from one of the more affluent gentlemen in town. Eliza wouldn't be surprised to learn that everything he owned was stolen. Rumors said that once upon a time, he would lure his crew members in by posing as an upright businessman, only to later reveal his dastardly nature when they were in too deep to back out.

27

Russell's already pale complexion nearly matched the hue of the snow blanketing the ground outside as he bumped into the wood-paneled wall and braced himself against it, shaking his head vigorously. "No, no, that ain't it. I want in. it's just..." He rubbed a hand along the back of his neck and licked his dry lips. "Well, stealing a whole herd of cattle in the dead of night right before a big storm isn't gonna go unnoticed in a town as small as Wolfspell. What happens if we get caught?"

Bennie's smile widened, though Eliza hadn't previously thought that was possible. A dangerous kind of mischief danced in his eyes, and a new crop of gooseflesh rose all over Eliza's body as he bared his teeth, looking similar to a wolf having finally cornered its precious prey. "That's the beauty of doing the job now, Russel. The storm will hide most of our activity, and if it doesn't..." he fingered the shiny black pistol he always kept tucked in the left side of his belt. "Well, they don't call me Bullettooth for nothing."

Eliza stumbled back, clamping her hand over her mouth as bile crawled up her throat and her stomach plummeted. She knew her brother had been up to many nefarious things since his partnership with Bennie had begun. Still, she had never heard them discussing one of their plans in person before, and she shuddered to think how many people Russel had let step in the way of that treacherous barrel. Even if he'd never done the deed himself, which she guessed he hadn't by the horrified look on his face, thank God, innocent people had likely still died on his watch.

The floor split up from under her in the room spun. Eliza used every ounce of her strength to keep her balance as the truth washed over her with disturbing clarity. Russel had never been her favorite person, but she couldn't stomach the idea that he might actually be in league with such a ruthless, heartless bandit.

The sharp, guttural sound of a throat clearing behind her sent her plummeting back to earth. The hair on the back of her neck shot up, and she froze, her nails digging into the gap between the ridges of the door frame of the bedroom, which was just a few steps away from the study and gave her the ideal vantage point.

"Well, well, what have we here?"

The gravelly voice, filled with an eerie kind of giddiness that made her heart race and her blood run cold, came from the doorway directly behind her and belonged to none other than Dan "Danny" Mason, Bennie's right-hand man and the second most-wanted bandit in town. "Looks like we have a spy in our midst." She spun around to find a man with tan skin, bushy brows, and bright green eyes just as menacing as Bennie's sneering at her. He stepped into the light.

Eliza's eyes widened, and she threw up her hands as she fumbled to think of an explanation. "What? No. I was only— Ow!"

He grabbed her arm, nearly ripping it from her shoulder in the process. "Wait, stop!"

His nails dug into her still-cool flesh as he marched forward and shoved open the office door until it slammed against the wall with an ear-shattering bang. He threw her roughly to the ground, and her knees burned as they collided with the hardwood. She slammed her palms against it to catch herself, wincing at the sting that radiated up her arms.

"Look whom I found sneaking around by the door," Dan snarled, glaring daggers at Russel. "It seems Russell's little sister here ain't as much of a wallflower as he led us to believe."

Eliza caught her breath and sat back on her haunches, brushing off the skirt of her dress as best she could. She peered at her stepbrother. He said nothing, but if looks could kill, she would have been dead instantly.

She cringed, fully expecting Bennie to whirl on his apparently untrustworthy business partner, but her heart stopped when his steely, murderous gaze settled on her instead. "Well, well, well, what do we have here? A little mouse thinks she can wander into the lion's den?"

His lips twisted up into that menacing sneer again, and Eliza shivered. She tried her hardest to push herself to her feet, only to crash back against the floor. "Please, Mister, uh, Bullettooth, sir, I was only trying to—"

He laughed a bone-chilling laugh, and Eliza's apology tapered off. "You can't sweet talk me, girl. I know what you're doing. You send your brother to get us to trust him, then you turn around and give all my secrets up to the sheriff."

Eliza shook her head frantically, eyes pleading with Russel over Bennie's shoulder. "No, no, I swear, it wasn't like that."

Bennie rolled his eyes. "Lie all you want. It ain't gonna delay your fate much longer. He stepped forward, his hand outstretched like claws as they reached for her. Eliza whimpered and leaned back.

Wrestle, still pale as a ghost but seeming to have regained at least an ounce of his sanity, weaseled his way between them just in time. "Bennie, wait! My stepsister may act like a biddy, but she ain't no tattle tale. No matter how annoying she may be, she won't go to the sheriff," he tossed the desperate look over her shoulder and met Eliza's eyes. "Will you?"

Tears rolled down her cheeks, and her breaths came in short gasps. "N-no. No, never. I-I swear." She stuttered out the answer between pitiful, racking sobs, wrapping her arms around herself as if they offered some kind of protection from the terrifying scene unfolding before her.

Bennie clicked his tongue, the deadly look in his eyes brightening. "You know, as your friend, I'd like to believe you, Russell, but as a businessman, that ain't a chance I'm willing to take."

He pulled the pistol from his holster, but before he could so much as raise it to his waist, a burst of energy shot through Eliza faster than any bullet. She clambered to her feet, shoved Danny to the side, and raced blindly out of the house toward the stables. The frigid air gnawed at her exposed skin, but she barely let it resister even as it seeped into the depths of her bones.

She freed Natalie from her stall as footsteps crunched the snowy ground. She barely had time to catch her breath or wipe away the frozen tears before they became icicles against her cheeks. Instead, she flung her leg haphazardly over the horse's backside and held herself up. She hadn't ridden bareback since before her father died. She had no reason to, but now it was her only hope if she wanted to survive. She kicked her heels as hard as she could into Natalie's flanks, and with a mighty, petrified neigh, horse and rider thundered out of the barn.

"Eliza?!"

Her heart ached as she caught a glimpse of Perry out of the corner of her eye as she raced past him in the pasture. His head shot up, and he met her eyes for the briefest of moments, his own normally soothing brown ones wide with fear and confusion. "What happened? Where are you going?"

A small part of her wanted to turn back, but her heart catapulted in her throat as she caught the leaving silhouettes of Bennie and Russel racing through around the barn after her. She plunged through the gate that led to the entrance of the ranch and darted into the woods nearby, riding off as if the devil himself was on her heels.

Chapter Two

Wolfspell, Montana

December 18, 1860

Alexander Swanson frowned and rubbed the scruff at the edges of his bushy brown beard with his thumb and forefinger, surveying the contents of their root cellar. He and Nathan Lane, his most trusted ranch hand, had been harvesting, pickling, drying, and doing everything they could to preserve as much produce as possible to carry them through the coming winter. Last year's crop had been more than enough to feed his little family, but things were looking a little more dismal this year. Which, of course, was the last thing he needed with such a record-breaking winter storm on the horizon.

A familiar set of footsteps clopped down the stairs, and Alexander frowned at the long line of soggy prints trailing behind Nathan as he approached Alexander's side. His teeth chattered as he stamped what seemed like a hill's-worth of snow from his boots. His normally black hair had almost turned stark white from the snow.

Alexander raised an eyebrow. "It's coming down pretty good out then?"

Nathan nodded with a little laugh. "You could say that." He rubbed his arms to warm himself.

Alexander's frown returned as he glanced once again at the dwindling piles of produce. "Well, the last harvest wasn't as good as I would've liked. I think it'll last, but it might get a little tight come planting time."

Nathan smiled tightly but squeezed his shoulder. "Don't worry, if there's anyone who knows how to make something out of nothing, it's my mother. She'll help you figure out how to make this last longer."

Alexander's lips curled upward. "And thank God for that. I don't know what I would've done if she hadn't been around to help me this past year. The twins probably would've led me into an early grave."

Nathan smirked. "Nah, you would've figured it out."

Alexander chuckled and ran a hand through his unruly crop of brown hair. It was down to his shoulders now, and he still had no desire to cut it, despite his mother's protests. "Maybe," he conceded. "But I'm glad I don't have to."

Nathan clapped him on the back and shook his head. "No matter what happens, you know my mother and I always got your back."

Alexander nodded. "That I do."

They worked in the cellar for a while longer and reorganized some of the smaller piles to make more room. Eventually, Nathan remembered that he was supposed to bring some more potatoes to his mother and his cheeks turned red when he mumbled out the request with a flourish. He glanced at the sun above him, which looked as if it was about half past noon by this point. Then his eyes darted back to the house as if he expected his mother to come traipsing out, yelling with her shoe in hand.

"Kind of hard to make potato soup without potatoes, isn't it?"

Nathan narrowed his eyes and snatched the potatoes from Alexander's arms a little harder than necessary. His over-the-top reaction, however, only succeeded in making his boss laugh harder. "Oh, shut your pan, Swanson," he hissed. Mama's gonna tan my hide if I don't get these. I gotta move lickety-split."

He stumbled under the weight of the root vegetables and bent to pick up more until they were piled from his stomach to his chin and he could barely walk more than a few steps without wobbling.

Alexander watched him expectantly, doing his best to temper the smirk threatening to twitch its way onto his features. He gestured to the cellar stairs. "Guess you better skedaddle then," he said with a laugh.

Nathan mumbled something unintelligible under his breath as he stumbled resolutely but ever so carefully back up toward the land of the living. At the last minute, Alexander cupped his hands around his mouth and called out, "Tell your mother I'll be in shortly. I'm just gonna go check on the feed for the animals."

His ranch hand grumbled, which Alexander took as a confirmation, shaking his head ruefully and turning back to his work.

Twenty minutes later, he had finished the arduous task of organizing all of the produce and had moved on to checking the various grains, oats, chicken feed, and hay bales they kept for the livestock. He had enough food to last at least another few weeks.

As he climbed up into the loft and inspected the hay bales, his wandering mind reminded him how much his nieces used to love playing up here. They treated it like their own little clubhouse until that fateful night, just a year and mere days from this very moment.

Thinking of them simultaneously brought a bubble of mirth to his lips and made a lump rise in his throat. His brother-in-law and her wife had come to live with Alexander on the Swanson property just after his father died of a heart attack when he was only fifteen. When his brother-in-law's wife became pregnant with not one but two babies, Alexander was beyond thrilled to receive the news.

The family had worked together as co-owners, and though the house often felt cramped with all of them living under one roof, including his mother, Alexander didn't think he could've asked for a better way to heal his broken heart. But as December 21st crept closer, Alexander couldn't quite keep away the melancholy cloud following him around. Just four days before Christmas last year, tragedy struck again.

***

On December 24, 1859, Alexander snuggled down beneath the blankets of his large bed, sandwiched between his four-year-old nieces. Effie's blonde curls were lying lazily against Alex's chest. She fought to keep her eyes open as her head dripped onto his shoulder, and she stifled a yawn.

Alexander smiled as he glanced down at her, tearing his eyes away from the book in his hand and running the fingers of his free hand through her hair. "You can go to sleep, you know," he whispered as he gently brushed a curl behind her ear.

Effie stirred lightly, rubbing away the sleep that had already begun to form in her bright blue eyes and shaking her head resolutely. "Nuh-uh!" She whined sleepily, even as she snuggled deeper into her uncle's side. "Don't wanna sleep. Gotta hear the end of the story."

He chuckled and kissed her hairline before turning back to the book. "All right, if you say so, Effie-Belle. But remember, the faster you go to sleep, the faster St. Nicholas will come."

Effie hummed and flopped one tiny arm over her uncle's stomach.

He grinned. "Whoa!" Suddenly, the right side of the bed began bouncing like a bucking bronco. Emma, Effie's older sister by exactly ten minutes – her *mischievous,* identical sister – still sat on her knees. Her eyes were wide and filled with exuberance. Where her sister couldn't seem to stay awake, Emma barely sat still. Instead, she wiggled out of her uncle's embrace and began treating the mattress like a trampoline. "Uncle Alex, I don't want to go to sleep. I'm not even tired yet!"

Alexander laughed and tapped to the now empty spot beside him. "Well, come settle down here, and maybe you will be by the time I finish reading."

She slid her tongue out and rolled her eyes, but one sharp look from her uncle nipped that behavior in the bud, and she crawled beneath his left arm. He hugged her to him from the side and gently tickled her nose.

"Good girl," he praised. "Now, where was I?"

He traced his finger over the pages of the book for a moment before he found the right line. "Oh, here we go!" He cleared his throat and, putting on the most dramatic voice he could put on, and continued reading *A Visit from St. Nicholas.*

On the last line, he made his voice extra deep, ending with a belly laugh as he tickled Effie's stomach.

She shrieked with laughter. "Uncle Alex, you're funny. Father Christmas doesn't sound like that!"

"Oh really?" Her uncle asked, a teasing note coating his words. "And how would you know? Have you ever met him?"

Emma pouted briefly before looking away. "No," she grumbled. Then, suddenly, as if someone had an annoying lit lamp over her head, she whipped back to face her uncle, eyes wide and innocent as she clasped her hands together.

Alexander chuckled, mentally steeling himself for whatever outrageous request his niece was about to make. It was a rare occasion on which he could openly refuse those adorable puppy dog eyes of hers, but tonight, there was still so much to do, and it was already way past her bedtime.

"But maybe I can this year?" she asked, pitching her voice up at the end until it turned into a question. "Please, Uncle Alex? Can I stay up just a little bit later on Christmas Eve?" She pinched her thumb and forefinger together and emphasized the word little, crawling into his lap and coming so close that their noses were touching.

He rubbed her nose gently, but resolutely shook his head as he ruffled her hair. "Nice try, Em. You know the rule. When does St. Nicholas come?"

Emma groaned and flopped back against the bedsheets but perfectly recited the line from the poem that had been their house rule since the twins were born. "On Christmas Eve. When all little girls are snug in their beds, with visions of sugarplums dancing in their heads."

Alexander nodded and tapped her nose again. "Exactly." He carefully unwound her sleeping sister from her position beneath his left arm, which by now had gone partially numb from the pressure of holding her weight. She stirred but never quite regained her sister's level of consciousness. Once Effie was settled, he rounded the opposite side of his bed and scooped Emma up, maneuvering her beside her sister and pulling the covers up to her chin, exactly the way she liked them. "Get some sleep, Emma. I'll see you in the morning. Sweet dreams."

Emma whined a little but eventually relented after reaching for another hug around her uncle's neck. "Oh-kay," she groused. But then, the moment she thought he wasn't looking, she flipped back onto her pillow with a contented sigh.

Alexander smiled as he put out the oil lamp and bid them good night one more time.

"Love you, Uncle Alex," the girls chorused simultaneously, though sleep colored their words.

Alexander's heart swelled, and his grin grew. He didn't think he would ever get tired of that, no matter how many times he heard it.

"Love you more, munchkins. Merry almost Christmas."

Even now, thinking back on that moment, just hours before everything went up in flames, a strange mixture of wistfulness, love, and dread filled his chest. If only any of them knew what was coming.

To this day, Alexander still wasn't sure what had woken him from his blissful, deep slumber that night. All he remembered was shooting up in bed, covered in a sheen of sweat, with his chest heaving and an eerie air of panic sweeping over the room. He remembered how his gaze had darted left and right, searching desperately for anything out of place, anything that might explain the inconceivable knot of dread twisting in his stomach.

At first, he'd found nothing. Then he heard it.

A bone-chilling scream reached his ears all the way from the east wing of the house. He would recognize it anywhere. Alexander vaulted out of bed without a second thought. One million thoughts swelled in his mind, each more terrifying than the last. He had only heard his sister scream like that only once— when she was the one to stumble across their father's body after his apoplexy.

The thought alone made Alexander's heart crawl into his throat, and he never stopped praying as he reached for the door handle.

He hadn't registered its heat until after it had already seared at his flesh, and even then, as he'd swallowed a curse under his breath, he hadn't had time to think anything of it as he flung the door open. He was greeted by a blinding sheen of smoke.

The next few hours were a blur for Alex. He remembered how his throat had closed up. He remembered fighting to keep his eyes open as a burning sensation filled them with tears. He remembered feeling his way through the smoky fog and covering his mouth with his shirt as he coughed and weaseled his way through the house until he reached the east wing where his brother-in-law, sister, mother, and nieces were staying, only to find both rooms haunted by flames nearly fifteen feet tall.

Every day, he wished he'd had just ten more seconds. Ten more seconds to think and devise a better, more sensible plan that would've ended up with everyone alive.

His niece's room was the closest and the furthest away from the monstrous ignition. Knowing they would likely be helpless when it came to their door, he'd barreled inside, picking them up in one fell swoop. Emma barely stirred, but Effie had woken up immediately and clung to his nightshirt.

"Uncle Alex?" She sniffed and looked around with wide, terrified eyes. "What's going on? Where are mommy and daddy?"

"Shh!" Alexander hugged her closer and let her bury her face in his shirt. "It's all right, Effie-Belle." He had done her best to soothe her, rubbing her back even as he dashed frantically toward the nearest exit. "Everything is going to be all right." And yet, even as the words had left his mouth, his tongue turned to sandpaper, and his throat dried. He knew, beyond a shadow of a doubt, that nothing would ever be all right again.

He managed to dash back inside one more time, rescuing his disoriented mother by the skin of his teeth, but could do nothing but stand and watch as the flames licked and conquered every corner of the east half of the estate, taking his sister and brother-in-law with them as they rose into the chilling clear air of the morning sky. By the time the sheriff and firemen arrived, only ash was left.

***

His growling stomach anchored Alexander to the present, and he dug his fingers into his palms, forcing the vivid flashback from his mind. A year later, he could still smell the smoke and feel the warmth on his skin and clothes. The scar on the inside of his left hand, which he got while grabbing his doorknob to thrust himself into the chaos, still hadn't fully healed. Every time it started to scab over, he would scratch at it until it opened again. It seemed only fitting that he had a physical wound to match the one on his heart.

After taking another minute to shake himself free, he climbed down from the loft and returned to the house to join the rest of his family for lunch. Perhaps potato soup would be just what he needed to warm his soul and body.

The aroma of rosemary, garlic, carrots, and freshly roasted and peeled potatoes immediately tickled Alex's senses as he stepped into the brightly lit kitchen.

Nathan sat in an armchair in front of the fireplace, inspecting some of the vegetables he had hung there to dry.

41

"Oh, Alexander! You're back! Good!" Marie Lane, Nathan's mother and a stout woman in her late thirties, wore a purple frock with a white apron strapped around her waist. Her bouncing black curls, bright green eyes, and sun-kissed skin made her a near-mirror image of her son. She looked up from where she stirred a pot of steaming soup at the stove and wagged a wooden spoon in Alexander's direction. "The girls and Nathan tell me you've been working yourself to the bone since four o'clock this morning. It is far past time for a good meal."

Alexander snickered as the motherly reprimand made him feel like a scolded boy again, but he obediently marched over to the table and took a seat next to his mother. "Thank you, Marie. It smells delicious."

"Why, thank you." She smiled as she ladled a large spoonful of the fragrant liquid into a bowl and shuffled over to the table to sit it in front of him. "Eat up. And if you're still hungry, you can always have more."

The smell alone was enough to make Alexander drool. He picked up his spoon gratefully and took a long sniff. "Thank you again, Marie. You know how much the girls and I enjoy your cooking."

"At least someone appreciates it." She tossed a mock glare toward her son, who only rolled his eyes and made a sarcastic remark.

Abruptly, Marie turned away from the stove and waved her spoon in the air again. "Girls! Come away from there and get your lunch!"

That's when he noticed the twins.

Alexander had his third spoonful halfway to his mouth and nearly dropped it when he looked up to discover the twins much too close to the drying fire for his liking.

"Emma! Effie!" He didn't shout the words, but they were loud enough to make them jump. "What are you doing? You're not supposed to be that close to the fire!" He scrambled from his chair and drew them backward. "Come sit with me and eat your lunch. Miss Marie made a wonderful potato soup."

Effie nodded quietly and scrambled into her seat, which had been adorned with an extra cushion on top of it to allow her to reach the table. Emma crossed her arms and stamped her little foot defiantly. "No! I don't wanna eat yucky old soup!"

Alexander heaved a sigh and rubbed his thumb and forefinger across his forehead. He loved his nieces dearly, but this was not what he needed today. "Emma Fuller!" He's scolded sternly. "You know better than to talk to Miss Marie that way! Now apologize and come to eat your lunch or no dessert for you tonight."

Emma paled a bit at that disastrous threat. She swallowed back any remaining retort that might have been dancing on her tongue and immediately scurried to follow her sister's example.

Alexander nodded approvingly and picked up his spoon again. "That's better. Now, what do you say to Miss Marie?" He raised an expectant eyebrow.

Emma bit her lip and ducked her head slightly when the older woman came over with a warm, much smaller bowl of soup. "Sorry, Miss Marie," she muttered, sounding genuinely contrite.

The older woman laughed and tossed Alexander a sympathetic smile. "It's okay, dear. Being cooped up inside all day would make anyone a bit cranky."

The rest of lunch passed without incident, and later that afternoon, Alexander rode out to check the fences and make sure they were reinforced before the snow came down any harder. He took advantage of a small break in the weather to venture down one of the more scenic paths, which was even more gorgeous in the winter despite the chill soaking into his clothes. To his relief, everything seemed to be up to standard. But just as he was about to approach the end of the trail and turn back for home, he spotted a gorgeous but unfamiliar gray mare grazing on a patch of grass that somehow remained unmarked by the snow.

Slowing his mount, he approached it carefully, clicking his tongue softly to gather its attention without spooking it. Eventually, the horse looked up, and he reached out to stroke its muzzle.

"Hi there," he whispered. "Haven't seen you around here before. Do you have a rider?"

The horse kicked and pawed at the ground with its front hoof. It let out a long neigh and craned its neck to the left. Frowning, Alexander leaned as forward as he could without losing his balance. He sucked a breath, but it caught in his throat as he glimpsed the edges of muddied fabric on the solid white ground. He rounded his mount to the other side of the frightened horse and felt the color drain from his face.

A girl who couldn't be much younger than him, with bright, flowing, coppery red hair, a heart-shaped face, full lips, and skin almost as translucent as the snow laid unconscious on the hard, freezing ground.

Alexander's pulse raced as he dismounted and scrambled over to her, crouching.

"Miss?" he croaked out as an anvil settled in his stomach. "Miss, can you hear me?" Swallowing, he reached out and gently shook her shoulder, but still received no response. A sickening feeling rose in him. No. He wouldn't let anyone else die on his ranch. He bent down further, feeling her neck and the underside of her wrist in an attempt to detect her pulse.

At first, he felt nothing, but then, it was there; so faint he almost missed it.

He listened again, waiting breathlessly for his senses to reveal they had only been playing a trick on him. Sure enough, she had a pulse.

She was alive

Oh, thank God! He prayed quickly and wasted no time heaving her into his arms, cradling her like he would a bride, and mounting his horse as best he could with her. He dug his heels into his horse's sides, grabbed the gray mare's reins as he passed, and together, they cantered toward the house.

Chapter Three

Snow tumbled around her like a cascading waterfall, its flakes entangling her unruly, knotted hair. Farther and farther Eliza rode, with no sense of direction or safety anywhere in sight. After a while, the cold seeped so heavily beneath her bones that it felt as if her fingers and toes ceased to exist. She had no hands to grasp the reins with, and her vision was blinded by a seemingly endless sheet of white, fogged by grayness which slowly overtook her until she scarcely felt anything but the burning cold gnawing at her skin. Her eyelids dropped with exhaustion until finally, she slumped over, puffed out one last, dizzying breath, and surrendered to the weightlessness.

Down, down, down she sank, the icy black nothingness piercing like daggers. But with each increase in depth, the world became a little warmer, a little more inviting, until it felt as if the warmest woolen blanket she had ever had the pleasure of wrapping herself in cocooned her in an impenetrable safety bubble.

Somewhere off in the distance, thank giggles rose upward to her ears, but no matter how hard she squinted, she couldn't find the source. Then, a soft voice called to her.

Lizzie...Lizzie... come home to me.

She squinted harder into the darkness, the fuzzy and long-forgotten memory dancing at the edges of her mind. That voice. She knew it. It was soft and familiar, gentle and kind, and it felt, more than anything she had experienced in her eighteen years of living, like home.

A smile blossomed on her face, and she waded through the seemingly endless void toward the melodic, hypnotic sound.

Lizzie... Lizzie... It continued to singsong, the sound like ambrosia to her ears. Closer and closer it came until she recognized it with a jolt that made her feel as if her whole world had turned inside out.

"M-Mother?" She breathed the word, so foreign yet so sweet, on the tip of her tongue. She tasted it, cautious as if it would disappear the moment it fully left her lips.

Indeed, as soon as the last syllable rolled off her tongue, a blinding light obstructed the ghostly figure that was starting to come into view. She vanished and giggled, high-pitched and jubilant, and sounded louder and louder in her ears.

The sound echoed around her, throbbing through her skull and swelling to a crescendo until—

***

Misty rays of scattered sunlight filtered through the frost-covered window. Lizzie stirred and groaned sleepily as her blurry vision slowly came into focus. When it did, her lips, which, thankfully, had regained their feeling, morphed into a small 'o' at the sight of two adorably pudgy, heart-shaped faces and buttery blonde hair peering down at her with wide, curious blue eyes. The girl on the left gave a tiny squeak as she nudged the other in the ribs with her elbow.

"Em, look," she hissed, her eyes darting back and forth between the other child's befuddled features and Lizzie's face. "She's awake."

The second girl, Em, gasped and shook the first one's shoulder. "I knew she'd wake up!" she squealed, clearly trying her hardest to perform an effective whisper and failing.

Lizzie winced a bit as the piercing timber of their voices glided over her eardrums, but Em took no notice as she cupped her hand near the side of her mouth. "Do you think she's going to be our new aunt?"

The first girl laughed harder this time. "I don't know, Em," she whispered back. "But I hope so. She's really pretty."

Em nodded, and Lizzie felt her cheeks warm. "Uh-huh." She took the other girl's hand and scrambled off the bed, leaving her sister no choice but to follow. "Come on, let's go tell Uncle Alex we woke her up."

"Okay!" The first girl's features came alight with enthusiasm, and together they raced from the room.

Lizzie took advantage of the peace to let her gaze wander around the room. Nothing in her line of sight seemed even remotely familiar. Not the pale white walls— though they looked more cream in the dark, sullen winter light-covered in intricately painted yellow flowered wallpaper surrounded by green vines. Not the matching polka-dotted sheets and pillowcases with lace trim, which felt as luxurious as silk when she ran them through her fingers. Not the diverse array of light brown ash and pine furniture—a dresser, nightstand, vanity, and even a coat rack near the full-length mirror on the far wall. It all looked cozy and homely compared to her old bed chambers.

The memory came in disorienting, disassembled pieces; a dusty, broken window she had to drape a sheet over whenever the weather worsened, a ratty bed frame that looked like it should have been replaced years ago, and a dresser that was missing one of its legs. Nothing else existed in the room, tugging at the corners of her subconscious. Though she had no idea where or when that familiarity had been replaced with the cheeriness that surrounded her now, she was certain beyond a shadow of a doubt that this room, and whomever it belonged to, was not hers.

She especially didn't recognize the photos, which had been carefully arranged in pristinely kept frames all around the room. A man nearly six feet tall, with rugged features, muscular biceps, and a broad, sturdy frame, crouched between the two little girls who had woken her not ten minutes earlier in one of them. She couldn't tell the color of his wavy, shoulder-length hair or lively eyes, but the wide, toothy smile he wore made her heart skip a beat.

"Good, you're awake!"

With a start, Lizzie's gaze snapped to the looming silhouette filling the door frame on the far side of the room. Her eyes darted between the real-life figure in the photo as if he had stepped out of it and straight into her reality. Her breath caught in her throat, and her heart hammered in her ears as she took in his perfectly chiseled stature, visible even beneath his thick woolen sweatshirt and long pants. In the flesh, his gray eyes sparkled even more than they had in the picture, and despite the disarmingly frigid weather, Lizzie found her palms beginning to sweat.

"I... um..." She stumbled for words and did her best to keep her eyes centered on the strange man's stern features. "Wh-where am I?" she finally managed, digging her fingers into her hands beneath the covers.

The man opened his mouth to respond, but before he could, the two girls – twins, she guessed, judging by their likeness – raced beneath his left arm and bounded up on the bed again, rocking it hard.

Lizzie laughed, steadying herself and suddenly feeling like she had boarded a runaway mine cart. "Whoa!" She threw her arms out in an attempt to brace herself, laughing all the while.

"See, Uncle Alex?" one of the girls chirped. "We told ya she wasn't still sleeping." She gave the man, Alex, a giddy, gap-toothed grin, and Lizzie's heart melted at the sight. She mirrored it with a grin of her own but shrank back upon registering the grim look on the girl's uncle's face.

Alex, so they called him, seemed anything but amused. He planted his hands firmly on his hips, and his already serious features morphed into a stern scowl as he looked at the girls. "I can see that, Emma. But what have I told you and Effie about disturbing our guests?

Both girls hung their heads. One rocked back and forth on her feet while the other fiddled with her hands clasped in front of her. "Um... Not to?" the slightly taller one replied, words a clear, chipper sound that made Lizzie ache even more.

"Right. So, what did you think you were doing when you decided to disobey me?"

"But Uncle Alex!" the shorter one whined. "We weren't trying to cause any trouble! We just wanted to help the pretty lady wake up."

Effie nodded along vigorously with her sister. "Uh-uh! So you could give her true love's kiss and then get married, like in the fairy tales!"

Lizzie's mouth dropped. She nearly choked on the sip of water she had taken after finding a glass filled with it on the nightstand next to the bed. "E-excuse me?"

Alex's eyes bulged for half a second before his glare turned steely. "Effie Henrietta Fuller! You know better than to say stuff like that in front of strangers!" he roared. Lizzie swallowed a gasp and quelled a little shiver as his voice boomed through the room.

But Alex didn't seem to notice, instead flicking one finger toward her while maintaining eye contact with his niece. "Apologize! Right now!"

Effie's lower lip quivered, and she sniffed a bit as tears came to her eyes, but she obediently spun around and whimpered, "Sorry Miss."

A minuscule amount of tension loosened from Lizzie's shoulders upon witnessing the little girl's crestfallen face. "It's quite all right, sweetheart," she said softly, returning the glass on the nightstand. "I know you didn't mean any harm."

The little girl shook her head empathetically. "'Course not. Em and I want Uncle Alex not to be sad anymore."

Alex choked out a harsh laugh, and Lizzie swore she saw a flicker of pain dance in his soft gray eyes when their eyes met for a brief second before he stepped forward and placed a hand on each of his nieces' shoulders. "All right, girls, that's quite enough. Now, run along and help Miss Marie with the laundry while I talk to Miss... um..." he shifted uncomfortably as his tongue darted out to lick his dry upper lip, and he ran a hand down the back of his neck. "I'm sorry, Miss, I don't believe I caught your name."

Lizzie inhaled deeply, searching every corner of her subconscious for anything that would give her a little glimmer of information about who she was. But all she found was that soothing, singsong voice that seemed to have pulled her back from the depths of darkness. Her mother. "L-Lizzie," she finally stuttered out, the word feeling sweet as honey and rough as sandpaper on her tongue. "I think... I think my mother called me Lizzie."

Alexander smiled that dazzling smile again, though this one held a slight edge of endearment. Lizzie sucked in a breath, ashamed to think how grateful she was not to be standing at that precise moment, for otherwise, her knees would have gone weak.

"Very well." Alexander extended a hand, and when she took it, weak as her grip was, a hot current zipped along her nerve endings. "I'm Alexander Swanson, miss." He dipped into a little bow, and she giggled. "But you can call me Alex."

Swanson... The name tickled something in the back of her mind. That was the name of a well-known ranch property on the other side of town. Which meant whatever else had happened to her out there – of which she could only recall scattered bits and pieces no more pleasant than nightmares haunting her – at least she hadn't lost her way. If she was still in Wolfspell, she could discover the truth. How had she gotten there? And, for that matter, why?

"Alex." Testing the name on her tongue sent a shiver down her spine, and if she didn't know any better, she could have sworn his smile grew a little wider when he heard it. "I like that." She ducked her head and fiddled with a loose thread in one of the quilted stitches of the comforter. "I must confess, I don't remember much before arriving here... but... I'm pretty sure you saved my life. So, thank you."

A charming, pink blush colored his cheeks, and he squeezed her fingers once more before releasing them and letting her arm fall to the bed.

"Don't mention it."

Chapter Four

December 19, 1860

An awkward silence settled between them, and Alexander shifted on the balls of his feet.

Come on, you clumsy saddle slicker, he chided himself inwardly. *Say something!*

He opened his mouth and finally mounted the courage to make eye contact once more. The heat that crept up his neck as he did so wasn't helping matters in the least.

Before he could crack a witty remark to break the tension, though, Lizzie's grumbling stomach did it for him.

They laughed together, hers as light and tinkling as jingle bells and his a hearty guffaw. He was careful to temper it the moment her cheeks turned scarlet.

"I'm sorry." She ducked her head and placed a hand on her stomach in lieu of meeting his eyes. "I guess I'm a little hungry."

He nodded and offered what he hoped was a tender smile. "I imagine you would be. You gave us all quite a scare there. Marie and I weren't sure you would make it for a while."

He could have sworn he saw her smile falter. "Your wife?"

Alexander felt his hands begin to itch. "Oh, she's my neighbor and temporary housekeeper. Also known as the one who did the real work nursing you. I just brought you out of the cold."

Her eyes widened, then she slapped her hand over her mouth. "I passed out in the snow?"

Alexander shook his head solemnly, then cocked it to the side.

Why does she seem so surprised?

"You did. I was running out to fix my fence, and that mare of yours caught my attention. I might never have found you if it hadn't been for her. So really, it was just a case of right place, right time."

Lizzie let out a long exhale and ran a hand through her long red hair. "Wow..." she murmured. "I wonder how long I was out there." She said it softly, almost as if she didn't want anyone else to hear her, but Alexander was far too close, and the sentiment sent alarm bells ringing. "Wait, you mean you don't remember?" A sliver of suspicion crept up Alexander's spine, but he pushed it away upon taking in Lizzie's distraught expression.

"I wish I did. The last thing I remember is..." Her eyes grew misty, and she changed direction, staring off at something he couldn't see on the other side of the room. "I was... riding. I wanted to get in one more ride before the-the s-storm hit, and then..." She trailed off to a stuttering stop, and Alexander's uncertainty increased when she refused to meet his gaze again. After another long, stifling moment, Lizzie dropped her shoulders, defeated, and brushed the hair out of her eyes. "I'm really sorry; I truly don't remember how I got here."

Alexander swallowed the feeling in the back of his throat and cut a hand through the air. "No matter. We can figure it out later. First, let's get you something to eat."

Lizzie nodded.

"I'll be right back." Alexander turned on his heel and strode from the room. As he ventured down the stairs, the events of the past few hours tumbled about in his mind. Though his initial instincts had compelled him to rescue the strange girl from a slow, painfully deadly fate, her apparent lack of memory had planted a seed of doubt in his mind. However unlikely it seemed, he wanted to believe her explanation. He wanted to believe she was telling the truth, that she had suffered some major injury during the presumed fall from her horse. It wasn't implausible, given how slick and hard the ground was now. Still, neither was that the hardest story to come by if she needed an alibi to move ahead with some other, more nefarious motive.

Like what?

The sense of reasoning his parents had ingrained in him since birth asked. As much as they encouraged his inquisitiveness, they learned just as quickly that they would also have to teach him how to temper it, or else the questions would never cease.

I found her passed out next to a horse in the middle of a snowstorm on a property she wasn't familiar with. Even the most thickheaded thieves wouldn't attempt something this deep into the winter.

That simple bit of logic made the gears of seemingly endless possibilities grind to a halt in his mind, and he held on to that feeling as he re-entered the kitchen.

"Ah! There you are!" Once again, Marie commanded her domain with an air of grace and poise. This time she was bent over the washing basin while a pot pie was baked in the oven. "And how is our patient?"

Despite all his worries, Alexander smiled at the question. "Well, Marie, it appears the twins were right. She is awake, and she's asking for food. I was hoping I could bring her some of that delicious potato soup you made earlier."

A smile blossomed on the older woman's face, and she gestured toward the back door. "I just sent Nathan to the poorhouse in town with the leftovers."

Alexander pressed his lips together and snapped his fingers. "Shoot!"

Marie chuckled and then bent down to open the oven. "But she's more than welcome to a piece of this pot pie. As soon as it cools."

An eager pair of blue eyes peered over the countertop, and Marie gently whacked Emma's hand with the back of her wooden spoon just before she could burn it on the hot pastry.

"Ah, ah, missy. You know the rules. No eating until everyone sits down for dinner."

Her lip jutted out in the adorable pout that, nine out of ten times, her uncle found irresistible.

"Please, Uncle Alex?" she begged, going over and hugging him around his left

leg. "Can't we eat some now?"

He laughed, picked her up and rested her on his hip. "Not yet, munchkin. If you try to eat it now, you'll end up with a big ole blister on the roof of your mouth. We don't want that now, do we?

Effie clamped her lips closed and shook her head.

"Right. So, I'm afraid we all must wait a little bit longer."

His niece nodded but craned her neck to see around him, focusing on the stairs. "But, Uncle Alex, what about the pretty lady in mommy's old bedroom? Did she say she was hungry too?"

A sickening feeling twisted in Alex's stomach. He hadn't expected either of the girls to notice that he had ordered Marie to make Lizzie comfortable in his sister's childhood room, but he supposed he should have known better. Those two were too curious for their good. Turning back to the conversation, he winked at Effie. "You're right. I did. But she's going to have to wait too. If the pie isn't cool enough for you to eat, it's not cool enough for us."

Effie nodded again, leaning her head against Alex's shoulder and tangling her fingers in his hair. "Oh-kay!" she huffed. "But can you at least tell us who she is? We tried to ask Miss Marie what happened, but she just told us we had to talk to you." She sent a withering glare in the kindly housekeeper's direction, and Alexander had to bite his tongue to keep from laughing. "All right. Let's find your sister, and I'll tell you both. Knowing her, I bet she's just as curious as you are."

They wandered off, finding Emma playing with her toys in the twins' shared bedroom. Alexander occupied the room just to the right. He had moved them there almost immediately after the fire and had no intention of letting them be away from him ever again.

"Hey, Emma," her sister crowed, still clinging to Alex's shoulder. "Uncle Alex says he's finally going to tell us about the pretty lady before dinner."

"Really?" Emma's gaze snapped to meet her uncle's.

"Really. But only if you clean up this mess and come into the living room first." The little girl nodded and began thrusting all of her toys back into the toy chest pushed against one of the far walls. Effie squirmed to be released from her uncle's grasp. "I'll help, I'll help!"

A few minutes later, the room was indeed clean – or as clean as it could be for a room that belonged to two five-year-old girls – and they were snuggling on the couch with Alex's arms wrapped around them.

"So?" Effie prompted, practically bouncing out of her skin with nosiness. "Who is she?"

"Yeah," echoed Emma. "Miss Marie just said you found her outside, but where? I've never seen her before."

Alexander laughed. "Well, as a matter of fact, Emma, I hadn't seen her before either. She's going to be a new friend for everyone."

Effie's forehead crinkled. "But if you've never seen her before, how'd you know she needed to be rescued from the snow?"

Smiling, Alexander repeated the afternoon event, adding as much room for elaboration as possible; he knew how much his nieces adored story time. By the time he was done, they were just as enamored with their new houseguest as Alexander had been when he first saw her – though he would never mention a word of it to the twins for fear that they might start planning their wedding! He couldn't help this well of pride from bubbling up in his chest. As concerned as he was about keeping his little family safe, which would always be his priority, the more he talked about her, the more he knew that following his instincts was the right choice. He had meant what he thought out there on the trail. No matter what it took, he wouldn't have let anyone else die on his property – not if he could help it. Luckily for Lizzie, in this case, he could.

Almost immediately after finishing the story, Marie announced that the pie was ready to eat and served each of them a heaping helping. Alexander declined his for the moment, asking her to leave the pie in the oven while he went upstairs to check on Lizzie.

He meandered down the hall and up the stairs to the second door to the right of the landing. Then when he reached it, he tapped lightly.

"Lizzie?" he called. "I'm sorry it took a little longer than I expected, but I've got some dinner for you if you're still hungry?"

"Alexander?" his mother replied. "Is that you?"

His brows shot up into his hairline, and his hand hovered over the brass doorknob, not daring to open it just yet. *What is Mother doing up here?* Last he'd heard, Marie assured him she was enjoying sewing some kind of winter scarf in her room. "Come on in, dear. There's no need to be shy. I'm just checking on Maggie. She tells me she's caught the flu!"

Alexander's heart lurched in his throat. He ran a hand down his face and took a deep breath to study his pulse, which had suddenly started thudding erratically.

"Oh, no. Not now!" he hissed. He silently cursed the doctors for being unable to help him treat his mother's ailing condition. She was diagnosed with dementia shortly after Maggie and her husband died in the fire. These episodes were common occurrences in the beginning, but Alexander thought she was beginning to improve... until she started confusing Lizzie with Maggie. Although they shared almost nothing in common in looks, Lizzie had his sister's quiet, gentle demeanor, which may have been enough to fool his mother's mind in its ailing state.

He all but burst into the room, half expecting Lizzie to be angry or, at the very least, thoroughly confused and maybe even a little bit frightened by his mother's response. To his utter amazement and great relief, the girl only smiled indulgently as his mother leaned forward and took the cup of water from the nightstand, tipping it to her lips.

"There you go," Louise assured her, padding her hand and using soothing tones she typically only reserved for the twins on her lucid days. "Don't worry now; just keep drinking that, and you'll be better in no time. Everything's all right now. Mother's here."

Lizzie obediently sipped the water before putting up her hand to signal that she'd had enough. "I'm fine, thank you. I think I'll feel better after a little more rest." She yawned, and Alexander couldn't tell whether it was real or fake. Either way, it gave him the opportunity he needed, and in four quick strides, he was at his mother's side. He placed the pot pie next to the water and held one finger up to signal he'd be back in a moment. Then, he gently lifted his mother by the arm and guided her out of the room. "Come on, now, Ma. dinner is ready, and we should let... Maggie..." the word caught on the lump in his throat, but he managed to push it out to keep up the façade. The last thing he needed right now was for her to get wind of the truth and work herself into a tizzy. "We should let her get some rest," he amended, doing his best to keep his tone level and soft.

The lines around Louise Swanson's eyes crinkled, and she hesitated. Alexander's frown deepened, and to his surprise, Lizzie persuaded his mother to agree. She reached out and squeezed Louise's hand, giving her a warm, genuine smile. "I promise I'll be fine in the morning."

Alexander watched in awe as his mother's stance softened, and her expression melted into tenderness. "Oh, I... all right... If you're sure."

Lizzie nodded and opened her mouth to reply, but Alexander interceded, not wanting to put any more burdens on this person he barely knew than he already had.

"Come along, mother, you heard her. Marie made chicken pot pie, your favorite."

"Oh?" Her faraway expression came alive again. She pushed to a stand from where she had drug the armchair next to the bed and allowed him to guide her toward the door. Just before he could help her over the threshold, though, she cast one more worried look over her shoulder at the girl in the bed, who, to Alexander, was becoming more and more mysterious with each passing moment. "Does she still have a fever?" Louise asked with a note of motherly concern coloring her words.

"Yes," Alexander supplied. "But you heard what she said. She'll feel better in the morning."

That seemed enough to satisfy his mother, at least for now, and he was finally able to lead her downstairs and put her in Marie's hands for dinner.

When he returned to Lizzie's bedroom, he found her still sitting up against the pillows, the plate of pot pie in one hand and a fork in the other. She stabbed another forkful and blew on it for a moment before slipping it into her mouth. She chewed, eyes closed blissfully, and leaned against the pillows in ecstasy.

He smirked as he positioned himself against the doorframe. "Enjoying that, are we?"

Lizzie's eyes popped open, and she swallowed much too quickly, placing the back of her hand over her mouth. "Oh! I'm sorry! I didn't realize anyone else was in here."

Alexander straightened. "Don't worry about it. Marie is a wonderful cook."

Lizzie nodded enthusiastically and gestured to the plate. "She is. I can't remember the last time I've had a homemade meal like this."

That suspicious feeling returned, and Alexander stepped closer. "What do you remember?"

After swallowing another bite, Lizzie shrugged. Her blue eyes were inquisitive, and her bright copper hair stood out against her pale skin. "It's the strangest thing. Everything feels like it's there, but it's all in bits and pieces. I know my name and a few details about my family, but that's all I can say with certainty. I still can't remember how I got here."

Alexander hummed and ran his hand along his beard. "I see. Well, anyway, I just wanted to check on you. And apologize for what happened with my mother. I'm sorry. I had no idea she knew you were here, let alone that she would come to seek you out."

Smiling around another forkful, Lizzie waved a hand and placed the utensil on the half-empty plate. Once she had chewed and swallowed, she looked at him with kind eyes. "It's okay. I understand. Better than you might think. As I said, I don't remember everything, but I remember bits and pieces. Your mother acts a lot like my grandmother did when I was younger. I think they had the same condition..."

Alexander nodded. "Dementia," he echoed.

Not many people had heard the term, let alone know someone afflicted with it. He placed his hand against the bottom bedpost and leaned into it. "I'm sorry your grandmother had to go through that," he said quietly.

Lizzie blew out a long breath, suddenly much more solemn, "Yes, it wasn't a very pleasant time. As I'm sure you can imagine." Her eyes darted back to the door as if she expected Louise to come waltzing in again any minute. "But she always used to say that everything happened for a reason, so maybe this was one of them."

Alexander bristled slightly but did his best not to show it outwardly. He wasn't at all sure he agreed with that theory. To this day, no one knew what had started the fire that killed his sister and brother-in-law, but no matter the cause, he didn't think he would ever see a time when he could justify their deaths with reason. He backed away from the bed a couple of steps, cleared his throat, and brushed his hair behind his ear. "Right, well. Enjoy your dinner." He gestured half-heartedly to the plate. "Marie will be up to check on you again in a while, but in the meantime, holler if you need anything."

For the beefiest of moments, Lizzie looked mildly crestfallen by his sudden gruffness, and a sliver of guilt wheedled its way into his mind. Why did he always have to take such good moments and suck the joy from them with thoughts like that?

Before he could think to apologize, though, the emotion vanished, and he half-wondered if he had imagined it. Instead, Lizzie wore a smile he was almost certain she had forced and said, "I will. And thank you again. For dinner and for, well..." she bit her lip and looked at the window as a shudder rippled through her. "Everything else."

Alexander softened. "Of course. I'll take you into town in the morning. Perhaps the sheriff will know what happened, and we can get this sorted out before that storm rolls in."

She nodded, and Alexander retreated down the stairs.

So much for a quiet start to the holiday season.

Chapter Five

December 19, 1860

Lizzie's sleep started peacefully enough. The fresh, roasted vegetables, tender chicken fragrant herbs, and fresh pastry made for one of the best and most satiating meals in her recent memory. True to Alex's word, Marie came up to check on her about half an hour after he had left. She had brought up a new book, a romance, claiming it was "something to entertain yourself with." She smothered a laugh as she thanked the kindly housekeeper and neighbor. While she didn't hate romance novels, she wasn't a big fan of the 'damsel in distress' lens through which they often portrayed women. She would much rather find a partner to whom she could be considered an equal.

Thankfully, the book also came with a glass of warm milk and honey. While she didn't think she needed any more slumber-inducing food to enjoy a good night's sleep, especially after everything she had gone through today, even if she still couldn't remember what that was – she had to admit the taste of the pot pie took her back to her childhood. When sleep finally claimed her, it was fitful. More images than she could process whirled through her brain.

A beer-bellied man in his early twenties, snoring on a beat-up old couch with a whiskey bottle dangling from his hand. A much kinder-looking older man with a healthy crop of blonde curls and just the slightest beard covering his chin. His kind eyes were hidden under a cowboy hat, but she could tell by the left lines around them that he was a real jolly, fatherly fellow. She guessed by his attire – a well-loved work shirt and a pair of grass-stained trousers – that he was likely a ranch foreman.

A beautiful Palomino horse with the brightest hazel eyes she had ever seen. The closer her dream self crept, the louder the horse whinnied. She reached out to hug it, and it leaned into her touch. When it turned to the side in its stall, Lizzie realized with a strange swell of pride where the animal's glow came from. She was pregnant. And due very soon.

Then finally, terrifyingly, came the pistol. It glistened like newly polished silver on the holster of a man who couldn't have been more than twenty and had the stature and demeanor of a hardened criminal. He had medium-toned skin, eyes so dark they were almost black, and a scar over his left eye. He stomped toward her, one arm outstretched, its fingers curled into a claw-like shape, while the other rested on the pistol.

"Nowhere to run, girl," he snarled. "You know too much of my business, and now you're gonna get exactly what's coming to you."

He unclipped the pistol from its holster.

"Bennie, wait, please! I swear on my life, I won't tell." Lizzie begged. She recognized the name as a match to one of the most-wanted criminals in Wolfspell, and her sobs came faster when she realized it did indeed belong to him.

"Wish I could believe you," the bandit said with an indignant laugh, "but all I got is your word." The safety clicked off. Lizzie willed herself to run with every ounce of energy she had left, but her boots were immovable no matter how hard she tried. Solid and heavy as any boulder, they felt like they were stuck to the ground by wet cement.

He aimed the barrel between her eyes. Lizzie squeezed them shut, praying for a quick and painless end.

When she opened them again, she was no longer staring down the barrel of a pistol. Instead, she rode on the back of a gray mare, the same one she realized that Alexander had said he found her next to lying in the snow. She flicked the reins as hard as possible against the galloping horse's nick, pushing her weight into her heels and leaning forward as far as she could. She craned her neck and squinted through the seemingly endless foliage, unsure of what she was looking for.

"Damnit," Bennie's voice hissed behind her. "Damn you, Russel, you promised me she wouldn't get away again!"

Lizzie's heart nearly stopped, but she mustered the courage to glance over her shoulder for only seconds. Sure enough, the beer-bellied man from earlier now stood next to the wanted bandit, sharing his menacing sneer.

"Don't worry," he said, placing his hand on Bennie's shoulder, even as he made direct eye contact with Lizzie. "If I have anything to say about it, she won't get far."

Lizzie didn't think her throat could get any drier, nor did she realize that she could take even one more ounce of fear coursing through her veins. She shivered as her teeth began to chatter. She could tell the beer-bellied man meant the look to seem menacing, but something else danced there too. A note of...caution ? Regret? Warning? She didn't know. Either way, she understood enough to deduce that whoever he was, he wasn't the leader of whatever operation was causing her to flee for her life.

But even that wasn't what haunted her the most. Rather it was the murderous look in Bennie "Bullettooth" Boyle's eye that she couldn't shake free of. Even after her eyes had shot open a millisecond after she turned forward to face the seemingly endless darkness again, she saw them. Appearing around every dark corner, hiding in every crevice, crouching waiting patiently, or plotting the perfect way to execute her demise. And the worst part? She still didn't even know who she truly was or what she had done to deserve it.

***

Lizzie's eyes flew open. Sweat drenched her sheets despite the chill of the night, and no matter how hard she tried, she couldn't catch her breath. She shifted into a sitting position, glancing left, right, and center. By the grace of God, she saw no sign of Bennie in the room. But that didn't stop his image from haunting her dreams. No matter how many attempts she made to fall back asleep, each was more terror-riddled than the last, rousing her to wake with a thundering heartbeat and ragged breaths. Her fear increased tenfold when she remembered Alex's words. Perhaps the sheriff will know what happened.

No. She may not remember who she was, but now she knew why she had been running. She had the target on her back. Alexander was probably right; the sheriff probably would recognize her instantly. But even if he did, then what? She couldn't tell the truth! Bennie had confirmed that much in her dream, but even if he hadn't, she wouldn't have ended up in this mess if she hadn't felt safe going to the sheriff. And if she couldn't do that, then... She most definitely couldn't go back home, wherever that might be.

The only break throughout her anguished night had been the brief moment of familiarity that had made its way into her nightmare: the older man with blonde curly hair and a kind smile. His name danced on the tip of her tongue, taunting her with her inability to fully recall it. Luckily though, she didn't need a title to feel a connection. She didn't know how or why, but she thought that that man, whoever he was, was one of the few people she thought closest to. And maybe the only person who would be worried about her if she didn't return. Of course, she couldn't; if there was even a chance, her theories might be correct.

But, if she was right, that still left the biggest question.

Come tomorrow morning, where would her loyalties lie?

***

The sun rose way too soon for Lizzie's liking, and she had no choice but to force her body into a stiff cat stretch. She reached across the nightstand and felt for the book Marie had brought her the previous evening. For once, she was grateful for anything that might distract her from the disturbing visions nagging her hazy memory. But just as she flipped open the front cover to the first chapter and began to read, a light rapping sounded on the other side of her door.

"Lizzie?" Alex's voice was soft and soothing as it echoed through the wood, and despite the terror fighting to keep a grip on every fiber of her being, she found herself smiling at the already familiar, comforting sound. "Are you awake?"

She put the book aside, carefully flipped the pillow behind her head, put the book aside, carefully flipped the pillow behind her head, and rearranged the comforter that should be flat against the bed sheets.

"Come in," she called, her voice equally soft when she finally felt everything was as presentable as possible.

The brass door knob turned, and sure enough, Alexander stepped inside. He cradled a breakfast tray in both hands, piled high with a simple meal of toast, over easy eggs, and two crispy strips of overland trout. The sight alone was enough to make her mouth water. She sniffed the air appreciatively, and her grin grew. "That smells delicious." She eyed the plate hungrily, and Alexander blushed.

"Thanks. Marie can't come in today because of all the snow, and this is just about all I know how to cook." He winked as he set the tray down, and she smiled before the weight of what he had said fully registered.

Snow?

A strange mixture of excitement, dread, and relief washed over her as she clambered out from under the covers and scrambled over to throw open the curtains. The world was bathed in an icy sheet of white snowflakes.

"Yep," Alexander assured her. "Looks like that storm came a little earlier than we were hoping. Unfortunately, it also means no one else can go anywhere, so your trip into town will have to wait another day."

Lizzie placed her hand over her mouth to hide her impossibly large, giddy grin. "Oh, that's all right. I'm sure I can – Whoa!"

She lost her footing as the relief over what these circumstances meant untangled in her mind. For at least one more day, she was safe. She tried to take a step toward the bed but teetered as bile rose in her throat.

A strong arm about her waist was the only thing to keep her from crumbling to the floor, and she found herself weak to resist as Alexander scooped her up and gently put her back in bed. "Maybe you should be more careful exerting so much energy. You had a nasty fall yesterday, or so it seemed. Perhaps we should consider this little delay a blessing now that you have one more day to rest and recuperate some of your strength."

"Nonsense. Lizzie smiled despite the sweat that had broken out on her forehead. "You've done so much for me already. If I stay here for another day, the least I can do is pay you back by helping you out a little while Marie isn't here." She swung her legs over the side of the bed and tried again to push up, only to be thwarted by another tender push downward from Alexander's uncharacteristically strong biceps.

"Tell you what. You stay here long enough to eat breakfast, and when you are a little stronger this afternoon, I'll find something you can do." He raised a playful eyebrow and stretched out his hand. "Deal?"

Lizzie rolled her eyes, took his hand and made sure to be level in her eye contact. "Deal."

***

Despite that well-intended promise, it was only a few hours later when Lizzie, – long done with her breakfast and bored – ever so cautiously put one foot in front of the other to venture down the stairs.

When she reached the bottom, she got to a forked corridor. Surveying her options along the way to the left – mostly bedrooms, she guessed – a blocked-off area to the right, and the edge of a loveseat peeking out from which she could only assume was the living room in the center, Lizzie opted to head straight.

It seemed eerily quiet for a house with so many people. Unlike her still foggy memories, this room was dotted with an array of well-loved colorful furniture. A leather sofa sat in the center, flanked by two matching chairs and a square coffee table that had been sanded down and painted to look as if it were the color of a dark oak tree. Across from the coffee table stood a majestic all-brick fireplace framed in a more dark wood, with an inviting roaring fire crackling in the center.

She peered through the second doorway cut out from the far most wall behind the left seat, only to glimpse the modest-sized kitchen. Smiling, she untucked the romance novel she had brought from beneath her arm. She had planned on returning it, but a fresh cup of coffee and a bit of light reading sounded just as good.

As she stepped one careful toe across the threshold into the kitchen, she called out, "Hello?"

"Maggie?" Louise's perplexed voice replied.

Lizzie's stomach dropped, and a wave of sympathy came over her for Alex. His mother was still in one of her states. Glancing in all directions, she saw nary a sign of the ranch owner and decided to jump in. She wasn't sure how much of the Louise she met last night was from the past and how much remained here in the present. Her instinct told her that if the situation was reversed and it was her grandmother who so often appeared lost and confused, she would appreciate any kindness someone would offer. People talked about the strain dementia puts on a person afflicted with it. Still, no one ever mentioned the exhaustion and complicated emotions from watching them go through it.

Despite everything coming back in mismatched pieces, she knew one thing for certain; dealing with such a condition on her own was incredibly hard, and as long as she was here, Lizzie was determined to do whatever she could to help.

So she drew her shoulders back, pasted on a much more enthusiastic smile, rolled her shoulders around, and calmly walked into the kitchen. "Here I am," she replied, purposely avoiding calling herself the name Louise had given her last night. What was it again? Maggie? Whatever it was, she hadn't missed the pained look that crossed Alex's face when she said it, and as much as she knew it was better to play along when his mother was in a state like this, she had no desire to see that expression upon him ever again.

"What are you doing?"

Louise, still clad in her night clothes with her hair sticking up, lit up as she shuffled around and took in Lizzie's familiar form. "Oh, Maggie! There you are, dear! I've been looking for you everywhere!"

Lizzie smiled sheepishly. "Sorry it took me so long. I guess I slept in a little later than I thought."

An easy, heartfelt smile greeted those words. Louise shuffled over and gently cupped her cheek in her hand. Despite herself, Lizzie couldn't keep from leaning into the motherly touch. "No worries, dear, you're here now, and that's what counts."

Lizzie stepped back and smiled. "I am. Now, what are you trying to do?"

Louise turned and glanced around the kitchen; her puckered lips squinted eyes and increased brown returned. "Well, I, um, I was trying to make myself a pot of tea, but I can't seem to remember where we put it." She opened the drawer, then laughed a little when she discovered it was silverware. "I swear it used to be right there, but you know how your brother is, always rearranging things, looking for the best, most efficient way to get things done."

Lizzie froze and swallowed thickly. Was Maggie Alex's sister? What happened to her?

She knew better than to ask, so she shook the thought and sidestepped around the opposite side of the kitchen. "Don't worry. I'll help you look."

As she got to work, opening and closing every drawer and cabinet she could think of, the beginnings of a plan hatched in her mind. She had only been here two days, and it was already feeling more and more like a place she wanted to call home. From the girls' warm-hearted antics to Louise's kind spirit, this family felt like a family worth being a part of. Perhaps, if she could prove herself useful enough, Alexander wouldn't be so quick to send her away.

SALLY M. ROSS

Chapter Six

Other than the snow and wind beating down upon the windows, it was a relatively quiet morning. The twins, of course, were never ones to let him sleep in. Like clockwork, the sound of little feet pitter-pattering across his hardwood floor, which quickly turned into a muted shuffling and stifled giggles between hurried shushes, made Alexander crack one eye open.

Sure enough, two crops of unruly blonde hair peaked over the edge of his bed frame. Emma, whom he could only tell apart because she insisted on sleeping with her hair in a tight French braid, stood on her tippy toes to peer into the bed.

With his pillow over his head, Alexander kept as still as possible. Maybe if he didn't move, they would, for once, actually go back to their room and try again at a decent hour.

But, of course, that didn't happen. It never did.

"Well?" Effie prodded her sister in a whisper so loud their uncle cringed as it echoed through the rafters. "Is he awake?"

The little girl frowned and shrugged her shoulders. "Don't know." Alexander hid a smile as she bent down and crab-walked over to his side of the bed. "Uncle Alex?" She placed her small hand inside his large one that he purposely left hanging off of the bed. "You awake?"

Alexander groaned but wasn't surprised in the least when the charade didn't work. *Well,* he thought, *at least I tried.*

Every time they played this game, he would do whatever he could to get them to stay in bed just a little while longer. Usually, that involved letting them crawl in his sheets instead and a promise of Marie making flapjacks with fresh berries if they at least attempted to go to sleep.

"Too early!" he murmured into the downy fabric of his pillow. "Go back to bed."

Effie scrambled to her sister's side, pouting and pointing resolutely out the window. "Nuh-uh, uncle Alex, we want to go in the snow!"

His eyes popped open. He pushed into a sitting position and followed his niece's finger over to the window. Sure enough, it was frosted over, but even beyond the thin layer of ice, he caught a glimpse of the fat flakes tumbling from thick, fluffy clouds. They poured down like an avalanche and showed no signs of stopping. A harsh wind rattled the window panes.

Alex's frown deepened, and he ran a hand down his face. Despite its severity, he'd really hoped yesterday's storm had just been a warning shot, and Mother Nature would cut him a break long enough to at least get the girl back to her family.

But, of course, like with most things since his sister died, luck never seemed to be on his side.

"Uncle Alex!" Emma whined, pulling lightly on his arm. "Didn't ya hear us? We wanna go play in the snow!"

Looking down at her wide, pleading eyes, Alexander swallowed a chuckle as he extended his arms in a long cat stretch and let out a big yawn. "Not yet, Em." He gestured to the window as he threw off the covers and rubbed the last of the sleep from his eyes. "It's snowing too hard to go out and play now. Maybe when it calms a bit, we can build a snowman."

Emma pouted slightly while Effie clapped her hands. "Yay! Snowman!"

This time, Alexander couldn't stifle a chuckle. The mattress creaked beneath his weight as he pushed himself into a stand

and ambled over to his dresser to search for a change of clothes. After pulling a shirt over his head, he turned back to his nieces. "But first, how about we go get some breakfast?"

As if on cue, Effie's stomach growled, and they dissolved into yet another fit of giggles as they raced out of the room. "Uncle Alex! Come on!"

He shook his head as he pulled on a pair of work pants before scrambling after them. Kids. Where they got so much energy, he would never know.

Half an hour later, the eggs had been cooked, the overland trout had been fried, and four slices of toast were warming on another pan. Once the first two were done, he put two more in, then mounted the stairs to deliver his houseguest her breakfast.

He informed her they wouldn't be able to go into town to see the sheriff after all, and she looked surprisingly relieved to hear that. He ventured back down the stairs and made sure the twins were occupied with crafts and toys before heading out to complete as much work as he could before the snow forced him to slow down.

He started by shoving the walkway, which took him the better part of two hours. Thankfully though, by the time he was back to the porch steps, the once heavy snow had receded to a light trickle. On a hunch, he abandoned his shovel and instead made his way to the stables to saddle up a house.

He mounted a stallion and gingerly rode out the edge of the property, finding the snow much softer than he expected. Once at the tree line where his fields met the gravel road, he dismounted and carefully stepped over to inspect it. Though mostly still covered in an unmarred sheen of snow, it wasn't nearly as slick, compact, or deep as he anticipated. Riding through it wouldn't be easy, but it shouldn't put the horses or riders in any danger. Perhaps Lizzie would be able to get home to her family today after all. With the weather as bad as it had gotten last night, he knew they had to be worried. He couldn't imagine how he would feel if the same thing ever happened to Effie or Emma when they grew older.

Good news in hand, he returned the horse to the stables but kept him tacked up in anticipation of their upcoming journey. As he returned to his initial task of assuring the pathway to the house was as clear and safe as possible, the sky grew darker, and the winds became harsher once again. They licked at the few bare patches of skin on his wrists, neck, and ankles and whipped his long hair against his face so it stuck to the corners of his mouth.

They'd have to move fast if they wanted to beat the next storm.

He mounted the steps and twisted the doorknob. As he stepped inside, he headed for the stairs. He reached the top, landing in ten quick strides, and rapped three times on Lizzie's door.

"Lizzie? Are you there?"

No answer.

"I've got some good news about the snow. I know I said I wouldn't be able to take you to the sheriff until tomorrow, but there's a break in the storm now, and I think—"

Joyful peals of laughter ricocheted through the rafters, cutting him off.

"That's splendid, Emma!"

Alexander furrowed his brow as Lizzie's exuberant praise floated up from the kitchen.

He backtracked down to the third step and peered over the banister. Emma and Effie sat at the table, which, shockingly, was draped with his mother's old lace tablecloth. Small sandwiches cut in triangles sat atop it along with a pot of tea, which to Alexander's shock, Lizzie had poured into his mother's best china. Louise sat at the head of the table. Each of the twins had their own place setting and teacup, and Emma stood to the side of the table with her hand over the lid of the teapot to keep it from slipping off as she gently tipped it toward Lizzie's cup.

At her praise, though, Emma stopped pouring almost immediately, beaming instead.

"My turn, my turn!"

Alexander smothered a laugh as Effie jumped out of her chair and scrambled over, attempting to snatch the teapot from her sister.

"No!" Emma yanked it back and pouted. "I haven't finished pouring all my cups yet!"

Effie stomped her foot. "But that ain't fair! You did three, and I haven't got any!"

Lizzie frowned and let out a long sigh. "Effie, you can have a turn as soon as your sister is done with everyone at the table. Remember what we said about shar—"

She didn't get to finish.

Effie – clearly in no mood to be patient today – waited until her sister wasn't looking and swiftly slipped the pot right out from her hands.

"Ha-ha!"

Her sister whirled around and balled her fists. "Hey! That's mine!" She grabbed onto the spout, and Alexander's hand flew to his mouth as the pot went back and forth.

Once.

Twice.

On the third try, Emma pulled a little too hard, and Alexander braced himself, squeezing his eyes shut in preparation for the air-shattering crash. One heartbeat passed, then two, and the house remained surprisingly quiet. Cautiously, Alexander opened his eyes, only to see Lizzie, barely keeping herself on the edge of her seat, had leaned over and caught the pot by the handle just before it toppled to the floor.

Phew!

He entered the kitchen. "What is going on down here?"

"Uncle Alex!" The twins yelped in unison, and out of the corner of his eye, Alexander saw Lizzie take advantage of their momentary shock to put herself back into an upright position and gently set the thankfully intact teapot back on the center of the table.

She waved her hand nonchalantly in the air and tried to look unbothered, but Alexander didn't miss the way it shook slightly. "Oh, nothing. The girls, your mother, and I were just having a little tea party."

Alexander's lips quivered upward. "I can see that. It sounded like you were having quite the hog-killing time here!"

Effie nodded and pasted on a smile a smidgen too wide. "Uh-huh. Miss. Lizzie's really fun. She was teachin' us how to pour tea like princesses!" She raised her teacup with her pinky out, and Alexander smothered a laugh, raising a brow toward Lizzie.

"Princesses, huh?"

Lizzie's cheeks turned scarlet, and she ducked her head. "I was just trying to think of something to keep them entertained," she muttered.

Alexander nodded. "Looks to me like you did a mighty fine job." His heart skipped a beat as her gaze darted upward to meet his for a fraction of a second. He smiled, then his gaze turned slightly more stern as he fixed it on his nieces. "But I also heard two little girls that might need a reminder about how to share?"

The twins traded slightly stricken looks and shook their heads. "Nuh-uh, Uncle Alex. We are good."

Alexander let his gaze linger a moment before nodding toward his mother. "All right. You guys stay in here with Grandma; I need to talk to Miss Lizzie about something. No picking up the teapot until we get back, and if I hear any more trouble, the both of you will be spending five minutes in the corner. Is that clear?"

The girls nodded vigorously. "We won't, Uncle Alex!" Emma flashed her gap-toothed grin, and his heart melted. "Promise."

"Good." Then he looked at Lizzie and jerked his head slightly toward the living room. His brow furrowed when she swallowed a bit too hard and fisted the skirts of her dress in her left hand, but he shook away the confusion when she rose to her feet and followed him.

Lizzie's steps were stiff and wooden, entering the living room. As he took up one of the loveseats and draped an arm over its back, that suspicious tingle reverberated through his senses once again when she sucked in a breath.

"You can sit down, you know." Alexander shifted and watched with his lips pressed in a thin line as Lizzie took her time gathering her skirt to take a proper seat opposite him.

"You...uh... wanted to talk?" Her words shook, though he could tell by her clenched fists and deliberate speaking pattern she was trying her best to hide it.

Alexander's features remained creased, but he sat up, folding his hands in his lap and offering what he hoped was an easy smile in an attempt to ease the tension. "Yes. Well, first, I should probably thank you for the wonderful job you did cleaning my kitchen."

Lizzie blinked, and Alexander felt the laugh lines around his eyes crinkle. "You didn't really expect me not to notice, did you? When I left, it looked like a dust storm had a hit, and when I came back..." He laughed and ran a hand through his hair. "I don't think I've seen it that clean since before the twins were born."

Lizzie's posture relaxed, and she shrugged. "It was nothing. I was just trying to help. You did so much for me..."

Alexander held up a hand. "And I am so glad to see you're better this morning. Speaking of that, though, I believe I have some good news."

"Oh?" Lizzie sounded curious, but her darting eyes and fidgeting hands made Alexander run his fingers through the scruff of his beard. She looked more nervous than a cat in a room full of rockers and, as hard as he tried, he couldn't for the life of him figure out why.

"Yeah. The storm is letting up a bit, so if we hurry, we might be able to get you into town to see the sheriff today after all."

He'd been expecting such news would completely release any remaining tension coursing through her, but to his surprise, she straightened, swallowed again, and then held up her hand as she shook her head. Something glimmered in her eyes. Terror...trepidation? He wasn't sure. Either way, as her long red hair swung onto her face, he fought the urge to let his protective instincts rise to the surface.

"Oh no... I couldn't possibly... I mean, no wagon could get over the road in this weather."

Alexander studied her. "I wasn't planning on using the wagon. I was just going to lead you there on horseback."

Lizzie's frown deepened. "The snow is far too deep for that. The horses could break their legs."

Alexander scoffed. "And you know this how? Need I remind you which one of us was found unconscious yesterday because she fell off her horse?"

Lizzie's cheeks flamed. "That was an accident!"

Alexander crossed his arms. "You said you couldn't remember anything."

Her face paled slightly, and Alexander stiffened.

What is she hiding?

As quickly as it disappeared, though, her bravado returned. She straightened her posture, and Alexander was left wondering if he only imagined the panic-stricken look that had crossed her face moments before. Still, she said nothing.

Alexander barked out a laugh. "If you're such a rider, why don't you go get your mare from the stables? We can ride in town to see the sheriff, and you can prove it."

Lizzie's eyes widened. She sucked in a breath and opened her mouth. "I, um... you see..." She ran her hand through her hair, and Alexander smirked.

"What's the matter? Afraid of a little competition?"

That caught her attention. She stepped forward, her bright emerald eyes alight with a passionate fire, unlike anything he had ever seen. A strange heat rose in his core, but he did everything he could to push it down.

"Why I never—"

"Uncle Alex, Miss Lizzie! Come look!"

Alexander's eyes ripped toward the kitchen doorway where the twins had come rocketing through.

"What's all of the commotion?" He and Lizzie shared befuddled looks as they followed the scampering children to the window. "Look!" Effie placed one sticky finger on the frosted glass. "More snow!"

He groaned softly and ran a hand down his face. "I see." He put an arm around each of them and then turned to face Lizzie again. "Looks like you won't get to prove me wrong after all," he joked.

Once again, in contrast to what he had expected, Lizzie's posture completely relaxed. Gone was any trace of the state she had worked herself into only a few minutes ago. Instead, she wore a lazy but peaceful and teasing smile. "I suppose not. Well, not yet, at least."

Alexander frowned. Yep, she was definitely hiding something. But what?

A tiny, shy smirk of her own lit up her features as she rested her hands on the windowsill, and Alexander found himself pulled from his perplexing thoughts and resisting the impulse to reach out and touch them.

Butterflies fluttered in his stomach and heart, but he tried to ignore them. They only seemed to grow stronger the closer she moved. He let his eyes wander to her face again, drinking in every beautiful inch of her heart-shaped jawline, lively sparkling eyes, glorious copper hair that flowed down her back like a waterfall, and radiant, easy smile.

Land sakes! Pull yourself together, Alex!

But hard as he tried, he couldn't seem to tear his gaze away from her.

Chapter Seven

December 20, 1860

A seed of guilt had nestled within Lizzie's heart the moment her conscience urged her to think of any plausible excuse she could to avoid using the break in the snow as Alexander had suggested. But after her nightmare... Lizzie nibbled her lip between her teeth as she made quick work of tying back her hair and slipping into the same dress she had worn since she arrived there. Earlier that morning, it had been washed and laid out by the fire to dry.

Once again, she crept into the kitchen, and when she went to the window, the world was bathed in white. Snow continued to bat against the windowpanes and showed no signs of slowing down anytime soon. The kitchen was all but silent. This time, not even Louise ambled about to greet her. She peered out the diamond window carved into the door just off the side of the kitchen but, as expected, found no sign of Marie's wagon. She released a long sigh, surprised when her breath emitted a cloud of fog despite being indoors. She went in search of a blanket in an effort to warm herself, making a point to start the fire in the fireplace as she did. When she returned to the kitchen and still found it empty, she decided to take matters into her own hands.

Using the knowledge she had gained from helping Louise find her tea the other day, Lizzie managed to successfully locate a pot and spatula and the basic ingredients needed for flapjacks. She wasn't much of a cook, especially compared to Marie, but she could make a decent breakfast.

As she added the last of the ingredients to the batter, the uneven shuffling of footsteps behind her caught her attention. She placed the bowl down on the counter and whirled around, a soft smile gracing her lips at the sight of Alex's mother, once again still clad in her nightgown and bonnet, meandering in from the living room.

"Why, Maggie, you're up early." Louise's eyes crinkled and brightened, and Lizzie did her best to mold her features into a swift but genuine smile. She still didn't know why she hadn't been introduced to Alexander's sister, but thought better than her initial impulse to question it. Instead, she turned back to the stove and spooned a handful of batter onto a hot pan.

"Good morning," she said cheerily. She was satisfied to see her flapjack showing tiny air bubbles. "Did you sleep well?"

Louise nodded, then sniffed the air appreciatively and gently placed her hands on either of Lizzie's shoulders as she came up behind her. "My, that smells delicious. What are you making?"

Blushing, Lizzie diverted her attention to picking at the edges of the flapjack. She lifted it with the edge of her spatula and mentally patted herself on the back as it crisped up. "Well, I'm not much of a cook, but seeing as we're fending for ourselves today, I thought I'd try my hand at some flapjacks."

Louise gave a little laugh and squeezed her shoulder. "Nonsense. I remember how much you used to love helping me in the kitchen when you were little. Blackberry jam was always your favorite on flapjacks." She winked and offered an endearing smile. "There was a time when you would refuse to eat them without some kind of fruit preserve on top."

Lizzie returned Louise's smile with a sad one of her own as a pang zapped her heart and a lump rose in her throat. They had a whole life here—a family. And as much as she enjoyed pretending, she'd never truly belong.

"Maggie, dear?"

Lizzie blinked, only for Louise's perplexed frown to further twist the knot of emotions already entangling her insides. On the one hand, she wanted nothing more than to dismiss her horrible nightmare as just that. To move on and fully embrace the name her mother gave her–though she suspected it wasn't her real one. But on the other, even with the seemingly endless questions and imminent danger hanging over her head like a freshly sharpened ax, she couldn't shake the nagging feeling. Wondering who she was might drive her to the edge, but finding out the truth might get her killed. She just wasn't sure which was worse.

"Are you all right?"

Lizzie managed to shake herself free of the tornado of emotions just in time to save her flapjack from burning. "Yes, sorry. I'm fine. Guess I'm just still not feeling as well as I thought."

Louise leaned over and gave her a side hug, gently flipping the spatula from her grasp in the process. "Why don't you go sit down and let me take care of this? After all, you need your rest if you're going to get over that flu."

Lizzie bit her lip and played with the hem of the apron she had found hanging on a hook in the pantry door. She didn't think it would be safe to leave Louise here all on her own, but she did eventually agree to sink into a chair near the counter. It hadn't all been a lie after all, as the moment she sank onto the chair, she felt as if the world tilted on its axis.

It took another twenty minutes for the rest of the flapjacks to finish cooking, and though Lizzie had to step in every once in a while when Louise forgot what she was doing, she had to admit she enjoyed their time together in the kitchen. Louise even managed to teach her how to make that cranberry compote she had been bragging about, and to Lizzie's surprise, it was quite fantastic.

When the twins emerged from their room an hour later quickly followed by Alexander, his eyes nearly bugged out of his head at the sight of the freshly made pile of pancakes on the kitchen table.

"I wondered what kind of trouble you two had gotten yourselves into."

Louise shot him a glare and flicked her dish towel in the air. "It's much too early in the morning and too close to the holidays for you to start bickering. Maggie and I have been up cooking since before the rooster crowed. What have you been doing? Sleeping in, sounder than a bear in hibernation, that's what!"

Alexander whipped around and nearly dropped the coffee cup he had just finished filling at the counter across from the stove. Lizzie winced, realizing he must've heard his mother refer to Lizzie by his sister's name once again.

Emma and Effie, who had already scrambled to their seats and were elbowing each other in an effort to reach the center of the table and spear the top flapjack with their forks first, both stopped. They exchanged confused looks, and Lizzie sucked in a breath. Emma spoke first.

"Um, grandma?" Her voice was small and tentative as if a part of her wondered whether she should be correcting Louise in the first place, but she couldn't help herself. "That's not Mama. That's the pretty girl Uncle Alex rescued from the snow yesterday. Remember? Her name is Li—"

Lizzie's stomach dropped, and Alexander clenched his jaw. Seemingly as one, they turned to face Louise, whose eyes had glazed over, only for the cool, confident, motherly look to be clouded by one of abject confusion.

"What do you mean? Of course, this is Maggie!"

Alexander put his coffee cup down and shuffled to his mother's side, opening his mouth. But he wasn't fast enough.

Effie shook her head. "Nuh-huh, grandma. 'Member, Uncle Alex said—"

Lizzie's heart jumped in her throat. Her eyes went wide, and her hand flew to her heart. She wasn't sure how, but this reaction was all too familiar to her. She remembered her grandmother having the same response whenever she was in the middle of an episode and someone tried to take her out of it before she was ready. The last thing the twins needed to see was the aftermath of reality crashing down around their grandmother. Even if she didn't know what it was, she had a sickening feeling in her gut that whatever had happened to Alex's sister, it hadn't been pleasant.

Frustratingly though, a blip of memory stuck there, and as hard as she tried, she couldn't seem to knock through what it was she had done to bring her grandmother back to her without anything getting out of hand. She sent up a silent prayer of thanks when Alexander stepped in.

"Girls? Why don't you finish your pancakes and then go play for a while?"

Emma pouted. "Aw! Why can't we stay here with you?"

Alexander pressed his lips together but managed to remain calm as he blew out a long breath. "Because your grandma needs to rest, and I have to go check on the animals."

He led his mother down into a chair and served her a plate. She still looked mildly confused, and her inquisitive eyes never left Lizzie's, but she ate quietly and without complaint.

Effie slumped in her seat and moved the last few pieces of her pancake around on her plate with her fork. "Oh-Kay..."

Lizzie swallowed a little laugh as she shrugged and stuffed the last, largest bite of flapjack she could into her mouth. It was amazing how quickly their moods changed.

As if to prove her point, Effie's gaze drifted toward the window and the still cascading snow, and her mischievous blue eyes lighting up. "But when you get back, can we go outside and play in the snow?"

Emma also immediately perked up at this idea, and they both turned to their uncle with the widest, most adorable puppy dog eyes Lizzie had ever seen, complete with their hands clasped in front of their faces and their heads tipped slightly to the side.

"Please, Uncle Alex? Pretty please with sugar on top?" They sang in unison, the sound through the rafters as if part of a church choir.

Alexander went to the door and plopped his hat on his head, taking only a strip of trout from the plate Lizzie had laid out for him in lieu of sitting down. He took a bite and chewed slowly, and Lizzie's heart fluttered as he played along. The more she saw him interact with the girls, the more she wondered why she never saw his wife around. Someone had to have snapped him up already.

A playful smirk danced across his lips as he took his time swallowing, but when he finally did, he looked down at them and smiled. "Maybe. But only if you're good for our guest while I'm gone."

Lizzie almost choked on her bite of flapjack. When she could breathe again, she gave Alexander an incredulous look. "Me?"

"Her?" the twins parroted.

Emma put down her fork. "But she's a stranger."

Lizzie swallowed tightly. They weren't wrong. It had only been a couple of days since she arrived. Still, hearing it so bluntly and out of the mouths of babes, well, she couldn't say it didn't feel like a knife to her heart.

Alexander cleared his throat and looked at her apologetically. She shrugged and tried to appear unfazed.

"Girls, that's not very nice. I know we just met, but remember what we said yesterday? Lizzie's a new friend. She's going to be staying with us until we can get her back to town and find her family. Besides," he took his last bite and put down his napkin, "I'll only be gone for an hour or so." His piercing but curious gray eyes turned on her. Lizzie's fingertips went numb. "You don't mind watching them, do you?"

She took a long sip of her coffee, watching the twins out of the corner of her eye as they ate. Did it really matter if she didn't have much experience with kids? After all, they were only two little girls. How hard could they be?

"Of...of course not," she finally answered, then tried for an easy smile. "After all, it's only an hour, right? We'll be fine. Sure as a gun."

The moment she said it, she saw the twins exchange mischievous smiles out of the corner of her eye. If only she had had the good sense not to confuse optimism with confidence.

Chapter Eight

December 20, 1860

Less than an hour later, Lizzie barely remembered what confidence felt like. Alexander had scarcely left, and the twins were already running her ragged. When Emma had suggested they play hide-and-seek the moment their uncle was out of earshot, Lizzie should have known something was up.

She should've smelled the rat right away, but she scolded herself for being too caught up in her ambition to impress Alexander to notice. Instead, like a fool, she had eagerly agreed to the innocent game of hide-and-seek but insisted on cleaning up the dishes first.

Louise had gone back to her bedroom, saying she was going to start the new book Alexander had brought her when he'd ventured into town the previous week, and, at Lizzie's instruction, the twins had scampered off to their room to get ready for the day.

Sign number two should have been obvious when they bounded down the stairs in identical floral, long-sleeved dresses with matching stockings and their hair twisted into eerily similar, albeit messy, ponytails.

Lizzie had smiled at their matching, gapped-toothed grins and innocent poses as they each clasped their hands together and bounced on the balls of their feet while she dried the last dish.

"All right, girls," she had said after replacing the last pan in the cabinet and wiping down the counters. "Who wants to seek first?"

A final, and, looking back on it, most obvious clue should've been when both twins unanimously voted for her to be the first seeker among them. But Lizzie, knowing as little about entertaining little girls as she did about herself and having used her knowledge from helping Louise to re-create a tea party the previous day, was caught completely unaware. She simply spun around, covered her eyes, and began counting.

"Eight, nine, ten!" She opened her eyes and around the now empty kitchen before cupping her hands around her mouth and calling out, "Ready or not, here I come!"

Soft giggles reached her ears from beneath the stairwell, and Lizzie smirked.

"Hmm, now, where could those little girls have gone?"

She looked under the kitchen table, opened a few cabinets, and made a big deal of wandering into the living room and glancing under the couch and behind every chair before finally moving to the staircase. Each time she switched spots, the giggling got louder, but no one was there.

Huh.

Frowning, she pushed to her feet and stood as still as possible. Soon enough, her curiosity was satisfied when the pitter-pattering of tiny feet and muffled shushing came from the opposite side of the room. She scurried over to the tiny space between the doorway and the hall, but when she crept up and peeked around the alcove, only one pair of bright blue eyes stared back at her. "Emma?" Lizzie questioned as her brows knitted together.

The little girl giggled into her palm and swayed back and forth slightly when she shook her head. "I'm Effie."

Lizzie felt her cheeks flare as she sighed and combed a lock of red hair behind her ear. "I'm sorry, Effie; I guess I haven't been around long enough to tell you girls apart yet."

The little girl laughed harder, and Lizzie caught her eyes drifting just over Lizzie's shoulder, but by the time she turned around once again, the room appeared empty. *So that's how this is going to go, huh?*

She curled a brow in Effie's direction and crossed her arms. "You all think it's fun to play tricks on me, do you?"

Effie didn't reply, but her widening smile was answer enough. "Very well." She bent down to be on the girl's level and said, "Want to make a deal? You tell me where your sister is, and I'll..." She glanced around, looking for a prize that might appeal to a mischievous five-year-old. But just as an idea began to form at the edges of her mind, Effie resolutely declared, "Uh-uh, I ain't telling," and then scampered off again. Momentarily stunned, Lizzie could only stare after her before her sister's taunting reply brought Lizzie back to her senses.

"See, Emma, I told ya she couldn't find us."

Lizzie pressed her lips together and resumed her search. It would take a lot more than a little parlor trick to outsmart her.

The game went on like that for the better part of an hour before the twins finally grew bored, and by the time it was over, they had switched places so many times they'd half convinced her there were six of them rather than two. Only the temptation of lunch was enough to put a stop to their seemingly endless well of energy, and even that didn't last long.

Before Lizzie took her third bite, Emma was already up and out of her chair. She sprinted to smash her nose against the ice-dusted window and let out a happy little squeal. "Look, Effie, the snow stopped!"

"It did?" her fork clattered to her plate as she pushed back her own chair and raced next to her sister. As quickly as she took in the snow, she spun back to Lizzie. "Can we go build a snowman?"

"Please?" Emma chimed in. "Uncle Alex promised we could yesterday, but he didn't take us." Her lip jutted out in a puppy pout so adorable Lizzie couldn't resist even if she wanted to. She smothered a laugh and wrapped her arms around herself as a troubling thought occurred to her. The last time the snow stopped, Alexander threatened to take her to the sheriff. Would he do that again today?

Her eyes flicked toward the door to the back porch as if any minute now, she expected him to come stopping in and demanding she mount her horse for the impending ride. When a whole minute passed, she exhaled deeply and turned her attention back to the eager twins.

"We can go outside," she said, holding up a finger to temper the excitement about to boil over in their expressions. "But only after you change into something much warmer. The snow may have stopped, but it's still winter. We don't want you to catch a chill."

"Aww!" They pouted a little but eventually ran off to do as they were told while Lizzie cleaned the kitchen. As she ventured to her room to ready herself, she glanced to her left toward Louise's door. As she crept closer, she raised her hand to knock, then thought better. It was risky enough for the children to play outside like this. She was pretty sure Alexander would have her head if he found their mother out with them as well. One risk was more than enough for the day.

As she entered and started surveying the wardrobe she had opened in hopes of finding a coat, she stared at it in utter confusion. It contained nothing but clearly a loved girl's clothes. A knock startled her.

"Maggie, dear. What are you doing here?" Louise surveyed the room with glassy eyes. "The twins told me you're taking them out to play, but you can't possibly go in the snow dressed like that!" She clicked her tongue, and Lizzie blushed.

"I wasn't. I was only looking for a coat."

Louise frowned. "Well, you won't find it in there."

Lizzie tilted her head to the side, but Louise disappeared down the hall before she could ask anything further. When she returned, she was carrying a beautiful burgundy coat with black fur trim along the collar and the edges of the sleeves.

"Here you go. This should suit you much better." When she walked over and handed it to Lizzie, her breath caught in her throat as she reached out to finger the delicate fabric.

"No. I... I couldn't possibly..." An iron fist squeezed her heart. She didn't know how, but somewhere deep inside her, she knew this coat originally belonged to Louise's daughter, and the thought of slipping it on, even when she didn't really have any other choice, made her feel like the cat who had been caught eating the canary.

"Of course, you can, dear. They're your clothes, after all. Take anything you like."

Lizzie bit her lip as the inviting fabric slipped through her fingers. Louise looked so full of joy, so sincere. *I can't refuse now. That'll only confuse her more.*

"O-okay," she finally agreed, turning around and pulling her hair back to allow the other woman to drape the coat over her shoulders. As she shimmied into the sleeves, she couldn't deny how wonderful the velvety material felt against her skin.

"Thank you," she muttered, her eyes growing misty when she faced Louise again. She could barely remember the last time someone cared for her like this.

The woman smiled and gently patted her hand. "Anything for you, Maggie."

The lump in Lizzie's throat grew again as Alex's mother gently shoved her out the door. "Now, don't let those girls run you too ragged. And have fun."

Lizzie grinned and pulled the collar tighter against her neck. "Don't worry. We will!"

***

Mere minutes later, the twins were bundled up from head to toe, with cold snow soaking through their tattered gloves as they put all their weight into rolling the biggest snowball possible for the bottom of the snowman.

"Like this, Miss Lizzie?"

Beaming, she clapped her hands and grinned. "Perfect. Terrific job, girls. Now, I'll do the body, and you can work on the head."

They went their separate ways, though they remained in each other's line of sight. As she put the finishing touches on the snowman's midsection, she called over her shoulder. "Girls? How's it going?"

There was no response.

Lizzie froze. "Girls?" if she listened closely enough, she could almost swear she heard whispering, but it was lost in the howling sounds of the rustling wind. Glancing up at the sky, which was growing darker every minute, she frowned.

Looks like the snow is back. I better get them inside.

"Girls?" she spun around and looked out over the expansive yard. "Girls, where are you? It's time to go insi–" Her words were cut short as something cold and wet smacked her squarely in the center of her face.

"Pah!" She spat the snow from her mouth and glared in the direction it came from — only to spot the two mischievous troublemakers giggling just a few feet away, behind one of the many heavy pine trees that flank the house. "Gotcha!" Emma stuck out her tongue as her sister tossed another snowball in the air. This time, Lizzie jumped out of the way with seconds to spare.

"Oh, so you want to play it that way, do you?"

The girls exchanged looks as though they weren't sure if they should be scared or entertained by her tone. Lizzie smirked as she bent down to scoop up a snowball of her own. "There may be two of you, but don't count me out just yet!" she raised it over her head, and the twins shrieked with joyous laughter as they took off sprinting in either direction. Lizzie ran after the one closest to her, gently scooping her up to her chest and trapping the snowball down the back of her coat.

Effie shrieked. "Ah, no! S-so cold!"

Lizzie snickered. "Won't be playing any more tricks on me today, will you??"

Effie squeaked again and shook the rest of the snow out of her stockings. Lizzie smiled.

"Good. Now, let's go get your sister."

They continued on like that, with Lizzie switching teams periodically until it eventually dissolved into an all-out snow war in which no one knew who was winning or losing but neither did they care. Soon, they rounded the east side of the house, and everyone stopped short.

Lizzie nearly tumbled into the twins, bracing herself on one of either of their shoulders as they stared up at the charred remains of a house section Lizzie had not seen before.

"Wh-What is this place?" she whispered hesitantly. Another chill swept through her, but this time it had nothing to do with the cold. Something about this place seemed... haunted, solemn – like a grave site with no markers. She dreaded the question the moment it slipped from her lips, but her stomach dropped, and her heart crawled into her throat when the twins exchanged an all too familiar look; one she knew well. It was the same look she had in her eyes whenever she talked about her father.

Emma clasped her sister's hand before looking up at Lizzie and stating plainly, "Mommy and Daddy died there last year. In a big fire right before Christmas."

Lizzie's hand flew to her mouth, and her eyes welled up. "Good Lord."

Effie nodded. "We miss 'em all the time, but 'specially around now. Uncle Alexander doesn't celebrate Christmas 'cause of that. Think it makes him too sad."

Lizzie swallowed tightly. Her heart went out to Alex. She could only imagine losing a sibling or what the three little girls in front of her must be going through. Another piece of her memory came back to her at that moment, and she realized who the man standing next to Bennie "Bullettooth"

Boyle had been in her dream. Russel... who was he to her, a sibling? An old friend? An enemy?

Before she could think of something to say, a familiar set of heavy footfalls jogged up behind them.

"What are you all doing out here?"

Alexander's stern, chiseled features came into view despite the misty fog surrounding the house, and he looked anything but satisfied with their chosen method of entertainment. Instinctively, the girls cuddled themselves closer to Lizzie, and she stepped out in front of them just slightly.

"Don't be cross with them. This isn't their fault. We were having a snowball fight, and I chased the girls over here. I'm sorry if we disturbed it. They didn't mean any harm..." She paused, but when he refused to say anything, she couldn't hold it any longer. "They, they told me what happened... to your sister." She reached out to place a hand on his arm, but he turned away, and she finished... "I... I know there's nothing I can say, but for whatever it's worth, I'm truly sorry."

Alexander's hardened features softened by the slightest fraction. He pressed his lips together and scratched the back of his neck but refused to meet her eyes... "Yeah, well... what would you know about it anyway? You've only just arrived here, and you can't even remember who you are. You don't know nothin' about us or what we've been through."

Lizzie's temper momentarily flared, and she fisted her hands at her sides. She wanted to prove him wrong, to remind him he didn't know about her either, and he had no business telling her she didn't know about grief. But, hard as he tried to hide it, she saw right through his livid exterior. Hurt was written all over his face, and what wasn't managed to seep through in his tone. So, in spite of her every impulse telling her otherwise, she held her tongue. "I... I'm sorry. I was only–"

"It doesn't matter what you were trying to do. You still brought the girls out into the cold. They might get sick. There's no way for a doctor to get here with all the snow. After what you went through, is that really what you want?"

Lizzie bristled and straightened. "No, of course not! I only meant to find a way to entertain them; I didn't think..."

Alexander snorted. "And that's exactly your problem."

Lizzie scowled.

He gestured to the girls and then the house. "Take them inside and get them warmed up. I still have a little more work to do, but I'll be in shortly."

Again, Lizzie held her tongue, herding the girls toward the porch. "Come on. You heard your uncle."

Emma looked up curiously. "But why do we have to go inside? We weren't doing anything wrong."

Lizzie sighed and looked back at Alexander's receding form. "I know, I know. Maybe we can have another one later. Right now, we need to do what your uncle said and head inside."

As she stepped into the foyer, though, she couldn't help but look back, following Alexander until the fog obstructed him from sight. She would never have guessed he was bearing such a burden all on his own. As much as she was glad to be taking shelter in the safety of the Swanson estate for at least one more night, she also found herself wishing there was more that she could do to help him before she had to leave. But what?

Chapter Nine

December 20, 1860

Alexander paid little mind to the numbing feeling overtaking his limbs as he trudged back out toward the fields to continue unloading feed from the wagon. What was she thinking? Letting the girls play outside in this weather? Bringing them back to a tragedy he had hoped they couldn't remember? The nerve of that girl!

Why did I ever trust him to look after the twins in the first place? I barely know her!

Even if asked, he wasn't sure he could explain himself. Taking her in had made sense when it happened, but now? Now he was more determined than ever to do what he should've done in the first place: get her into town and give her to the sheriff as quickly as possible. After all, they were running a ranch, not a boarding house.

Alexander pressed his lips together. He had half a mind to turn back and take her immediately in his wagon, but the wind picked up again, whipping the brim of his hat down against his forehead. Unfortunately, the sheer force of will wouldn't be enough to get them into town safely. The storm showed no signs of passing soon, so they would have to brave the elements sooner or later, but if the wind continued to pick up like this, it would be far too dangerous tonight.

***

As Alexander marched up the steps to his front porch a few hours later, sweat beaded on his forehead despite the cold. He thought he had been used to running the ranch with only a small crew, but he hadn't realized until today how different that was from doing completely on his own. After a long day of hauling feed sacks, fixing broken barn siding that had been damaged from the storm, and doing everything he could to make sure all his livestock were warm and dry, exhaustion seeped into his bones deeper than any cold.

He still stood by what he had said earlier: it had been downright irresponsible for Lizzie to bring Emma and Effie out into the cold in such bitter weather. But a tiny part of him, one so small he didn't even want to acknowledge it at first, was grateful he hadn't sent her back as quickly as he had initially wished. He couldn't imagine doing all of this and managing his mother and the twins at the same time.

The cheerful sound of a crackling fire greeted him as he stepped into the flare, and his aching muscles immediately relaxed at its warmth. He sank gratefully into the armchair and held out his hands, as the twins turned away from their game of jacks and scrambled to him.

"Uncle Alex, Uncle Alex, you're back!"

He smiled through his drowsiness and gestured for them to climb on his lap. They both happily obliged. Emma and Effie nodded toward Lizzie enthusiastically. "We were bored, so she brought us out here to play!"

Alexander scowled in Lizzie's direction. "Did she?"

Eliza winced. "We built a snowman and had a snowball fight and played hide and seek and made biscuits for lunch and, and—"

Alexander laughed a tense laugh as he ruffled her hair, but there was no mistaking his pensive glare, which he shot at her when he thought the twins weren't looking. "Sounds like you had a really eventful day."

Lizzie swallowed. "You could say that."

Alexander's happy façade dropped when one of them sneezed. "Why did you think taking them to play out in the snow had ever been a good idea?"

He gave the girls a friendly pet on their bottoms and told them to go inside. "Miss Lizzie and I will be right there, I just want to talk to her about a few grown-up things, and I don't want you to catch a cold."

Lizzie winced, and the twins hesitated but moved to do what they were told as soon as Lizzie nodded. "Go on," she said. "I'll be right behind you. Or so she hoped.

Once they were out of it, Alexander turned to face, his hands on his hips. "I know the twins are a lot to handle, but after everything you've been through, I would hope you've all people would know not to bring them outside in such bitter weather." He tapped his foot impatiently as he waited for an explanation.

"Listen, Alex, I know you don't want them to get sick; I don't either, believe me. That's why I insisted we all get to know that before we ever even thought about coming out here. They had just been cooped up for so long, and they had so much energy. Toys and books were not going to be enough today."

Alexander sighed. "I suppose I should just be glad you are still in one piece, and no one has gotten sick. Yet."

Lizzie perked up a little. Maybe she was going to get out of this unscathed after all.

"But if you ever do such a thing again, I will no longer trust you enough to leave you with the twins unsupervised. You're still a stranger on my ranch, so as much as they may like you, as long as you are under my roof, my rules come first. Is that understood?

Lizzie nodded and hung her head, feeling thoroughly chastised. "Perfectly clear."

Alexander nodded. "Good. Now let's go inside before we freeze."

***

After dinner and baths, Alexander led the twins off to bed. As he tucked the comforter beneath Emma and Effie's chins and they snuggled deeper into the sheets, Emma asked, "Uncle Alex, is Lizzie gonna be our new aunt?"

Alexander choked as he inhaled, then did a double take when he caught his breath. "Wh-What?" *Where in the world did they get an idea like that?* Another coughing fit hit him, and he whacked himself on the chest to dislodge the block. "Em, what are you talking about?"

Emma bit her lip and suddenly found a piece of fuzz sticking up from one of the threads on the sheets very interesting, so Effie spoke up instead.

"Well, she's really pretty and super nice, and she likes to play with us,"

"Yeah. Emma piped up again, seeming to have regained some of her courage. "And you've been less sad since she came. Well, sometimes."

Alex's jaw dropped, and his eyes nearly bugged out of his head. He stayed there for a solid minute. *Lord, what am I meant to say to that?* He missed his sister and brother-in-law every second of every day, but he always tried his hardest not to let his own emotions filter into the way he raised his nieces.

But they're grieving too, a small voice reminded him. He wanted nothing more than to shield them from everything.

They had been through more than enough already. But he supposed, no matter what, he couldn't shield them from that. Still, his pride was more than a little wounded, as was his ego. Until now, he hadn't known he was so easy to read. In fact, most people he used to know, including Nate and Marie, would say the opposite. So how come his nieces, in all their child-like wisdom, could see through all the walls no matter how many he put up?

"Girls," he said slowly after giving himself a second to gather his bearings. "I'm glad you like Lizzie. I do too. But she's only been here a couple days. She cannot be your new aunt."

Emma tilted her head. "But why not? What about all the princesses and princes in fairy tales? They fall in love!"

Alexander frowned and ran a hand down his face. Maybe he shouldn't have let them read so many of those. "Em, those are just stories. Like playing pretend."

Her eyes went wide. "So, they're not real?"

Again Alexander shook his head. "Love is real, but it doesn't happen like it happened in the stories. It takes more than just a few days."

Or at least, it's supposed to. Then again, no matter how hard he tried, Alexander couldn't seem to banish Lizzie's caring, empathetic expression from his mind.

Effie shrugged. "So, ask her to stay longer!"

Alexander mustered a smile and tweaked her nose. "I can't do that either, munchkin. She has a family to go back to, remember? As soon as the snow stops, we're going to take her into town so she can go back home."

107

And it will be like none of this ever happened. Alexander wasn't sure if he felt relieved or saddened by that. On the one hand, his mother and nieces had been happier than he had seen them in a long time. And so had he. But on the other... She was a complete stranger. He couldn't just let her waltz in here and uproot their entire lives!

"But—"

"No more buts." He put a gentle finger to Emma's lips and put out the oil lamp on their night table. "It's time for all good little girls to get snug in their beds and go to sleep." They quieted, and Alexander kissed each of them lightly on the forehead before getting up. "Good night, girls; I love you."

"Uncle Alex?"

He stopped. "Yes, Effie?"

"Will you tell us a story? One about mommy when she was a little girl?"

Alexander exhaled but shifted his weight and sat back down on the bed. His heart ached every time he thought of his sister, but he knew whatever he was feeling, her children had to be feeling it tenfold. "Of course. Now, which one should I tell." He snapped his fingers. "Oh! I know. Did I ever tell you about the time your mama was seven years old, just a little bit older than you, and we almost had to call the fire marshal because she climbed so high up in a tree to rescue a cat?"

The girls giggled in the darkness.

"Nuh-uh," Effie replied.

"Tell us!" Emma chimed.

Alexander smiled. "All right. So one spring..." But he didn't get more than a few sentences in before...

Crack!

The sound was so loud and echoing that all three of them jumped. Effie's lower lip trembled.

"Wh-what was that?"

Alexander scowled and glanced at the window. Snow was tumbling down again, thick and unrelenting. He shuddered at the thought of the damage it would do overnight. "Don't worry, girls," he said softly, "Everything's gonna be all right. I'm just gonna go outside and see where that noise was. I'll be right back, I promise."

They whimpered but didn't protest, and Alexander didn't have time to wait any longer. He grabbed his coat and dashed to the front door. The snow was heavy and constant but, thankfully, hadn't gotten bad enough that he wasn't able to see. He glanced around and at first saw nothing suspicious until his eyes landed on the stable. A giant branch at least twice as tall and three times as wide as he had cracked away from a nearby oak and landed with a thud in the middle of the roof of the stable. The center was nearly dead caved in, and the terrified whining of the horses echoed over the ranch.

Alexander cursed under his breath and readied himself to charge inside just as another voice called out to him. "Alex? what happened?"

He walked down the porch steps, spun around, and squinted. "Lizzie?" The blurry figure nodded.

"I heard cracking, so I— Heavens!"

She gasped as her eyes landed on the stable's collapsed roof.

Alexander pressed his lips together. "Yeah, you can say that again. Have to get the horses out of there and into the barn before the whole thing caves in on 'em." He stuffed his hands in his pocket. "Thing is, I don't know if I'll be able to do it on my own."

Her pensive expression grew determined. "Then let me help."

Alexander gaped at her. "Wait a minute, you know how to wrangle a—" but she was off and running for the building before he could finish.

***

"There you go, fella, easy now."

Alexander watched in bewildered amazement as Lizzie's calm demeanor, soothing voice, and gentle pets helped soothe even the most terrified of his stallions as they led them out of the stables and into the safety of the barn. When she led the last one, Storm, a wild gray and black spotted animal, over the threshold, he shoved the barn door shut with a metallic clang and spun to face her.

"I reckon that's the last of them."

She smiled, and his heart jumped again. "Seems like."

"You know, you're really good with horses. Did ya... did you grow up on a ranch too?" He rubbed his gloved hands together in an effort to stay warm, and his brow creased when a flicker of recognition followed by the smallest twinge of terror passed over her features before she glanced away.

"Oh, I, uh... I don't remember."

Alexander frowned. "Lizzie?"

"It's late. I mean early. I mean," she flushed and combed a piece of hair behind her ear. "We really should be getting back to bed. Good night, Alex."

The sound of his name on her tongue was enough to set hundreds of butterflies the flight in his stomach, but even then, he couldn't quite detract from the inkling of suspicion slowly growing somewhere inside him. He didn't know how or when it started happening, but as she passed by him without another word, he began to wonder if Lizzie knew more about her past than she was letting on.

Chapter Ten

December 21, 1860

When Eliza awoke the next day, her whole body was thrumming with restless energy. Like the day before, she was the first one awake and downstairs, but unlike yesterday morning, this time didn't feel relaxing and serene, but far too quiet and empty. She did her best to occupy herself with chores, brewing a fresh pot of coffee, cleaning every speck of dust from the kitchen, and making sure everyone's clothes were put away. Well, everyone's except for Alex. She didn't get the sense that he would appreciate her invading his privacy without his consent.

At first, she wasn't sure what had caused the feeling of discontent. She couldn't really explain it, but ever since she had woken up—not much of a task, considering the leftover energy from the impromptu horse rescue in the middle of the previous night had left her tossing and turning until dawn— she felt like she wanted nothing more than to crawl out of her own skin.

Slowly, memories of her former life were beginning to trickle back, and she didn't at all enjoy the picture they were painting. The only bright spot was that she seemed to own a ranch, but even that wasn't much of a comfort, considering her only living family was a brother to whom she wasn't very close. And he seemed to have somehow managed to catch himself up with one of the town's most devious criminals. For reasons Lizzie still did not understand, had deduced that must have placed a target on their backs.

Each new revelation only heightened her desire to prove herself useful. It had become about so much more now than simply caring for her own safety. She had missed this. The family, the closeness, the feeling that they would do anything for each other. It was something she had only the vaguest inkling of. This was the first time she could really recall experiencing it in person, even though she felt as if most of her big questions about her past had been answered as the holes in her memory kept slowly sewing themselves together.

Louise was like her grandmother come alive again, and the girls–though she still felt somewhat helpless when it came to taking care of them–she found their antics more charming and entertaining than she did annoying. After learning of the tragedy they faced, losing not one but both of their parents at an age they would soon be barely able to remember... Well, she wanted to do everything she could to make the remainder of their holiday special. And Alex... well, Alexander was a mystery. An intriguing, infuriating, perplexing mystery with a heart that she suspected was bigger than anyone knew. She hoped she would have time to witness him reveal it before she had to leave them.

As she finished putting away the twins' toys, she heard someone moving inside the house and expected Louise to be the first one to greet her. Instead, her teeth chattered as a frigid breeze whistled through the back door as she poured herself her first cup of coffee. She hugged her arms around her and looked up as Alexander stepped in, shaking snow from his shoulders and stamping it from his boots. A few flakes were even caught in his beard, and his normally tan cheeks were chapped and red from the cold.

"Oh, Alex." She pushed herself up from where she'd taken a seat at the kitchen table and scurried over to the kettle to pour him a steaming mug of his own. When she returned with it and held it out, he wrapped his hand around it gratefully. As their fingers brushed, she pulled back slightly when a shiver ran up her arm. A small gasp escaped, and she pulled it back, rubbing furiously at the goosebumps that had risen on her skin. If anything, though, at least she could blame the cold. "You're up early."

He smiled and blew some of the steam away before joining her at the table. "I needed that." He took a long sip, and when he swallowed, his eyebrows rose, and curiosity swam in his gray-blue eyes.

She shrugged, keeping her gaze on the wooden grooves on the table and tracing one of them with her finger. "What?"

"You remembered how I like it?"

Heat crept up Lizzie's neck, and she tried to bite back a smile. He had told her two mornings ago when he found her puttering in the kitchen while he was on his way to feed the cows. She couldn't tell if he was simply shocked or genuinely touched, but either way, she couldn't help the pride that swelled in her chest. "I may not remember much about my past, but I can still make new memories."

Alexander's features softened slightly. "Well, thank you. I can't remember the last time anyone made coffee for me."

Lizzie grinned and reached across the table but stopped just short of taking his free hand, which was now resting on the table. "I can do a lot more than make coffee, you know. If you'd let me, I'd like to help with the stable. How are the horses?"

Alexander ran a hand through his hair. "They were okay. Better than they were last night, anyway. But they can't stay in the barn forever. Luckily, I think I have enough supplies here to fix the roof. At least temporarily until we can get back into town."

"Let me help," she insisted again. Alexander held up his hand and shook his head.

"No need. There's a lot to do, but I think I can handle this one on my own. I've got Nathan too. If you really want to be useful, though, do me a favor and entertain the girls and my mother again today. But no going outside, any of you. The weather is much too unpredictable now, and I don't want any of you getting a chill or getting hurt on the ice."

Lizzie had half a mind to argue but swallowed the impulse. With Christmas so close, this home, the first one she found herself looking forward to in longer than almost as far back as she could remember, was the last thing she wanted to lose. Besides, if yesterday was any indication, Alexander had a point. If he was going to fix the roof before anything got worse, there was no way he could do that and mind his nieces and his mother all at once.

"All right," she conceded, draining the last of the coffee from her own mug. "I'll watch them. If you change your mind, let me know."

Alexander's lip quivered and his mouth puckered as though he had just swallowed something sour. If she didn't know any better, she could swear he was trying not to laugh. "Don't worry, I will."

***

Eliza nearly slumped into the loveseat. She propped her elbows against either armrest and put her head in her hands. She thought yesterday had been an adjustment, but compared to this morning? Their little game of hide and seek felt like a friendly jaunt to the Christmas market.

"Marius? Marius, where are you?" For what seemed like the umpteenth time that morning, Louise wandered into the living room from her bedroom and lightly squeezed Lizzie's shoulder. "Maggie, have you seen your father? I can't find him anywhere!"

Guilt twisted Eliza's insides, and her heart went out to the woman as she forced herself to smile. She hadn't been lying to Alexander earlier when she said she knew the best way to get Louise through one of her episodes was to play along, but when it was something like this, something where she knew deep in her heart that her husband nor her daughter would ever be coming back, well, to say that was difficult would be an understatement.

Nevertheless, she stood firm in her convictions and forced a smile. "He'll be home soon; he's just out making sure all the animals are safe after the storm."

Louise laughed. "Oh dear, this is nothing. Why... Did I ever tell you about the blizzard that hit us when I was a little girl? That storm felt like it went on forever, and by the time it finally stopped, the whole town looked like it had been caught in an avalanche."

Eliza shook her head and sat back as Louise took a seat on the opposite couch. As far as she could recall, this was the biggest storm she had seen in her eighteen years, but she knew it was far from the worst, and she thought it might be interesting to hear the first-hand account from someone who was actually there.

Louise smiled and sat up a little straighter, folding her hands in her lap. "Well, it all started when I was about eight or nine or so. Not too much older than the twins are now. The papers had been speculating that this winter would be harsh. All the farmers spent weeks buying extra feed, lamps, fixing the fences, the creaky stable doors, and everything else they could find on the ranch, to be as prepared as possible. They checked their animals' health and made sure they had adequate blankets and supplies if needed. They even gathered extra kindling and coal to be sure they had extra for the fires. No matter what they did, no one could've predicted it. The papers have been saying there would be a lot of snow, but nobody accounted for the ice."

"My papa didn't believe what everyone was saying. Called the papers hogwash and refused to do anything until Mama insisted they take it seriously. But even then, he made a fuss about it. See, we hadn't had a hard winter in a long time, and they predicted one every year back then, so Papa thought this would be just like every other time."

"They would say it would get real bad, they would say everyone should stay inside and bring their animals into a shelter when they could, and then we'd wake up the next morning, and nothing would be different. In fact, he was crooked as a Virginia fence about the whole thing, as my mama would say. He was so determined to prove the weather report wrong that one night, he made the mistake of letting the cattle roam the pasture, thinking we had at least one more day until the storm hit us big."

Eliza gasped and leaned forward a bit. "Oh no! What happened?"

Louise got that far-away look in her eye again, as if she were traveling back to her girlhood and could see it all unfolding right in front of her. "Well, for one thing, the blizzard rolled in hard. When we woke up, the snow was so thick we could barely see our hands in front of our faces, and Papa couldn't even step outside without falling into a hole that was waist-deep.

Eliza put a hand to her mouth and shivered. "But what about the animals?"

Louise's expression grew grim. "They got the worst of it, I'm afraid. See, with the storm also came a giant stampede of cattle huntin' for food. The problem was it was the middle of the night, and no one had any extra to gift. One herd broke straight to our fence and ate all the saplings Mama had planted that spring."

Eliza shook her head. "Oh no!"

Louise nodded. "Aye. Papa said they must've been bawlin' for food, but by the time he and the ranch hands went to check on 'em, the whole new herd that had been smart enough to take a shelter in the barn after the fence broke had nearly frozen to death.

Eliza crossed her legs beneath her and leaned a little further forward. "Good grief, that's awful."

Louise hummed and glanced out the window. "Mm. I sure hope this storm ain't as bad as that one. It's already lasted so long!"

Eliza reached over and gently squeezed Mrs. Swanson's hand. "It'll be all right, Louise. It's almost Christmas, and I'm sure the storm will pass soon." She pushed herself to her feet. "Tell you what, why don't you go back to your room and finish that book you were reading, and I'll tell you the minute Alexander gets back."

Louise smiled. "Thank you, dear, I'd like that."

Satisfied that Louise was occupied, Lizzie ventured toward the twins' room, only to find them fighting over one of their dolls.

"Emma! You said I could be the princess," Effie whined, reaching across her sister's lap for the rag doll Emma was clearly holding out of Effie's reach.

"You have to rescue her from the tower first!"

Effie pouted. "I'm tired of playin' rescue, though. Wanna play Rapunzel." She lunged for the doll again, knocking her sister over in the process.

"Oof! You pushed me!"

"Girls!" Eliza clapped once, and both of them turned to look at her. "What is going on here?"

"Effie keeps trying to take my doll!" Emma whined.

"Am not!" Effie defended, "I was 'posed to have a turn!"

Eliza exhaled with a long sigh and stepped between them before things could get any more heated. "I think it's time both of you take a break from toys. Why don't you go draw a picture?"

Emma rolled her eyes and crossed her arms. "Don't wanna draw!"

"Yeah," her sister piped in. "Drawing's boring."

Eliza giggled in spite of herself and shook her head. "All right. Well, why don't we..." she racked her brain When suddenly another long-forgotten memory came into focus. Baking cookies in the kitchen with her father. It was something they did every year before the holidays, and she always loved it.

"Oh! I have an idea!" A smile spread across her face as she gestured for the girls to get up. "Follow me."

"Where are we goin', Miss Lizzie?" asked Effie.

"What's your idea?"

"It's a surprise," Eliza replied, doing her best to keep her own excitement out of her words. She didn't want to get their hopes up if she couldn't find what she was looking for, but since Alexander's mother still lived with them, they had to have an old cookbook somewhere around here. "Just follow me, and you'll find out soon."

The girls scampered along after her, and they hurried into the kitchen. Eliza searched as fast as she could, banging around the doors and cabinets.

"Whatcha looking for?" Effie asked.

Eliza ignored her, squatting down to check the cover under the sink. "I know I saw one... ah-ha!" She bounced, holding the leather-bound recipe book over her head like a trophy. "Girls, how would you like to make some Christmas cookies?"

Emma and Effie's eyes sparkled, and they let out adorable little squeaks as they bounced on the tips of their toes. "Yay, cookies!"

Eliza beamed. Relief washed over her. She was hoping for that reaction. "Great. So let's get going. Emma, I'm going to read the recipe to you, and you find all the ingredients we need, okay? Effie, why don't you look for the baking pan and the mixing bowls?"

They got to work straight away. To Eliza's surprise, they made a rather good team as they continued sifting, scooping, and stirring ingredients until the smells of cinnamon, ginger, and nutmeg permeated the house.

"Mmm." Emma sniffed the air while Eliza flipped the dough onto the floured counter and began rolling it out so they could cut it into little gingerbread men. "Smells good!"

Her sister nodded. "I don't 'member ever trying gingerbread before, do you, Em?"

Emma shook her head. "Nuh-uh."

"Don't be silly!"

Everyone turned toward the door from the living room. "Grandma!" the girls squealed.

120

"Louise!" Eliza grinned. "I hope we didn't disturb you too much."

Alex's mother shook his hand and gently swatted the girl's hands away when they tried to hug her with sticky, flower-covered fingers. "Not at all. I was thrilled to sense those smells again. You know, girls, your mother used to love making gingerbread around Christmas. And thumbprint cookies and shortbread." She laughed, lost once again in a memory, but Eliza was just relieved that this time at least, it seemed to be a happy one. "She would make every kind of cookie she could get her hands on."

Eliza's brows shot up, and she exchanged surprised looks with Alexander, but he shrugged and mouthed, *Go with it.* Eliza tried her hardest to regain her composure, but it really was remarkable seeing Louise so lucid.

Emma wrinkled her nose. "Really? Don't 'member that."

Louise smiled sadly and cupped her granddaughter's cheek. "You were probably too little, but I promise you Christmas time was the best time of year when it came to your mother and her delicious baking."

Eliza handed the gingerbread man cookie cutter to Effie and let her step out twelve imprints in the dough. "Well, I don't know if mine will be as good..."

"Of course, they will, dear. They were your recipe, after all."

Liopened her mouth, then blinked and snapped it shut, realizing she still must think of her as her daughter. "Right, well, we better get these in the oven. Don't want them to still be baking when your uncle gets home."

An hour later, everyone gathered around the now clean counter once again to decorate their own ginger person.

"Let's make ours look like twins," suggested Effie. Her sister readily agreed and reached for the bowl of icing

"Let's do the hair first."

Eliza watched contentedly as she continued piping her own decorations, which, to no intended plan of her own, was beginning to look remarkably similar to the twins' handsome uncle. Maybe she could bring a little bit of Christmas magic back to this family after all.

Chapter Eleven

The sun hung low in the sky when Alexander finally managed to climb down from the roof and head back toward the house. When he nudged the front door open, the soothing scents of ginger, cinnamon, and a twinge of smoke mixed with a blend of spices he couldn't quite name tickled his scenes. He froze, feeling for a moment as if he finally understood what happened to his mother whenever she was lost in one of her episodes. If he didn't know any better, he could swear he was back in time. Two years ago, to be exact. The closer he ventured to the kitchen, the more he expected to see his sister standing at the counter, happily baking away as she babbled with her then-toddler twins.

Instead, what he did find sent a bittersweet paying of gratitude through his heart. The twins were indeed baking, but it was Lizzie, not Maggie, who was at the helm of it all. Eight gingerbread men still sat on a cooling rack near the stove, but four of them had been taken off to be decorated. He tried to be as quiet as possible as he crept closer, not wanting to disturb the holiday tradition for his nieces. But the squelch of his boots against the floor caught their attention, as it always did. They dropped their piping bags, successfully spewing buttercream all over the counter in the process, and raced to his side.

"Uncle Alex, Uncle Alex, look what we made!" Effie held up two gingerbread girls with globs of icing down the sides of their faces and big dots for the eyes. It was clear they were meant to be the twins. Her sister, however, held out a single gingerbread man with a large beard, and his big red mouth turned downward.

"What a beautiful job, girls. But," he pointed to the gingerbread man and looked at them inquisitively, "Who is this?"

123

"It's you, Uncle Alex," Emma supplied.

He blinked and leaned back a bit, stuffing his hands in his pockets. "Me?"

Effie nodded. "Yeah, you've been sad, so we made your cookie sad too."

"Oh." A pit grew in Alex's stomach. The twins had obviously put a lot of work into their creation, and they really were good, especially for five-year-olds. But still, was that really what they thought of him? He worked hard. He kept a roof over their heads and food on the table, and he always felt bad whenever he would snap at them, but he hated to think that they always saw him as the same, sad picture. "Thank you, girls." He took the cookie and promptly bit off the head of the sad gingerbread man, determined now more than ever to change their minds.

"Mm, delicious." He offered them a cheeky grin.

Emma laughed, and Effie pursed her lips.

"You ain't supposed to eat his head first."

"Oops." Alexander just shrugged, and when a musical giggle reached his ears, he caught Lizzie's eyes and strode over. "They really are delicious, you know," he whispers softly.

Lizzie blushed as she played with the lace hem on her apron. "Thank you."

He nodded. "You're welcome. There's just..."

She cocked her head. "What?"

"You've got a little..." The confused look in her eyes increased as he pointed at his own cheeks. Without thinking, he rolled his eyes and softly brushed the pad of his thumb over the spot of flour dusting her cheek. Her skin was smooth and soft, and he couldn't help but lean in a bit when she shivered pleasantly beneath his touch. Their eyes met, and his breath caught in his throat. How had he never noticed before? Her eyes were a bright, emerald green, filled with empathy, curiosity, and something else. A tenacious, fighting spirit that made his heart race and his walls crumble just a little easier every time they met his. His thumb lingered on her cheeks, and, to his delight, she raised her hand to entangle it in the back of his longer hair. Neither moved an inch closer, but Alexander could do nothing to stop the wave of wanton rushing through him.

Until a throat cleared behind them. "Well, well, congratulations to the happy couple. How long have you two been husband and wife?"

Alexander's mouth dropped open, and both of them sprang apart before facing his mother. Lizzie hurried to correct her. "Oh, I, um… we're not…"

Louise's smile turned mischievous, and she winked. "Maybe not yet. But mark my words, dear, one day soon—"

"All right, Ma," Alexander swiftly stepped between them and tried to ignore the sound of his nieces giggling in the background. "I think it's time for you to take your medicine now. Why don't we go find it?" As he led her from the room, he caught Lizzie's eyes again, and this time her whole face bloomed scarlet.

***

Dinner that night was a simple affair. Stew made from soft leftover vegetables and beef broth and the last of the bread with a small ration of butter. Louise retired early, claiming it had been a long day, and it wasn't too long after that when Alexander suggested his nieces do the same.

"Aw! But Uncle Al-ex," Effie stomped her little foot for emphasis and drew her features into a sour pout. "We ain't tired yet."

Alexander crossed his arms and raised a brow. "I don't remember asking if you were tired, Effie-Belle. Now, march. Or else, no cookies after dinner tomorrow."

Effie whimpered but looked down. "Oh-kay!"

As they trotted up the stairs, he saw that Lizzie couldn't help but smile as she finished rinsing the dishes.

He shook his head as he paddled after them. They may be little minxes, but they sure were cute.

Thirty minutes later, he descended the stairs alone, only to find Lizzie threading two needles between some yarn beside the still crackling fire. He walked over and leaned casually against her chair. "What are you doing?"

Eliza smiled up at him as she set the knitting needles on her lap. "Oh, your mother gave me her old sewing kit since she never uses it anymore. It looked like she had started a scarf in her room but never got around to finishing it."

Ah, so that explained the project.

"I thought I would try to help her out—Ow!"

Alexander frowned. "What happened?"

She shook her head and lifted her left hand, then gently sucked out her pointer finger. "Oh, nothing." When she pulled it away from her mouth, Alexander noticed a small red spot on the tip. "I just pricked myself."

"Oh!" He leaped up almost immediately. "Let me help with that." He strode into the kitchen and rummaged through the drawers for a roll of bandages.

Eliza smiled and covered her mouth with her hand as he held them triumphantly over his head as if they were a trophy. "Got them."

Eliza gave him a tight-lipped smile as she shook her head. "Really, it's not that bad. I just pricked my finger."

"Still." He sat across from her and held out his hand. Her cheeks flushed red as she obediently gave him her injured finger. "Better safe than sorry." He tore off a small piece of the bandage and wrapped it around the tip of her finger. "There."

Eliza admired his handiwork and looked at him again. "You really didn't have to do that."

"Sure I did. It was the least I could do after what you did for the twins earlier today." This time, Alexander made sure to let his smile reach his eyes.

"That was... very kind of you," he managed around the lump in his throat. He couldn't remember the last time anyone had done anything like that for him or his family. "Almost as kind as making those gingerbread cookies this afternoon. I'm sure it wasn't an easy task with the twins underfoot."

Lizzie laughed but grinned as she shrugged. "It was fun. Besides, Louise said Maggie..." she looked away, and Alexander's heart bounced. "Um, your sister... She said she used to make them all the time when the twins were little."

Alexander hummed and scratched the back of his neck. "She did. She..." He swallowed again. "Maggie loved Christmas. Baking, caroling, decorating.... All of it. She always lit up a room, but around the holidays... Most kids think it comes from Saint Nicholas, but for me... It was always her who brought the real Christmas magic."

"Well..." Lizzie fiddled with the ball of yarn attached to the unfinished scarf. "I know it's not the same, but... I'm glad I was able to recreate that for them."

Alexander blinked away a wet film over his eyes. "After she died..." he trailed off, then shrugged. "Well, the magic died with her, I guess."

Lizzie frowned and reached out to take his hand. Against his better judgment, he let her. "Maybe you can find it again."

Alexander shook his head. "I've tried, but...." He looked away but found himself gripping her hand tighter. "No matter what I do, it's never the same."

"It'll always be different," she said softly, running her thumb over the top of his hand in soothing circles. "But I bet she'd rather that than see you and the girls grieve forever. Christmas is supposed to be a time for togetherness, and I hope I'm not overstepping here, but that seems to me like you all need that more than ever."

Guilt stabbed at Alexander's heart. "Maybe," he mused. She had a point, much as he hated to admit it. With the twins being so young, how could he possibly create new memories for them without completely erasing the old ones? He didn't worry just for them, but for him too.

Alexander contemplated that thought as he tossed and turned into the wee hours of the morning.

Chapter Twelve

December 24, 1860

Despite Alex's bitter and miserly attitude around the holiday, when Christmas Eve arrived a few days later, Eliza was more determined than ever to bring some Christmas magic back to the ranch. She knew one day soon she would have to admit the truth and return to her real life, but in his short time with the Swanson family, she had come to care for each and every one of them even though she was staying there under false pretenses. She shuddered to think what they, and especially Alex, would make of her when they found out the truth, even if she wasn't one hundred percent certain of it yet herself, but she tried not to think about it as she wandered down the stairs. Today was Christmas Eve. It should be happy, joyous, and above all, magical. Everything else could wait.

When she made her way into the sitting room, she found the fire in the fireplace had long been extinguished and promptly went in search of a match to relight it.

That done, she prepared a simple breakfast of eggs, toast, and some dried fruit. The Swansons surprised her once again when the twins were the first ones down the stairs.

"Good morning, girls!" Eliza said brightly. "I've made you some breakfast." She gestured at their two smaller plates on the table, and the girls sprinted toward it.

"Mm, looks good." Emma's eyes widened as she caught sight of the steaming mug next to her plate. Is that..." She peered over the top of the cup, and a wide, cheesy smile appeared on her face as she looked at Lizzie. "You made hot cocoa?"

Eliza laughed and shook her head as she sat down. "Well, It is Christmas Eve, after all, so I figured we all deserved a little treat." She took a tentative sip of her own and sent up a silent prayer when she discovered it was neither too bitter nor sugary, as she had to use the last rations of cocoa to make it.

Effie yipped and swallowed a giant gulp of hers, moving the mug away to reveal a very chocolatey mustache. "Mmm, yummy! Thanks, Miss Lizzie,"

"You're welcome, Effie." She handed the little girl a napkin, stifling a laugh when she immediately wiped her face.

"It's really good," Emma added, cupping her own glass in both hands and gingerly bringing it to her lips.

"I'm glad." Eliza took a bite of her food and chewed slowly before continuing. "And I have one more surprise. I was hoping after breakfast, you girls may help me gather some holly, mistletoe, pinecones, and cranberries so we can decorate the sitting room. What do you think?"

Effie was already nodding enthusiastically before Eliza even finished her sentence, but her sister looked a little more skeptical.

"But we don't celebrate Christmas, 'member? Uncle Alex might get mad."

Eliza reached over to brush a blonde lock that had fallen into Emma's eye out of the way.

"Nonsense, it's Christmas! And no matter what, no house should be without decorations on Christmas."

"Yeah, Em," Effie said, "Don't you want the house to look pretty, like when Mama and Daddy was here?"

Eliza tensed slightly as she saw the little girl's face, but to her surprise, her trepidation, while not gone, was now mixed with something closer to excitement. Emma peaked up at Eliza again and fiddled with her hands. "You sure Uncle Alex won't be mad?"

Eliza nodded. She couldn't promise he'd be happy with her idea, but after their heart-to-heart by the fire, she highly doubted he would find it in his heart to be cross with his nieces. Especially today. Besides, who could say no to such sweet faces? "Promise. And if I'm wrong, you just leave your uncle to me, all right? I'll make sure you don't get in trouble."

Emma smiled. "Okay. If you're sure, then... Let's go." In a flash, the little girl had hopped off her chair and raced toward the door. "Come on, come on! If we want it to be a surprise, we have to get going before Uncle Alex wakes up."

Eliza chuckled. "Oh, so it's a surprise now?" She shook he head, amazed at how fast their attitudes could change. Then again, from what she knew, these girls were nothing if not resilient.

Emma rolled her eyes. "Of course! If we decorate the house, it can be like our Christmas present for him."

"Awesome!" Effie cheered, raising her fist.

Eliza beamed. She hadn't thought of decorations being equivalent to a present; she had truly just wanted to make the house more festive. But if Emma considered it a gift, who was she to argue. "That's a great idea, Emma." She walked over and squeezed the younger girl's shoulder as she gathered their hats, gloves, and scarves. "Let's go."

It took them about half an hour to gather everything they needed from the fallen trees, and Eliza had to creep down to the root cellar for the cranberries, but braving the cold was more than worth it when she caught sight of the twins' sparkling eyes and beaming smiles at the sight of the decorated sitting room, complete with candles perched among the pine garlands and ready to be lit once the sun went down.

Alexander ventured down the stairs precisely a few minutes after everyone had finished hanging the last string of popcorn and nestling the last sprig of holly between the bare spots in the garland hanging from the stair banister and fireplace and draped across every piece of furniture they could find. The twins, wanting the full effect, crouched between the couch and the window and repeatedly shushed each other in between fits of laughter.

The distinctive sound of pine needles rustling between his fingers, followed by a perplexed "What on earth?" in Alex's smooth baritone, told all three of them he would soon be within spitting distance of their minor holiday miracle. The twins grew uncharacteristically stilled as his heavy footfalls crept closer and closer to the hiding spot. When he finally entered the living room, Eliza stood in the middle of it, hands folded and watching with bated breath as he took in the sight.

"Good grace!" He exclaimed with a laugh. "What... what happened in here?"

It was then the twins decided to make their grand entrance, springing out from behind the couch and spreading their arms wide as they yelled, "Surprise!" before bounding over the cushions and hugging either one of their uncle's legs.

He laughed and bent down, hefting both of them up in one arm apiece. "Morning, munchkins," he said and then gave each a kiss on the forehead. "What's all this about?"

"Lizzie thought it would be fun to decorate for Christmas," Emma explained, her gaze fliting briefly to Eliza's. She smiled reassuringly and gestured for Emma to continue. She opened her mouth but couldn't think of anything else to say, so her sister jumped in.

"And it was." Her already huge smile grew even bigger, which, seconds ago, Eliza would've sworn was impossible. "Do you like it?"

For the first time, Eliza witnessed Alexander Swanson completely at a loss for words as he spun in a circle and took everything in. His smile was watery and unsteady, and unshed tears swam in his eyes, but he blinked them back and hugged his nieces tighter to his chest. "I love it."

Eliza looked, and a sudden wave of adoration swept through her as he buried his face in their hair.

Effie was the first to wriggle away. "Uncle Alex, you're squishing me!"

A wet laugh emitted from his throat, and Alexander loosened his grip to let her climb down. "Oops, sorry, munchkin."

Soon enough, her sister seemed to want to be free of the hug as well, and with both of his hands free, he strode to the center of the room and clasped Eliza's hands. When they touched again, that same shiver of pleasure rippled through her, more intense this time than it had been before.

"You did all this?" His wonderment was clear in his tone, but Eliza found herself utterly unable to do anything but nod.

Alexander barked out a laugh and ran a hand through his hair, which was still mussed and sticking up. And yet, somehow, Eliza still found it utterly irresistible. So much so that she had to keep herself from doing the very same thing.

"But how?"

Eliza shrugged and nibbled on her lower lip, casting her eyes downward for the smallest of moments. "Well, I did have a little help." She gestured to the twins, and Emma scampered over.

"Yeah, Uncle Alex! Lizzie made Effie and me into Christmas elves."

Her uncle smiled and ruffled her hair. "And you did your jobs wonderfully. We already had a white Christmas, but thanks to you guys, now we'll have a pretty one too."

Emma nodded before running off happily. As she did so, Alexander caught Eliza's eye again and mouthed *Thank you.*

She responded with only a soft smile, but her heart glowed. Maybe the great Alexander Swanson had been wrong about something after all. There was some Christmas magic left in him still.

***

Dinner that night was a simple but satisfying meal of venison, mince pies, roasted veggies, biscuits, and roast potatoes. Everyone ate their fill, and the conversation flowed easily. Even Louise seemed in higher spirits. She was thankfully no longer fretting over the whereabouts of her husband but still muttering phrases like, "Maggie, pass the gravy," and "Girls, listen to your mother." Eliza didn't miss the way Alexander flinched every time, and halfway through the meal, Eliza reached over from her spot on his left, and gently placed a hand on his arm.

He jumped a bit at the sudden contact, and his mouth dropped open momentarily, but he didn't pull away. Eliza counted her blessings as she sucked in her breath, her heart thundering in her chest at the victory, however small it was.

When the last plate had been licked clean, Eliza smiled, replaced her cloth napkin on the table, and pushed back her chair. "Anyone have room for dessert?"

As expected, the children's already contented expressions lit up at the notion. Eliza swallowed her laughter at their excitement as they nearly toppled their chairs backward, raising their hands.

"Me, me!" Effie squealed.

"Do we have any more gingerbread men?"

"Not this time, Emma," Eliza replied. "But I think I'll have something you'll like even better." She disappeared into the kitchen and returned moments later with an ornate serving platter holding a dome-shaped pastry speckled with currants and cranberries and topped with orange slices and holly.

Eliza's neck and cheeks grew hot, and everyone *oohed* and *ahhed* over the creation. She set it down on the table and gathered her skirts to take her seat. Alexander let out an audible gasp.

"Christmas pudding!" the twins chorused.

Louise looked just as gob smacked. "Why, Maggie, you haven't made this in years!"

Eliza smiled. "I found the recipe in the cookbook we used for the gingerbread the other day and thought it would be a nice surprise." She dropped her voice to a whisper. "I hope I got it right."

Alex's sent her a grin that made her feel ten feet tall. "I'm sure it'll be delicious," he said as he began carving and serving the treat. "But how did you find the time?"

Eliza simply winked. "I have my ways."

Everyone dug in, and to Eliza's relief, both Alexander and Louise said the pudding was the best they'd had in a long time. After everything was cleaned up, they returned to the sitting room, where Louise wandered to the bookshelf. She pulled out an old, well-loved leather-bound volume and turned the cover, reading *A Christmas Carol,* toward Alex.

I know it's been a long time," she said, ambling over and clasping his hand. "But would you consider it?

Alexander sighed but looked around. Eliza was surprised to find herself just as enraptured by the request as the twins. She had heard of the book but had never gotten the chance to read it herself. For some reason, she had a sneaking suspicion Alex's deep voice would fit the narration perfectly.

Three chapters in, she discovered she was right, but the chime of the clock striking ten cut him off mid-sentence.

He finished the paragraph, then promptly closed the book and smiled down at his nieces, who, though they were trying their best to hide it, were nodding off with their heads in their hands. Alexander placed the book on the coffee table and pushed to his feet.

"All right, girls, bedtime." He tried to scoop them up as he had done earlier that day, but Emma squirmed away, and her sister followed suit.

"No! Please, Uncle Alex, can't we stay up just a little bit longer?"

Alexander sighed and ran a hand down his face. "Effie-Belle, Emma, come on now, you know the rules."

"But it's Christmas!" Emma protested. She leaped out of his reach once again and scurried off down the hall.

A frown creased Alex's features, but he followed her at a slow pace. "Em, please don't do this. Not tonight. We've had such a good day, and you're old enough now not to be causing such a—"

But before he could finish, she reappeared, cradling a small velvet box. Eliza watched Alexander grow stiff, and her heart dropped.

"Where did you get that?"

***

Emma just giggled, and he was left with no other choice than to follow her back to the sitting room.

"Emma?" Her grandmother asked. "What you got there, sweetie?"

Emma unfastened the clasps on the box to reveal a beautifully polished, gleaming silver harmonica. The occupants of the room seemed to gasp as one, and Alexander did his best not to cringe as his niece spun to face him.

"If we hafta go to bed," she bargained. "Can we at least hear a song first?"

"Great idea, Emma!" Effie chirped.

"Oh, that would be wonderful," his mother added, wiping a stray tear from her eye. "It's been so long since you played."

Alexander sighed but still held up his hand and tried to back away. "Girls, I really don't think—"

"Please, Uncle Alex?" Emma begged, clasping her hands together and fixing him with the biggest puppy eyes. "Pretty, pretty please, with sugar on top?"

Her sister soon joined in, but Alexander was determined to stand firm. He hadn't played since the year before Maggie died, and, as wonderful as all of them may have been, there had been enough changes for one Christmas Eve. "Girls, I love that you want to hear me play, but it's so late and—"

"I...wouldn't mind hearing a song." Eliza said, her eyes glittering in the candlelight.

Her mouth ran dry as he accepted the instrument and plopped into a seat.

"Okay," he agreed breathily. "But just one."

One soon turned into so many he lost count, but Alexander no longer cared. Eliza did her best not to let his mind wander from the current moment as she watched his nieces link arms and dance around in a circle in the center of the room. She sat just behind them, laughing and clapping. After a few tunes, even his mother joined in for a dance, though she was quickly tuckered out.

When his lips were so dry he could no longer play a note, Alexander finally declared the festivities had ended. Eliza turned to him with a wide smile.

"That was wonderful! Thank you so much! For tonight and for everything else. This is the best Christmas Eve I've known in a long time."

Alexander blinked. "You remember other Christmases?"

***

Oh no.

What now? Eliza knew the fantasy couldn't last forever, but she couldn't spoil it tonight. Everything had been so good, and it was the happiest she had seen Alexander since she arrived. Her eyes blushed, her brow furrowed, and her spine stiffened as she struggled to form the words. "Well, you see... I uh..."

"Caroling time!" Effie's shriek nearly burst her ears, but before Alexander could ask anything further, Effie started belting *Silent Night* in a high, shrill soprano. Emma soon joined in, followed by his mother, and the question was forgotten as they sang merrily into the night.

Chapter Thirteen

On Christmas morning, Alexander Swanson awoke feeling like a new man. He couldn't quite put his finger on the reason, but somehow, he felt more like himself that morning than he had since his sister died. He did his best to take his morning routine slow, not wanting to spoil the feeling of serenity that had washed over the house. As he thrust open the curtains, he grinned. There was not a cloud in sight, and the freshly fallen snow, though its layers were probably still deep enough to reach up to his midriff, sparkled in the early morning sunlight.

He had an extra skip in his step as he made his way down the stairs and wasn't at all surprised to find the twins sitting eagerly in front of the fireplace and ogling the pile of presents sitting there. Lizzie and his mother sat there as well, each of them occupying an armchair with steaming mugs of coffee in their hands. A third mug sat untouched on the coffee table, and he picked it up, tossing a grateful smile toward his house guest before starting with his nieces and bending down to give them each a one-armed hug.

"Mornin' girls!" he said softly as he kissed each of them on their cheek. "Merry Christmas!"

"Merry Christmas, Uncle Alex," they chorused, returning the gesture and peppering either side of his face with their own wet, slobbery kisses.

Out of the corner of his eye, Alexander caught sight of Lizzie with a hand cupped over her mouth, trying to stifle her giggling despite her shaking shoulders.

He tossed her a playful smirk even as his cheeks burned. "They always do this on the holidays."

Lizzie swallowed and tried again to hide her mirth but was unsuccessful. "Oh, don't mind me," she sputtered through her laughter. Actually, I find it quite adorable."

"Sure, you do."

Well then, let's see how funny you find it when you're the one being kissed. For a split second, his gaze flickered over to a sprig of mistletoe hanging above the fireplace. Seeming to move of their own accord, his feet wandered over to it, but his conscious mind caught up with him a millisecond before he could grab it.

His eyes darted back to Lizzie again, and while he could no longer deny he found her very beautiful, he constantly reminded himself that she had a real home, a real family to return to. If he let himself run away with such wild thoughts, there was no telling what he might do. So instead, he tore his gaze away and focused on his nieces.

"Come on, munchkins. Let's go see what we can whip up for breakfast, and then we can come back here and open presents."

To his surprise, and the twins' palpable delight, though, no one had to wait that long. The moment his mother was up and roaming, he passed around plates of freshly fried bear signs he had made on a whim. Lizzie passed around three mismatched boxes, though they were all tied with an elegant ribbon.

"Lizzie..." Alexander put his box down and took a moment to fully drink her in, as well as to marvel at the kindness of the gesture. "You didn't have to get us anything."

Lizzie simply shrugged as she placed her napkin in her lap. "Of course I did. You all have been so kind to me over the past few days. A small gift was the least I could do."

For a moment, everyone simply sat there. Alexander knew he couldn't speak for all of his family, but judging by the bewildered looks on all of their faces, he would venture to guess they were all equally bewildered by the kindness. "Th-thank you," Alexander finally muttered.

Lizzie smiled and nibbled on her bottom lip. "You're quite welcome. Now," She flailed her hands around theatrically and gestured for them to open the lids. "What are you waiting for, Christmas?"

Peals of laughter echoed around the table, but eventually, every one of them carefully untied the bow and set the ribbon aside. The twins allowed their uncle to help, and the apparent delight on their faces when they discovered the new pair of patchwork gloves at the bottom of each box made Alexander's heart soar.

He held up his own pair, which were red, gold, and white, and stared in wonderment at the tight needlework. Then he remembered how Lizzie had explained his mother had given her the old sewing kit and gaped at her. "Wait a minute, did you make these?"

She blushed, and her beautiful copper hair fell over her face, but she nodded. "Let's just say your mother's scarf wasn't the only thing I was working on these last few days."

Alexander gave a rueful chuckle. "I should say not."

He ran his fingers over the fabric and relished the soft texture. "The cross stitching is amazing. I can't believe you did all of this in only a couple of days."

Again, she only shrugged.

Just then, Alexander felt a tug on his sleeve and looked down to see Effie holding out her own pair of brand-new gloves. "Uncle Alex, Uncle Alex, look at mine. Aren't they pretty?"

Alexander nodded. "They sure are. What do you say to Miss Lizzie?"

A single prodding was enough for the little girl who launched herself straight into Lizzie's arms. And though surprised, the girl caught her with ease and grace the likes of which Alexander had never seen. "Thank you, Miss Lizzie, for my nice present. Merry Christmas." She wrapped her arms around the other girl's waist, and Lizzie hugged her back just as tightly. Alexander felt his eyes grow misty, but he pushed the threatening tears away.

When the girls had disentangled themselves, Effie turned toward him. "Uncle Alex, when can I use my new present?"

He chuckled and wiped his mouth with a napkin. "I don't know, Effie-Belle; how about now?"

Effie brightened immediately. "Really? You mean, we can go outside?"

Alexander nodded again. "Now that the snow has stopped, I was thinking we could take the day, and all go down to the lake to do some sledding. What do you think?"

"Sledding?" the girls echoed.

Again, their uncle nodded, and they both shrieked with laughter. "Yeah! This is the best Christmas ever!"

Alexander continued to laugh and exchanged a rueful look with Lizzie across the table. "I'll take it they want to go then?"

Lizzie grinned and pushed back from her seat. "I'll pack up some sandwiches for lunch so we can stay out longer."

***

Once everyone was sufficiently clothed for the weather, they ventured out toward the lake. Even Louise had decided to come, and Lizzie wasted no time looping her arm through his mother's every time they approached an icy patch. "Here, hold on to me. That way, you won't slip."

Each time Lizzie guided her, his mother seemed to grow more and more at ease receiving help. On the one hand, Alexander was beyond thrilled that she had found a kindred spirit in the girl, but on the other, it made him dread the day when he would have to explain to her why Lizzie was no longer there. He only hoped that she would have had at least one or two lucid days by then. That way, he wouldn't have to reexplain his sister's death all over again.

By popular request, and because everyone else insisted that they didn't mind, Emma and Effie went first, each of them taking turns and sometimes going down both at once as Alexander trudged back and forth, up and down the hill with the sled trailing behind him. He pulled them through the snow, listening to their joyful laughter as though hearing it for the first time. They laughed and played for most of the morning, and by the time the sun reached its midday peak, everyone's cheeks were pink from the cold.

As Emma pushed her sister down the slippery slope for what seemed like the one-hundredth time that day, Alexander leaned back and pressed his hands into the freshly fallen snow. He tilted his head toward the sun and closed his eyes, letting the warmth bathe his already chapped skin.

"Penny for your thoughts?"

He opened his eyes to find Lizzie staring down at him, and his lips eased into a slight smile. "Oh, nothing. I was just..." He trailed off and watched the twins for a moment longer, delighting in their carelessness as their shouts of joy echoed through the pine trees. "I just wish Maggie could be here to see this. To see them. They're growing up so fast, and I..." He looked away. "I don't know. Holidays are just hard without her. I'm beginning to think they always will be."

Lizzie sighed but sunk down into the snow next to him, placing a gentle hand on his shoulder. "She may not be here physically," she said, cautiousness evident in her words. He gave her a small nod, though, and she continued. "But I would be willing to bet almost anything that, wherever she is now, she's smiling."

Alexander sighed. "I hope so."

"I know so," she said, and the words carried a surprising amount of power behind them. "You're doing a wonderful job with them. I know I've only been here a few days, but I can already see that much."

His gaze met hers again, and this time, he couldn't even try to hide his unshed tears. "Thank you." He sniffed. "I think... I think I really needed to hear that. Sometimes I feel like no matter what I do, it will never be enough."

"Just be there for them," Lizzie insisted, reaching over to clasp his hand. "Trust me. I may not remember much about my past or my family, but I know one thing for sure. What a child needs, more than anything, is just love. Pure, unconditional love. And no matter what, you, Alexander, have it in spades."

"Thanks." The word was shy but sincere. If only it were that easy to believe.

A silence settled between them, and Alexander shifted. It wasn't exactly tense, but it wasn't insignificant either. Though she had only been here a few days, Alexander couldn't deny how his heart skipped a beat every time Lizzie drew nearer. He glanced down at her hand, which she had set just inches away from his on the snowflake-peppered blue blanket they had draped over the ground. His fingers twitched, and he dared to scoot his own hand a little bit closer, but reigned himself in just before their fingers touched.

What are you doing? You can't get close to her! You said yourself she has to go back home!

Alexander frowned and started to pull his hand back. No matter that, he couldn't remember when he had felt as alive and joyful as he did with Lizzie in the house. Her curious green eyes, always searching for the next adventure, never failed to make his heart feel like it was tap dancing in his chest. He hadn't seen his mother or nieces this happy since before Maggie had died. True as all of that may have been, it was also utterly irrelevant. Lizzie had a family, a real family, waiting for her. And—

A serendipitous breeze interrupted his brooding.

Lizzie gasped beside him, and when he turned to face her, he couldn't help the sly smile that turned up the corners of his lips. The snow had begun to fall again, though this time, it was light. Snowflakes danced around her, catching themselves in her beautiful copper hair and bathing her in almost ethereal winter light – it was as if she were the Spirit of Christmas itself come to life. The breeze whipped her hair against her cheek, and when she reached down to brush it out of the way, her eyes lingered for a second too long on Alexander's hand, which was still outstretched.

For the briefest of seconds, their eyes met, and Alexander could've sworn he saw a tinge of desire swimming in Lizzie's exuberant gaze. It vanished as quickly as he blinked, though her cheeks remained slightly pinker than they had been only a moment ago.

Alexander raised a brow and bent one knee to drape his arm over it. "Cold?"

"Hmm?" She turned to him and flashed one of those bashful yet mischievous smiles but never failed to make his mouth dry and his knees grow weak. "Oh, no, I—" A shiver rippled through her, and she reluctantly removed her hand from where it still sat next to Alexander's to tug her coat a little tighter around her shoulders.

Alexander knew that was due to his hesitation and mentally kicked himself for it.

You fool! He mentally chided himself. *She wanted you to hold her hand! Why didn't you just do it?*

Of course, he came up with excuses, but none of them seemed as intelligent now as they had a few minutes ago. Shaking the thoughts away, he pushed to his feet and held out his hand. okay, so he missed one moment. That didn't mean he couldn't make another.

"I know something that might warm you up."

Lizzie cocked her head and eyed him suspiciously. "Do you now?"

He winked and offered a little smirk. "Do you trust me?"

In lieu of answering, Lizzie allowed him to help her to her feet, and he felt as if he was walking on air as they descended the hill toward his destination.

"Where are we going?" Lizzie laughed.

The smile stretched his cheeks until he thought they might snap as he turned back to face her. "You'll see!"

They walked a little further until he stopped promptly at the sled. Its once sparkling red paint was now well-loved, and the seats appeared empty as the reigns fluttered lightly in the winter breeze.

Concern passed over Eliza's face, and she glanced around. "Where are the girls?"

Laughter rumbled in Alexander's chest as he pointed down the hill. Eliza followed his finger and smiled when their giggling bubbled up from the nearby snowbank. Emma and Effie were helping each other make snow angels.

"Looks like they found something else to do." He winked and bent down, picking up the reins and turning slightly to hold them out in Eliza's direction. "All the more reason to take a turn of your own."

Eliza sputtered another laugh and shook her head, putting her hands up. "Who, me?" She backed away a few steps. "Oh, no. I couldn't possibly—"

"Of course you can!" Alexander smiled wider until he felt his dimples protruding on his cheeks.

Lizzie bit her bottom lip to hide her smile, and Alexander's heart jumped. Her cheeks pinkened a little further, and this time he couldn't quite convince himself it was all from the cold. He held out the reins once again and shook them a little.

"Come on. It's fun! No better way to get into the Christmas spirit."

She took a few tentative steps forward but still eyed the sled as if it were a wild bronco that was going to buck her the moment she tried to sit on its back. Alexander's lips puckered, but hard as he tried, he still wasn't quite able to quell the tiny smirk that made its way onto his lips. "What's the matter? he chided gently. "Scared?"

She searched his face for the briefest of moments, and Alexander's eyes softened.

"What?" Lizzie sputtered. "That's preposterous. Why would I be...."

Butterflies fluttered in Alexander's stomach. *So, she's not invincible after all.* For some undefinable reason, the thought made his insides warm. Sledding was an odd thing to be nervous about, true, but he was just glad he was finally beginning to see the vulnerable side of Lizzie. Dropping his shoulders along with any hint of bravado, he smiled gently and held out his hand again.

"Come on. Let's just go down once. I'll be right behind you the whole time, and if you don't like it, we can stop."

Lizzie's eyes darted down to the freshly fallen snow, and she bit her bottom lip and nibbled for a second before finally nodding.

When she accepted Alexander's outstretched hand, and their fingers touched, ignited currents brighter than anything he had ever felt zipped up and down his body from the tips of his toes to the top of his head. The feel of her soft, delicate hands in his sent a pulse of passion through him. As her fingers laced between his, he traced every inch of the way they fit together with the pads of his fingers. To his surprise, her palms were a bit rougher than he had expected and covered in nearly as many calluses as his own hands. He thought back to the previous night when she hadn't hesitated to run through the barn and help him save the horses despite the danger of possibly being snared by another fallen tree. Perhaps she was a rancher after all.

The wanton feelings only intensified when after some careful instruction, she straddled the front of the sled, and he climbed on behind her. As he did so, her long hair brushed against his cheeks, and the soothing scent of lavender engulfed his scenes and made his every nerve-ending tingle. His heart tap danced against his rib cage for the smallest fraction of a second. He was afraid she would hear it. He wrapped his arm securely around her waist, feeling her suck in a breath as she sank into him. They came together like two perfect puzzle pieces, and Alexander held his breath.

He wrapped his arms securely around her waist and gently guided her hands to the other side of the leather reins at the front of the sled. "Put your hands over mine." A ping of embarrassment washed everything when the last word of the sentence came out in a low growl. He opened his mouth to apologize, but to his astonishment, Lizzie only threw her head back and laughed. Then she turned to face him over his shoulder just enough to offer a shy smile in return.

"You know," she said, and Alexander's pulse sped up once more at the purr in her words. "I've never actually gone sledding before."

He smiled even as a sheen of sweat began to drench his brow. "Well, there's no better time to learn." He moved her hands to the proper spots one more time and gently flipped the reins. They sailed off downhill, and Alexander's whole body tingled as Lizzie's musical laughter echoed through the snowy Christmas air.

"This is amazing!" Lizzie squealed.

Alexander chuckled and called over the slight howling of the wind, "I'm glad you like it!'

She beamed over her shoulder, and her eyes sparkled like a child who had just got her favorite Christmas present. "I love it."

As they coasted to a stop, she turned and blushed. "Thank you for going with me, Alex. That was the most fun I've had in...." She trailed off and shook her head. "I don't remember how long."

Alexander's heart felt like it was going to burst in his chest. "Anytime."

He endorsed her wishes three more times, but even as much as Alexander enjoyed seeing the complete unfiltered giddiness on Lizzie's face, he couldn't quite quell the nagging voice in the back of his mind. Lizzie had said she had never gone sledding before, but if she couldn't remember who she was, then how did she remember that?

He looked at her again out of the side of his vision, studying her every move for any hint of uneven posture, shifting eyes, or any other sign that something was out of place with her story, but found nothing. In the few days that she'd been there, Alexander had found more than one or two holes in her story, particularly in how well she knew to take care of his mother.

"Uncle Alex, Uncle Alex!" The twins' exuberant shout cut through Alexander's somber thoughts as they raced for the sled. "We saw you going down the hill! Can we have a turn with Miss Lizzie?"

Alexander laughed and ran a hand through his hair. "Well, I suppose that's up to her." He winked at her with a raised eyebrow, and she giggled. "Of course! They switched spots, and she gathered the fabric of her dress to make room. "Climb aboard."

Alexander stood and they quickly switched places. With Lizzie in the back, the twins sandwiched against each other in the front. As he had done for her, she wrapped her arm securely around Emma's waist, but they didn't quite reach far enough to wrap around Effie's as well, so Lizzie guided her sister to do it instead. "Is everyone holding on tight?"

Alexander took his position at the head of the sled and pulled all three of them back to the top of the hill one more time. A myriad of questions still lingered in the back of his mind, but he did his best to push them away. After all, it was Christmas. Everything else could wait until tomorrow.

Chapter Fourteen

They spent nearly the entire day on the lake, and dusk was beginning to settle over the ranch when they finally returned to the ranch. Eliza had intertwined her arm with Louise's again, cautious that the older woman remained safe, especially in the dark. They lingered a few feet behind Alexander and the twins, but Eliza could barely make out their silhouettes as they crossed the threshold into the front yard. As they approached the steps to the house, Louise reached over and patted Eliza's arm.

"Lizzie, honey, I don't know what you did, but I wanted to thank you. I hadn't seen Alexander or my grandchildren this happy since before my Maggie died. I didn't think I'd ever live to see the magic of Christmas on the Swanson Ranch again, and I've never been so happy to be proven wrong. I don't know what kind of angel brought you to us, but I thank the Lord every day that he did."

They skidded to a stop. Eliza's eyes nearly bugged out of her head, and she turned to face Alexander's mother. Her jaw dropped. She opened and closed it a couple of times, feeling like a fish out of the water as she tried to process what the woman had just said. "You... you called me Lizzie," she finally stammered. Louise laughed a little, and her smile widened.

"Why, of course, I did, dear. That's your name, is it not?"

"I... um.... well, yes."

Lord help me, she's lucid!

But how much did she remember? Eliza didn't want to say too much for fear of confusing Louise, but her heart thudded a little harder in her rib cage as she realized she was witnessing a genuine Christmas miracle.

Louise nodded and squeezed her hand. "And what a lovely name it is."

Despite herself, Lizzie blushed. "Thank you."

She kept her voice just above a whisper as her eyes darted toward Alexander's disappearing silhouette for a moment. Did she tell him? As much as she knew it would make him overjoyed to find his mother lucid, Eliza once again knew better than to think this would last. After all the joy they had today, she didn't know if she could bear seeing his heartbreak if she was right.

They started moving again as a million scenarios raced through Eliza's mind, but before she could come to any decision, a large yawn seized Louisa, and she stretched her arms out and arched her back. "Well, our day at the lake wore me out." Her bright eyes became weary again as she twisted the doorknob and stepped inside, only a few paces behind Alexander and the twins. "I think I'm going to retire a bit early. Will you tell Alexander and the twins I said good night?"

Eliza nodded and tried for what she hoped was an easy smile. "Of course."

Louise returned it. To her surprise, she spun around and wrapped Eliza in a warm, if a bit fragile, hug. For the briefest of seconds, Eliza stiffened in her arms. It had been a long since anyone hugged her like this, with such a motherly touch behind it. But eventually, she allowed herself to relax into the embrace and even wrapped her arms around the woman to hug her back.

"Thank you again for such a wonderful day." Louise placed a soft kiss on Eliza's cheek, and she felt tears prickle at her eyes but pushed them away.

"You all have done so much for me," she managed around a thick lump in her throat. "Making today special is the least I could do to repay you."

Louise smiled sadly, and the faraway look in her eyes returned. "Oh, Maggie." she cupped Eliza's cheek, and it took every ounce of strength she had to choke back a sob. "Family never owes family. I hope next year's Christmas will be half as magical as this one."

With that, Louise went up the stairs, leaving Eliza alone with nothing but her thoughts and the lingering, dwindling light of the Christmas candles Alexander must have lit on their way into the house. They were in the garland up the banister and around every surface they had been able to find until they reached the sitting room. As she admired their warm glow, Eliza couldn't help but entertain the nagging thoughts in her head. Now that Christmas was over, what was she to do? Surely Bennie and Russel would be after her soon. Even if she got lucky enough that they didn't find her, sooner or later, Alexander would make good on his promise to take her into town to see the sheriff. The cozy little bubble she built for herself, not to mention all the people whom she was slowly beginning to consider more of a family than Russel ever could be, would be in great peril.

The haunting thought played with her throughout the night as she boiled water for the girls to bathe.

"Lizzie?" Effie asked when they were halfway through their bath, and Eliza had done little more than give them simple instructions. "Are you okay? You always play a game with us a bath time."

"Huh?" Eliza took a deep breath and did her best to free herself of her melancholy stupor. "Oh, I'm sorry, girls. I guess I'm just a bit tired today. All of that sledding."

Emma beamed from where she sat in the water next to her sister. "Yeah! It was the best!"

Eliza opened a towel, and Emma held up her arms obediently. As she dripped onto the kitchen floor, Eliza laughed and tweaked her nose. "I'm glad you had fun. What was your favorite part?"

They went on chattering as they each clamored into their pajamas, and Eliza found herself, for what felt like the millionth time, being unbelievably grateful Alexander and his family had stumbled into her life. Or rather that she had stumbled into theirs.

Twenty minutes later, when everyone was all clean and settled in the living room, reading, playing a game, or, in Eliza's case, starting on another sewing project, the back door of the kitchen opened. At once, everyone jumped up and scrambled into the other room.

"Just me."

Eliza's hand flew to her heart until she recognized Alexander's familiar silhouette in the doorway.

"Oh!" She took a breath and laughed. "It's you! Where have you been? We didn't even hear you leave. And the girls were wondering when you were going to be back to say good night."

Alexander ducked his head but smiled slightly as he held something behind his back. "Sorry. Didn't mean to spook anyone. I just went out and did some foraging. I thought we deserved one more Christmas treat." Emma and Effie stood on their tiptoes around either side of Eliza's skirts eagerly.

"What is it, Uncle Alex?" Effie asked.

His eyes shown as he drew his hand out from behind his back and revealed an entire bucket full of chestnuts. "I went digging under the chestnut tree. I thought we could roast these before you girls go to bed for the night. What do you say?"

"Yummy! Chestnuts!" Emma shouted.

Eliza and Alexander laughed, and she wasted no time sprinting off in search of the necessary supplies for a chestnut roast.

Ten minutes later, they were all settled by the fire, watching as the first chestnuts sizzled in the heat.

Eliza watched in fascination as Alexander stirred them and scored the skin before finally taking them off the stove and peeling them. He set the first plate between the twins, who immediately dug in. He proceeded to score twenty more with a sharp knife.

Emma grinned with her mouth full, and Eliza cupped a hand over her mouth to hide her giggling. In the waning light of the fire, the little girl really did look somewhat like a chipmunk with most of the nuts stuffed between its cheeks. "This is really good, Uncle Alex," she muttered around the mouth full of nuts. "Thank you."

Alexander laughed but nodded. "You're welcome. But next time, Em, chew and swallow before you speak, okay? We wouldn't want you to choke. And save some for your sister!" His laughter increased when he realized how empty the plate was, and Effie scowled.

"Uncle Alex, how come I didn't get any yet?" She stuck out her lower lip, and Alexander shook his head.

"Gotta be faster with a little squirrel like your sister around." Her scowl deepened, and he came over to ruffle her hair. "Tell you what, munchkin? The next batch is all yours, deal?" He held out his hand, and Effie shook it eagerly.

"Deal!"

Emma, on the other hand, glowered and stomped her little foot. "That ain't fair."

Her uncle only booped her nose. "Well, neither were you when you got all of the nuts before anyone else could have some."

"You know," Eliza chimed in, having been perfectly content to sit there and watch the exchange with a warm heart up until this point. "I've never actually had roasted chestnuts before. Do you think I'll like them?"

Alexander's lips parted a bit in disbelief or confusion. She wasn't quite sure which, but the twins nodded enthusiastically.

"Uh-huh," Effie said. "They're the best!"

"The best," countered her sister. "I wish we grew chestnuts all year long!"

"Alexander hesitated, stirring the chestnuts a few more times before turning to face her and tipping his head to the side. When the girl's attention was otherwise occupied, he said, "So, you know you've never had chestnuts before, and you know you don't know how to sled, or at least you didn't before today...."

He paused, and Eliza felt her heart climb into her throat.

Oh no.

He was going to ask her how much she remembered. She cringed inwardly and fought the urge to do so on the outside as well. What was she going to say? She could continue to lie and face the fact that she would have to learn to live with the gnawing pit of guilt that seemed to become an even deeper chasm every time she had to dodge one of Alexander's questions. Or she could tell the truth and risk putting them all in danger?

"Do you, do you remember anything else?" The question tumbled from his lips just as she feared it would. As he said it, he scooped a few freshly roasted chestnuts from the pan over the fire and carefully manipulated them out of their shells. Eliza stayed silent as he transferred them onto her plate.

Truth. On the one hand, it would feel so good to finally be rid of any pretenses.

Lie. On the other, she wasn't sure how many actually existed in the first place. In Lizzie's skin, she felt more like herself than she ever had as Eliza.

Truth. But then, was she truly being herself if it was all a ruse?

Lie. Alexander and his family took her just as she was. No expectations, no ridiculous preconceived notions of what a woman of society should be...

Eliza picked up a chestnut and chewed thoughtfully. Through happenstance or fate or whatever she wanted to call it, this adventure had given her the one thing she always craved. Acceptance. The only thing she could do to repay them was to be sure she kept them safe. So, as much as it pained her, there was only one option left.

Lie.

"Bits and pieces," she finally muttered, unable to meet his gaze as she swallowed. "I remember bits and pieces, but not enough to truly recall who I once was." Even as she said it,

159

she gritted her teeth against the pulsating ache of the ever-growing hole in her heart. She had to do this. It was the only way she could even come close to guaranteeing they would be safe. The less they knew, the better.

Alexander sighed and looked at her sympathetically.

Please, she wanted to beg. *Please stop being so nice to me. It hurts too much.*

Alexander's frown deepened, and she did her best to blink back the stampede full of emotions swirling within her. Luckily though, he seemed to mistake her guilt for missing her family. He reached over and squeezed her hand.

"Don't worry," he said in a soothing tone that made a few stray tears slip free from her eyes and slide down her cheeks. "As soon as the weather allows it, I'm going to take you back into town, and we're going to find the sheriff and get you home. Mark my words; if I have anything to do with it, you'll be safe and sound before New Year's Eve."

Maybe she imagined it, but Eliza could've sworn Alexander's voice hitched when he said that. She wanted to tell him how much she wished it could be different. How much she wished she could be different. The only people she cared about keeping safe were Alexander and his family.

If only you knew.

****

That night, the girls insisted on being allowed to stay up again, but no sooner than Alexander had agreed than they fell fast asleep on the carpet in front of the roaring fireplace.

Alexander watched adoringly until Lizzie finally nudged him gently with her knee. "Should we wake them or let them sleep?" she asked in a hushed whisper. Alexander leaned forward, closed *A Christmas Carol* , then placed it on the side table.

"As much as I don't want to," he finally decided. "We probably should. I don't want them to get cricks in their neck or anything sleeping like that."

Lizzie sighed. "That's what I figured. All right, let's try not to wake them. They didn't sleep enough last night as it was."

Alexander nodded and bit back a smile. How was it that she knew them so well already? As carefully and quietly as possible, they crept over to the sleeping toddlers. Alexander scooped up Emma, and Lizzie did the same to Effie. Step by step, they ascended the stairs and gingerly made their way to the girls' bedroom. Alexander shifted Emma, so she was cradled in the crook of his left arm and used his free hand to turn down the bed. They slipped the sleeping girls beneath the covers, and Alexander's heart skipped a beat when he leaned down to place a kiss on each of their foreheads and caught Lizzie about to do the same, only to restrain herself. As they tiptoed back out into the hall, their hands reached for the door in the same instant. When their fingers brushed, a lightning bolt zipped around Alexander's arm and down his spine. For a moment, he thought his heart would stop. He caught Lizzie's gaze for the smallest of seconds before she dipped her head and whispered almost imperceptibly, "Good night, Alex. Merry Christmas."

He beamed. His whole body sparkled like the glittering candles winding down the banister. As he went around blowing them out to be extra sure there wouldn't be another fire hazard, he felt as though he had clouds on his feet.

It had been a truly Merry Christmas indeed.

***

The question of what to do churned over and over in her mind as she tried in vain to fall asleep that night. She longed for her mother's spirit to come and lure her into the blissful sleep she had first experienced when she arrived here, but hard as she tried, she couldn't seem to find her anywhere. Instead, only the spine-chilling, blood-curdling features of Russel Rivers and Bennie "Bullettooth" Boyle stared back at her. The latter forever had that incriminating pistol strapped to the holster at his hip, and each time she dreamed of it, it seemed to grow bigger and bigger.

For what felt like the hundredth time that night, Eliza fled for her life. She crashed through the front door and darted for the stables, Bennie and Russel right on her heels. Only this time, when she turned around to look back, she found herself not staring at her own door but at the door of Alexander Stanton.

Bone-chilling terror unlike anything she'd ever felt before threatened to freeze every muscle in place, but a bright orange flash out of the corner of her vision drew her attention. She turned as heat licked at her skin and the few barren spaces on her arm between her wrist and her hands. Her heart vaulted into her throat as she took in the sight. Flames ten feet high licked along the side of the barn where Alexander kept the cattle, just a few feet away from the already charred east wing of the house. Out the back door, Bennie and Russel were slipping away, leading a herd of cattle out of the ranch. Part of her wanted to go after them, but a much bigger piece was filled with dread at the thought of what or who else might be inside the burning barn.

She cupped her hands around her mouth and yelled with all her might. *"ALEX! Alexander, where are you?"*

This was all her fault. She should've never stayed here as long as she did. She should've let Alexander take her back into town when he wanted to. If she had been brave enough to face her fate then, perhaps now, they would all be safe.

She listened and positioned herself in a running stance, her eyes darting every which way, looking for any sign of life.

Please, Lord, she prayed. *Don't let them be in there. Whatever happens to me, I deserve it. I led them here, but they, they're innocent!*

Eliza's heartbeat roared in her ears, and the howling wind swallowed any sound of life. One second passed. Then two. With each passing second, she was beginning to lose hope that she would ever see Alexander or the rest of this family again.

Then, suddenly, as if carried by an angel on a whisper of the wind, came the faintest yell.

"Lizzie? Lizzie, can you hear me?"

Emma! Or Effie! She wasn't quite sure, but at that very moment, she didn't care. If one was alive, the other had to be too.

"Girls!" She called out. *"Where are you? I'm coming!"*

"We're here!"

She listened, once again straining to pinpoint the origin of the sound over the roar of the wind. She spun in every direction until she finally realized – *"The house!"*

Somehow someway, their voices were coming from inside the burned-out portion of the estate. Eliza sprinted toward the ruins, piles of ash and dust, and what looked to be the remainder of the seating area and maybe a fireplace though now it was nothing more than charred rubble.

Eventually, she found them. Alexander had his hand restrained behind his back, and huddled protectively over the girls who were also tied up, but Alexander had made sure to put them behind him. Standing over him was none other than Bennie "Bullettooth" Boyle himself. And like every other time she'd seen him, that haunting, pristinely polished pistol dangled precariously from his hip. Strangely enough, her stepbrother was nowhere to be found. She assumed he had made a run for it.

"What do you want?" Alexander spat. *"I am only a simple rancher. I have nothing that would be of any value to a criminal like you."*

Bennie smiled and laughed coolly, his scar gleaming in the eerie moonlight overhead. *"See, that's where you're wrong, Mr. Swanson. You very much have something I want. But as soon as that little lady shows herself, I'll let you and your shavers here go free."*

Eliza sucked in her breath, hiding behind a charred pillar, or what was left of it. Confusion blanketed Alexander's features, but slowly, terrifyingly, realization dawned.

"You mean Lizzie? But what would you want with her?"

His cackling rang through the night again. *"Oh, is that what she's calling herself now?"* He clucked his tongue and shook his head. *"Eliza, you can come out now."*

She froze. How did he know she was here? Her mind was racing as she considered her options.

"I am waiting. Unless you want one of these sweet little girls to face your fate for you!"

One of the twins whimpered, and a sudden rush of protectiveness fueled by a red current of rage washed over Eliza. *"No!"* She dove into view, no longer afraid of this no-good thieving bandit. No matter how dangerous he may be, she wasn't going to let him harm the Swansons.

She stepped into the light with her shoulders drawn back defiantly. *"It's me you want,"* she growled. *"So take me and leave them out of this."*

Bennie grinned in a calculating, malicious manner that made goosebumps ride all over her body. *"I don't know. I may have come here for you, but a few extra victims never did anything to hurt my reputation."*

"No!" Tears sprang to her eyes, and she rushed over to throw herself in front of Alexander and the girls. *"If you want to hurt them, you're going to have to go through me!"*

Bennie shrugged and unhooked the pistol from its holster. *"Feisty as ever, I see. Your brother warned me you'd be trouble before he went on soft and checked out halfway through. But no matter now."* He uncocked the safety and aimed it between her eyes.

"Any last words before you meet your maker, Eliza?"

"Lizzie, no! What are you doing? What does that rat want with you anyway?"

She ignored the question, partially because she couldn't stand to lie anymore and because she knew she didn't have time to explain properly. She shook her head and remained firmly planted on the ground in front of them.

"Do your worst."

Benny's maniacal smile and the empty black void of the barrel were the last things she saw before her eyes flew open.

She sat up in bed, panting and heaving, and she waited for her eyes to adjust to the darkness. Slowly he recognized the familiar walls and the silken feeling of the sheets beneath his skin. She was at the ranch all right, but Bennie and her stepbrother were nowhere in sight. It was the middle of Christmas night, and she was safe.

For now.

Chapter Fifteen

December 26, 1860

"Uncle Alex," Effie whined pitifully just a few minutes after they finished their breakfast the next morning. "Do you have to go back to work?"

Alexander smiled but nodded. "You know I do, munchkin. Ranchers don't get holidays."

He winked at Lizzie across the table, who mustered up a forced laugh but didn't comment. Her silence gave him an uneasy feeling as if to provide validity to his thoughts from the previous night. He had thought he heard shuffling from her room in the middle of the night, but when he went to check on her, she had the blankets pulled over her head, and he decided it was better not to disturb her. Still, he had been more skittish than usual, and he barely attempted to make conversation with his mother, who by now had already retired to her room. Even so, Alexander found that monumentally uncharacteristic of the Lizzie he had gotten to know over these past few days. Part of him wanted to prod a bit deeper, ask her what was wrong. But the larger part, the part that went out, was still a bit too afraid to open that particular can of worms. What if his fears came true? What if the girl she'd been presenting her so bad this entire time was nothing more than a lick and a promise of whom she really was?

Effie's chair creaked across the floor as she angrily pushed away from the table and crossed her arms, drawing him back to the present. "Aww! But we wanted to go sledding again!"

Alexander sighed and ran a hand down his face. "I know, girls, but there's so much I have to do. I have to thrash and clean a large area of the field today, not to mention milking the cows again and double-checking the repairs to the stable. Hopefully, I can go into town soon to get some real lumber to patch up the last of the holes. Maybe Lizzie can take you, though?" He phrased it as a half statement, half question, shifting his gaze to hers as he spoke.

She nodded absentmindedly, but her eyes were far away, and she kept nibbling on her lower lip. "Sure," she replied listlessly. "I'll take you. Go and get your clothes on, and then we'll—"

"Yay!"

She didn't even finish the sentence before the girls were up and out of their chairs, running for the stairs and their winter outfits.

Alexander put his fork down and got up to carry his plate to the sink. As much as he wanted to know the truth, he wasn't sure if he could handle it. In nearly the week since she arrived here, Alexander couldn't remember there ever having been so much laughter and light in the house. At least not since Maggie died. But he knew she had to go back, and soon by the looks of the way, the snow slowly started to tumble to a halt outside the window that morning. He wanted to keep the magic of her presence around for as long as he could.

Still, he kept one wary eye on her the entire time he went about taking care of the rest of the dishes. Soon, only hers remained, and when she didn't get up to put it in the wash bin, Alexander exhaled. He took a seat opposite her at the table and braced himself. Then he opened his mouth. "Are you okay?"

She blinked, seeming only then to register his returned presence. "Oh, um, yes. I'm fine. Just a bit tired, I guess."

Alexander's brow furrowed as he scraped his beard. "Didn't you sleep well last night?"

Her eyes widened, and her cheeks paled a bit. She gripped the edge of the table, digging her nails into the wood. Alexander watched in utter confusion as the pit in his stomach grew. Something truly had spooked her last night. But what?

"I... suppose not," she finally answered. "I had, I had a nightmare." She swallowed convulsively, and Alexander could only guess that her throat had gone dry.

He raised his brow. "Oh? About what?"

Lizzie stayed silent but pressed her lips together.

"Was it..." His own breath quivered in his chest, and he inhaled and exhaled through his nose a few times to steady himself. "Was it something from your... from before?"

Lizzie looked as though she had seen a ghost. He could practically see the wheels turning in her head as she templated how to answer, and that alone was enough to indicate to Alexander that there was more to her story than what she had been admitting. He just didn't know how much. And if she chose now to reveal it, would he be ready?

After what seemed like an eternity, Lizzie finally pushed back her hair and met his gaze. She folded her hands in front of her on the table, but before she could say anything, two pairs of thundering footsteps trotted down the stairs.

"Okay!" Emma announced as they stepped off the bottom railing. Her sister followed soon after, and they twirled a little to show off their mismatched winter gear. "We're ready!"

The pronouncement broke the tension of the previous conversation, and in spite of themselves, both Eliza and

Alexander laughed. "Very nice clothing choices." Their uncle said, taking in the fact that the twins seemed to have purposely swapped one of each of their new gloves as well as their scarves and hats, so they were no longer color-coded as they had been the day before.

"Yes," Lizzie chimed in. Alexander turned to see some of the glow had come back into her cheeks though he suspected it probably had more to do with their distraction than anything. "You both look wonderful. Let me just help you with your boots, and then we can get going."

As she rose from her chair to help the twins tie their boots, which had become so unraveled, they were nearly falling off of their feet. Alexander took it as a cue to leave. He stood once again and grabbed his hat from the coat rack sitting next to the back door, tipping it lightly at the girls as he reached behind him to pull it open and let in a brisk winter chill. "It seems you've got things handled." He nodded to Lizzie, who smiled thinly and waved him off. "So with that, I'm going to get to my duties for the day. But we will continue this conversation tonight."

Lizzie's skin flushed again, but she nodded wordlessly with one hand behind her back.

"Uncle Alex," Emma asked again. "Do you really have to go?"

He snickered and wound his thumbs in his belt loop. "Yes, munchkin. I really do. I'll be back for lunch, though. Be good for Lizzie now, you hear?"

"We will!" The twins chorused as he turned and opened the door just enough to slip out. The overly angelic tone of the voices made him smirk. He would believe that when he saw it.

***

He spent most of the morning tiling his land, which was twice as hard as usual since Nate still hadn't been able to make it back to the ranch due to the weather. He only made it through about four or five acres, choosing to save the rest for when they had less inclement weather and more help. By the time he finished that task, every part of his body ached. Even so, he trudged toward the barn with the intention of giving his cows an extra milking. After feeding them, milking them, cleaning the milking pails, storing what he had earned, and finally cleaning the parlor of the mess he always managed to leave, no matter how careful he was, it was nearly time for lunch.

He wandered leisurely back to the house, stretching his legs and fully expecting the girls to be warming up from their snowy adventure with a bowl of stew or soup. Instead, to his horror, he nearly bumped right into Lizzie as she rocketed out of the house.

"Alex! Alex, where are you?!"

He braced her by the shoulders but wasn't quite fast enough to keep them from colliding completely. She sagged into him for a minute before stiffening again.

"Lizzie, what's the matter? What is it?"

She grabbed him by either arm. "Alex, I'm so sorry."

His blood ran slightly colder. "What happened? Is it the twins? Are they all right?"

"The twins are fine. They're inside playing."

Alexander felt a fraction of the tension leave his body, but not enough that he could consider himself anywhere near calm.

"Then what, what is it?"

Lizzie froze, bit her lip, and turned away before finally looking at him with tears welling in her eyes. "It's your mother. She's gone."

Alexander's ears buzzed. His mouth dried, and his vision narrowed. "Gone? What do you mean gone?"

Where would she go? His breathing came in gasping short bursts, and his palms grew sweaty. *No. Panicking is not going to help now.* He gritted his teeth and tried his hardest to even out his breathing, focusing instead on Lizzie's voice. Though from the looks of her ashen cheeks, wide eyes, and quivering words, she wasn't faring much better.

"I went to her room to check on her and let her know the girls, and I was leaving. Maybe ask if she wanted to go sledding with us. I knocked on her door twice, but she didn't answer. At first... I just thought she had taken a nap or something. But when I peeked inside...." She choked on a sob, and Alexander winced, equally overcome with the urge to reach out and comfort her, gripped by the iron fist squeezing his heart and filling his mind with thousands of terrible possibilities.

"Alexander, I didn't see her anywhere." He could tell it was taking everything in her to hold back her emotions, and even then, a few stray tears managed to slip down her cheeks. He resisted the urge to pull her into his arms and instead used the pad of his thumb to brush them away. She leaned into his touch, and for a moment, they simply stood there, basking in the assuredness of the other's heartbeat. But finally, as much as he didn't want to, Alexander knew he had to break the silence.

"What happened next?" He clasped her hand in his, using his own body as a shield against the wind whipping against both of them.

She took a quivering breath, blinked until her vision appeared clear again, and squeezed his fingers. "I looked everywhere, but I haven't been able to find her. I told the girls to wait inside after I searched every room. That's when I came to find you."

Alexander nodded, his resolve hardening. "It's okay. We'll find her." On impulse, he leaned in and placed a quick, chaste kiss on Lizzie's forehead. Her cheeks turned scarlet, and the tiniest of smiles slipped onto her lips, but it disappeared so quickly he wondered if he'd imagined it. When they separated, he immediately turned back to the task at hand. "You go back inside and keep the girls busy. Stay at home in case she comes back. I don't want them to worry that something has happened. I'll look for her."

Lizzie nodded but looked around uncertainly. "Alex, has this ever happened before? What if... What if she's not...."

Alexander stiffened and put a finger to her lips before she could voice his greatest fear out loud. "Don't. Don't even go there, or you'll make yourself sick with worry. She's on the ranch."

She has to be.

"But how do you know?"

He set his jaw. "I don't. But we can hope." Before she could protest any further, he jogged off in the section of the stables, armed with every intention of saddling a horse in case he had to search all the way to the edge of the Swanson property.

As he rounded the east wing of the house, however, he found he didn't have to. To his shock and heartbreak, Louise stood in the middle of what had once been his sister's bed chambers, wearing nothing but her nightgown and looking positively chilled to the bone. She was covered in soot and ash. Nonetheless, relief washed over him.

"Mother!" he yelled, upping his pace to as much of a jog as was possible in the still fairly deep snow. "There you are! We were so worried."

"Al...Alex?"

She turned around, and Alexander's heart stopped. Time came to a halt, and his stomach dropped to his feet. Her face was marred with tear tracks, and she had that familiar glazed look in her eyes. It was almost as if she was in the middle of another one of her states, but worse, somehow. He slowed his jog to a gentle walk, approaching her like one might a frightened animal.

"Is that you?" He took a step forward and stumbled. He rushed to her side just quick enough to catch her by the arm before she landed face down in the snow.

"Yes, Ma. Yes, it's me." He kept his tone sucked into the house. He said it hurt from injuries and tried to brush away some of the grime. Thankfully she looked unharmed but was definitely weakened and certainly much too cold to be out here. "What happened? What on earth are you doing out here?"

"Oh, you're here! My beautiful boy!" She threw her arms around him and hugged him so tight he could barely breathe. Alexander stiffened in her vice-like embrace. Those words. This hug. She had only ever acted like this once before – on the day Maggie died.

He swallowed back the lump in his throat and tried to temper down the fear threatening to overwhelm him. What was wrong with her? She had had episodes before, but never this bad. If she ever did dream of the fire, it was usually only a terrifying night terror that he could lull her out of within a few minutes. Of course, he would then spend the rest of the night wide awake, but somehow none of that was nearly as bad as seeing her standing here alone in the wreckage. She was just as confused and afraid and covered in the remnants of the fire as she had been when they escaped the house that night. Just how entrenched in the memory was she?

"Mother?" he asked carefully. "What day is it?"

She blinked, and he realized she was trembling even harder now. "There was...Fire! Alex, honey, we have to get away from the fire! So much smoke, soot, I can't..." She grasped at her throat and started gasping for breath. The current of trepidation washing over Alexander almost threatened to freeze him in place. He'd never seen her this bad before. He didn't even know where to begin to pull her out of this. His own trauma from the fire still felt so fresh and raw, and some days they were times when even he fought to remember that, as horrible as it might have been, it was over now. He suspected the impact from it would never fully heal.

Nevertheless, he managed to get just enough of a handle on his thoughts to reach out and gently place his hand on his mother's shoulder. "Shh. It's all right now. There's no fire. It's been put out."

She blinked, and confusion blanketed her features. "But Maggie and the twins! Oh, where are the twins?"

The ache in Alexander's throat grew bigger, and the pain in his heart hurt just as much as it had that night. Surrounded by all the remains of what once was and the potential for what should've been... Maybe Nathan was right, and he should've had this part of the house torn down long ago. After all, there was a reason he hadn't been back to it in such a long time. And yet a part of him thought that if he washed away the tragedy, he would also be washing away her memory. And that, that he just couldn't live with.

"Alex, come on! We have to go. We have to get the twins!"

She tried to pull him further into the rubble, but he gently but firmly held her back. As it was, he did his best to take his own pain and push it to the side. He could grieve later; first, he had to make sure his mother was safe and warm.

"The twins are fine," he said softly. "They're inside. Do you want to go see them?"

His mother tilted her head to the side. "They're okay? They... they weren't hurt in the fire?"

Alexander shook his head, thanking God that at least this part he could be truthful about. "No. Everyone is safe now. Come on, let's get you inside and get you warm, and then you can see the twins."

Again he tried to pull her away from the wreckage, and again she lingered behind.

"What about... What about Maggie and her husband? Where are they? I didn't see them!"

Alexander's chest constricted; he opened his mouth but didn't respond right away. He knew from experience and watching Lizzie's interaction with her that playing along was usually best, but in this one instance...he just couldn't. He was so tired of lying, and he couldn't do it anymore. Not with her. Not about this.

"Come on. Let's just get you inside. Everything will be better when we're no longer out in this cold." He desperately wished to offer her a better explanation, or any explanation at all, but he had nothing to give. This time though, thankfully, she went without complaint.

"Okay," she whispered softly. Alexander swallowed a sigh of his own at the disparity in her tone. At that moment, he felt less worthy than he had ever had in his life. He didn't even have the proper words to comfort her because he had no knowledge of when or where she thought she was. "Okay. Let's go."

Chapter Sixteen

December 26, 1860

When Eliza heard the front door open, the guilt eating away at her and making it impossible for her to focus on the book perched in her lap gave her the briefest moment of reprieve. Whether it was from the reoccurring dream and her ever-growing fear that Bennie and Russel would find her and somehow find a way to use her newfound family against her or simply from her utter incompetence and inability to find Louise, she wasn't sure. Probably both.

She sprang to her feet and practically launched herself at the door, relief flooding every nerve ending of her body when she saw two familiar silhouettes standing there. "Alex! Louise! Oh, thank the Lord, I was so worried!" Suddenly finding herself without a hint of decorum, she threw her arms around Alexander's neck and hugged him for everything he was worth, inhaling deeply to encircle herself in the safe and enchanting scent of pine, animal fur, and a distinct odor of barnyard must that she had come to love.

Only when she pulled away and turned to do the same to his mother did she take in her disheveled appearance from her set, ash-covered body all the way to her pale tear-stained cheeks and wide unfocused eyes. Eliza's hand flew to her mouth, and she glanced at Alexander for an explanation.

He shrugged and stuffed his hands in his pockets. Unable to meet her gaze. "I… I found her like that. She was, she was standing in the rubble of the old east wing of the house. The one… The one that…."

"The one that got destroyed in the fire," Eliza finished. Alexander could do nothing but nod, and her heart went out to him. "Oh, Alex. I'm so sorry. I don't know how she passed us. I didn't even hear her leave her room."

He took a deep shuddering breath, and she fought back the urge to go to him right then, not wanting him to feel smothered with too much comfort. "I have no idea that's where she would go. She's had episodes before. You've seen them."

Eliza opted not to reply, sensing that he had something he needed to get off his chest and not wanting to interrupt him.

"This... It was worse than that. Different. Something, something I've never experienced before. It was like... Lizzie, when we were out there, it was like she was reliving the night of the fire all over again."

Upon hearing that, Eliza no longer had a care for her impulses and walked over to him and gently wrapped an arm around his shoulder. "I can't imagine what that must've been like," she whispered, running her hand through his hair and thanking God the twins weren't around to hear this. "But she's safe now; you both are."

And after we get through this together, I'm going to do everything I can to keep it that way.

Alexander ran a hand down his face but nodded.

She inclined her head toward his mother and then placed a reassuring hand on his shoulder. "I'll get her cleaned up. You stay here and rest a minute. I'll be back as soon as we're finished." She left no room for argument and instead hurried to the sink to boil some water for a bath. That done, she gently guided Louise toward her bed chambers. "Come on, dear, let's go get you washed and changed."

"Maggie?" Eliza paused to let the older woman study her features, and win she recognized them, her face blossomed into a relieved smile. "Oh, thank goodness! I was so worried something awful had become of you during that horrible fire. I'm so glad to see you're safe!"

She wrapped Eliza in a bone-crushing hug which Eliza gladly returned, though for very different reasons. "I'm right here," she assured the woman, and she gently petted her on the back. He purposely avoided using either name to minimize further confusion. "Now come on, let's get you cleaned up and into bed. It's been a long cold day, and I think you could do well with a nice nap."

Louise happily obliged, and it didn't take long for Eliza to coax her into the tub after helping her remove her soiled nightgown. Eliza made sure to take her time as she gently scrubbed every inch of soot and grime from the older woman's body. When the only trace of the incident remained in the water of the wash tub behind the screen in her room, Eliza finally allowed Louise to step out and draped a soft cotton nightgown over her head. She placed some lavender oil on the pillow and drew back the covers until Louise climbed in.

She sat with her and listened to her tell stories about Alexander's sister when she was younger for another twenty minutes before the woman finally drifted off into a somewhat fitful but seemingly solid sleep. Only then did she gently stand up from her chair, tiptoe out the door, and descend the stairs to find Alexander sitting at the kitchen table with his head in his hands, taking deep, quivering breaths.

***

She held her breath and approached him cautiously. Taking the seat just to his left, she reached out and almost laid her hand on his back but stopped herself at the last second and set it on the top of the kitchen table.

"She's okay," Eliza said quietly, at a loss for what else she could do. "We had a nice warm bath. I put her in some clean clothes, and now she's taking a nap. Hopefully, when she wakes up, she'll feel better."

Alexander raised his head and looked at her through red-rimmed, glassy eyes. "Th-Thank you for all your help," he stuttered out. He raised his hand to his mouth, choking on another sob, but managed to hold it back as he wiped his cheeks with the back of his hands.

Eliza wanted nothing more than to pull him into her arms and remain that way until everything made itself right again. She scooted closer. After a few minutes of heart-wrenching silence, during which she thought of anything and everything she might be able to do to offer him even a sliver of comfort, but nothing seemed good enough, she finally sighed. "Alex, I hate to ask, but... What happened today? Has anything like it ever happened before?"

When he nodded, Eliza's heart crawled into her throat. "She... She has nightmares. Some of them have gotten pretty bad. She'll wake up terrified, then sleepwalk all around the house, looking for any signs of fire."

A torrent of emotions welled up in Eliza, but she knew better than to stop him. If this had been going on for as long as he said, she could only imagine the strain it put on him as Louise's sole caretaker for so long.

"The worst ones... The worst ones are when she looks for Maggie." He stopped as his chin quivered, and he pressed hands together before bringing them to his lips. "I... I honestly didn't think it could get any worse than having to explain what happened over and over again. But seeing her today, standing in the middle of the wreckage, looking just like she did that night... She was even wearing the same nightgown from that day. Did you know that?"

Eliza shook her head.

"I know, I know the pain will never truly be gone. Will have to live with what happened for the rest of our lives. But... I can't keep going back to that night, Lizzie. That terror? That helplessness?" He turned away from her, staring resolutely at the window. "I promised myself I would never feel that way again. And yet, every time this happens...."

"It's like you're losing her all over again."

Alexander nodded. "I don't want the twins or any of us to ever forget her. But I need to move on. I just... I don't know how."

Eliza stared at him, wishing more than anything he could take even a fraction of his clearly palpable pain away. At that moment, she felt as if she would bear the burden a thousand times over if only it meant she never had to see this sad, lonely, utterly distraught expression on his face ever again. Unfortunately, though, that wasn't real. The only thing she could do was be there.

Giving into her earlier instinct, she leaned forward and wrapped her arms around Alexander's muscular frame, surprised at how well they fit together. He didn't even resist, melting into her almost instantly. She ran her hand through his hair and murmured soothing words in his ear. A second later, she would forget what she had said.

After a few minutes, his head came to rest against her chest, and she felt his chest rise and fall almost in perfect rhythm with hers. Goosebumps rose on her arms as she took in the feeling rising from within her. She didn't quite have a name for it yet. It was warm and soothing and fiercer than anything she's ever felt. Never in her life would she have ever seen herself holding a man the way he held Alexander at that moment, but somehow, it didn't feel awkward or inappropriate or uncomfortable in the least. In fact, in the dim glow of the kerosene lamps, with the twins' voice drifting softly in from the playroom down the hall, and the remnants of the Christmas decorations still peppered around the room, Eliza couldn't think of a time in her life when anything had ever felt more right.

After an indeterminate amount of time, Alexander finally pulled away. When he did, though, his eyes were no longer red-rimmed, and his breathing was much more even. He seemed calmer now, steadier somehow. However, his cheeks colored when he cleared his throat and reached around to scratch the back of his neck.

"Thank you," he said with a rough but not unkind edge to his voice. "I didn't know how much I needed that"

Eliza offered a small smile and was briefly bold enough to twine their fingers together as butterflies took flight in her stomach. "Of course."

Alexander returned the smile, and Eliza felt her heart skip a beat.

"I'm supposed to be getting back to work now. But I'll see you for supper?"

He phrased it like a question, and Eliza smirked. "I'll be here."

She wasn't sure she ever wanted to be anywhere else.

Chapter Seventeen

December 26, 1860

As Alexander ventured once again into the now-waning sunlight, the feeling of Lizzie's arms around him lingered, leaving a prickling trail of heat along his skin and igniting a fire deep within his soul. He had never had a woman comfort him like that. No one ever dared to try and show any interest.

When it came to his mother in her condition, Alexander was more than used to people in town seeing her as a burden or a nuisance. He was almost certain none of his close friends or family would've had the courage to be there for him as Lizzie had been. He wasn't sure what to call the feeling rising from within him. After all, he

had known her less than a week, and one day soon, all of this would be nothing more than a pleasant holiday dream.

He saddled up one of the horses and rode out to another acre, resolving to turn over as much of the field as he could before the sun said that night. On the way out there, he found a few broken fences and returned to the barn to collect the necessary supplies to mend them. He gathered wire, planks, nails, and a hammer before riding back out to make the repairs. His hands were frigid beneath the gloves. Alexander blew on them and rubbed them together for warmth, but he could still barely feel them as he worked to set the proper planks in place. His mouth was full of nails, and the metallic taste was harsh as he pulled them out one by one to nail the fixtures in place. By the time he was done, his brow was once again sweaty, but nearly all of the fields had been tended to, and most of the damage caused by the storm had been remedied. At least for now.

He returned to the house to find Lizzie stationed at the stove, cooking up the pot of stew he had expected earlier. He peered into the kitchen and, to his relief, saw his mother sitting on the sofa, quietly reading a book to the girls who sat on either side of her. He wandered over to the stove and crept up behind them.

"Smells good," he said softly. "What are you making?"

She turned, startling a little before her expression melted into an easy smile. "I ventured down to the root cellar earlier today and found some vegetables on the verge of spoiling. There was a whole sack of potatoes that needed to be used, so I thought a nice thick soup would be the perfect thing to warm everyone up after such a long day."

Alexander removed his hat and went to place it on the coat rack alongside his boots and other equipment. "I can't wait to taste it."

About an hour later, Lizzie served the soup with fresh bread that she had baked. Everyone gathered at the table and bowed their heads as Alexander led them in saying grace. Once everyone's napkins were in their laps, they dug in. After his first bite, Alexander gave him a low whistle. "Wow! I knew you could cook, but you're gonna have to teach me how to bake like this."

Lizzie blushed, and Alexander's heart glowed. "I'm glad you like it. I'd be happy to show you sometime," she said.

She continued spooning steaming scoops of soup into her mouth, and they made idle chatter about his workday. Soon enough, he realized why the meal had felt so out of place. Out of the corner of his eye, he glanced at the twins, who were both staring listlessly at their still steaming bowls. Emma was stirring her spoon around, but it didn't look as if Effie had even touched hers.

Lizzie's brow furrowed as she turned to look at them more fully. "Girls? What's the matter? Don't you like your soup?"

"Not hungry," Effie muttered, swallowing convulsively and pushing her plate away.

Lizzie and Alexander exchanged worried looks.

"What's wrong, Effie-Belle? Do you not feel well?"

Effie nodded. "Too hot!"

"I'm old!" Emma complained, grouching.

Uh oh. Hot and cold?

An alarm went off in Alexander's head. *Lord, please don't let them have the flu.* Getting sick was never fun, but catching the flu in the middle of a Montana winter as harsh as this one would be miserable.

Lizzie's scowl deepened, and once again, he could practically see the wheels turning in her head.

"Does anything else hurt, sweetie?" She asked as she reached over to feel both of their foreheads simultaneously.

"My tummy feels yucky!" Emma complained. Her sister nodded.

"Uh-huh. And my head feels all stuffy."

"Aw, you poor things!" Lizzie drew her hand back and nodded faintly at Alex. "They are a little warm," she said softly.

"I was afraid of that," Alexander said. The last time they were this sick was before their mother died. He racked his brain for anything Maria had ever done every other time they've got a cold or something similar since then, but at that particular moment, he was drawing a blank.

Lizzie gently helped each of them down from their chairs and put an arm on each of their backs to study them as they slowly wobbled their way to the stairs. "Why don't you go up to your room? I'll draw you a nice warm bath, and then we will get you in some comfortable clothes and get you off to bed early." She half-winced at that last statement, expecting at least a fight or some mild protest. Instead, she was met with only murmurs of agreement as the girls obediently trotted up the stairs.

Alexander's eyebrows rose into his hairline. "Wow, no dinner and no fighting about going to bed early? They must be really sick."

His tongue darted out to lick his drying lips, and he searched the depths of his memory for everything he was going to need to take care of them properly. He scowled as Eliza's features puckered as if she was studying him.

"What?"

"Nothing. You've just always seemed so calm and collected. Even this afternoon, you didn't get rattled until long after you had already found your mother, and she was safe in bed."

Alexander frowned, and his gaze slipped to the floor. "Don't remind me. Living through that once was more than enough."

Lizzie cringed and combed back some hair from where it had fallen into her face. "I'm sorry. Perhaps that humor was ill-timed. It's just, well, I guess I never expected to see the great Alexander Swanson undone by something as simple as the winter flu."

His glare intensified. "I'm not. You just head up and help the twins draw their bath. I'm going to go see if we have any willow bark or meadowsweet in the cellar. That's supposed to help with fever, I think."

On his way out the door, he couldn't help with turning around, and a small smile played on his lips at the extra bit of sass it seemed to have infiltrated its way into Lizzie's step. "Don't worry about anything," she called down to him. "It's just a little cold. I'm sure the girls will be better in no time."

A few hours later, that little cold didn't seem so little anymore. The girls were up every hour. Between the two of them, Lizzie and Alexander were running ragged, bringing them wet clothes and tea, and continually emptying and washing the basins into which they expelled their stomachs.

"How are you?" Alexander asked, turning from his spot at the sink when Lizzie came down the stairs with the metal basin yet again. He took one look at her drawn features, ragged hair, and the large bags under her eyes and regretted the question the minute he had asked it. He frowned. "No improvement?"

She dropped the basin into the sink. She would empty it outside later. For now, she sunk her weight against the opposite counter. "Not yet. If we could only get their fevers to break, I know they would get better, but as it is, they're both still burning up."

Alexander nodded. "I know. If only there was a faster way to cool them down."

Lizzie steadied him for a moment, and then her eyes brightened. What about the snow?"

Alexander's lips puckered. "What do you mean?"

"I mean, what if instead of running down here every time we need something cool, we went outside and scooped some snow into the water basins? Then we could just dip the cloth inside, and when it melts, we'd have cold compresses ready."

Alexander tapped his chin. "It's a good thought, but I don't think the snow is fresh enough to be safe. We don't know what kind of debris may be in it. After all, the storm blew a lot of things around. We'll just have to make do with what we have for now."

Eliza slowly exhaled and quickly returned to the task at hand. That's how they spent the remainder of the night. If one of them wasn't running for supplies, they were cuddling the twins. Holding them seemed to be the only thing that would keep away the chills until the fever broke. The first time Lizzie tried to do so, Alexander was quick to question her since he didn't want her to make herself sick after what she had been through a few days ago. Yet she insisted on not letting the twins get too cold.

He leaned against the side of the door frame and watched fondly as Emma and Effie both nuzzled themselves into either side of Lizzie. It was little things like that, the littlest, most simple thing, that made that strange feeling that had started to come over Alexander earlier in the afternoon reared its head again. But only part of him wondered if you would ever truly be able to go back to his life without Lizzie.

Of course, I will! It was ridiculous to think otherwise. They barely knew one another, and she still had a home to go back to. *But I'd better take her soon.* Otherwise, he wasn't sure he would be able to stop himself from riding after her wherever it was she happened to go.

When they each sunk into kitchen chairs as the first signs of dawn peeked over the horizon, Alexander nearly collapsed. It didn't take long for Lizzie to do the same.

"When it rains, it pours," she joked.

SALLY M. ROSS

"Does it ever." Alexander tried for a smile that he was almost too tired to even make his lips curl upward. His adoration from earlier came back with a vengeance because even haggard and worn down from having been up all night, Lizzie somehow still managed to retain the vibrant personality that had drawn him to her in the first place. With her hair sticking up, her bright eyes a few shades duller than usual as she tried in vain to blink away the tiredness overtaking her features, and her pale skin a strange gray color in the morning light, Alexander still couldn't deny that she was the most beautiful creature he had ever seen.

The thought of continuing without her almost seemed too preposterous to consider. Though she had been staying with him for nearly a week, they still knew nothing about each other.

Falling in love with someone he barely knew was impossible.

Wasn't it?

If the incessant hammering of his heart against his rib cage or the fierce sense of protectiveness that seized him every time he sensed she might even be in the slightest bit of danger – or the way his moods seemed to light up every time she stepped into a room – were any indication, then maybe it wasn't that impossible.

But terrifying? Definitely.

"Penny for your thoughts?" Lizzie gently nudged his shoulder, and he startled out of his contemplation.

"Oh, um..." He looked away and shuffled his feet. "Nothing. I was just thinking. The snow should be melted enough in a day or two to bring you into town. Are you... Are you ready to go see the doctor and the sheriff?"

The tiny, impassioned part of him that had found a kindred spirit within the mysterious girl who had fallen off her horse in the middle of his property nearly begged for her to say no. But the larger, wiser part who knew better than to get close to anyone, especially someone with as many secrets as he suspected Lizzie to have, made him hold his tongue.

She paled, but nodded.

Relief flowed through Alexander, mixed with pangs of sadness and melancholy he didn't wish to acknowledge. He frowned and set his chin in his hand, propping an elbow on the table. "What is it?"

Lizzie focused on the floor. "Nothing."

"Lizzie." He gave her a long hard look until her posture deflated.

"It's just... I've been so happy here. I hate the thought of going away and maybe never seeing y'all again."

Alexander felt a bit better upon hearing that, but the pit in his stomach remained. "But what if you have a family of your own?"

Lizzie said nothing but a flash of trepidation lingered in her eyes. It was the same look she had this morning when she confessed she had a nightmare. As if he didn't have enough evidence already, her reaction confirmed it. She was definitely hiding something. More than that, she was afraid. But of what?

Chapter Eighteen

December 27, 1860

Every time she lied, guilt twisted around her insides wound a little tighter. But after everything they'd been through and everything that haunted any hope of getting a good night's sleep, Eliza was more convinced than ever that this was the right decision. No matter how much it hurt, she had to do everything in her power to keep them safe. Even if it meant never seeing them again when Alexander did finally make good on his promise to bring her into town.

She tried her hardest not to think about that, though, as the next morning, just as she had hoped, the twins were back to their usual, energetic selves. If she was right, and this one was, in fact, one of her last days with the Swansons, she didn't want to squander it on such negative thoughts.

As the four of them wandered to the kitchen late that morning, a scent of butter, fresh maple syrup, and sugar tickled Eliza's nose. She sniffed the air appreciatively and moved around the corner with a large smile.

"Louise!" Delight crept into her tone as she took in the scene before her. Louise, clad and an apron, a fresh pair of clothes, and spectacles she had never seen up until this point stood in front of the stove, flipping a freshly made flapjack onto a plate. "I didn't expect to see you awake this early! What are you doing? "

"Oh, Lizzie, There you are, dear!" Her exuberant smile matched Eliza's, and she set the spatula down and rounded the counter to come and wrap her in another one of her heartwarming hugs.

Eliza's heart leaped a little when she realized the older woman had called her by the proper name. She was lucid again. Wrapping her arms gratefully around Alexander's mother's thin frame, she sent up a silent prayer of thanks. She couldn't imagine a better gift than to be able to spend her last days with the family, truly being herself.

When Louise pulled back, she cupped Eliza's face in her cheeks. "Glad to see you're looking better. Alexander told me about the utter chaos that went on here last night with the girls and that dreadful stomach bug. I do wish you had come to wake me. Perhaps I could've helped."

Eliza laughed a little and gently squeezed her shoulder. "It was no trouble. And besides," She craned her neck to look at the kitchen again, which, well, much more a mess than she ever made, still smelled mouthwateringly delicious. "I'd say you helped enough just by making breakfast. What are you cooking?" She rounded the counter to the stove only to find not flapjacks as she had first thought, but a large plate of biscuits next to another skillet full of perfectly fluffy scrambled eggs.

Louise shuffled after her, grinning. "Nothing too fancy. I just thought you might want something light to settle your stomach. I have a toast, too, if the biscuits are too heavy."

Eliza shook her head and winked. "No. This all looks wonderful! I'm sure the girls will love it too."

She was relieved when, not ten minutes later, she found her assumption to be correct. Not only did the girls come bounding down the stairs nearly completely back to their normal state of constant energy, but they devoured biscuits and half a pile of eggs each in a matter of minutes.

"Glad to see you've got your appetite back," Lizzie said with a laugh as she sat down with her own plate.

Emma nodded vigorously around another mouthful of eggs. It was just the four of them that morning, as now that the snow was clearing, Alexander had gone out early to tend to the animals.

"It's yummy, Gramma!"

Louise beamed and gently petted her granddaughter's hand. "Thank you, my dear. But be careful now, don't eat too fast. We don't want you to get another tummy ache."

Emma scrunched up her nose, and her eyes widened as she pushed her plate away and shook her head. "No way, tummy aches are stinky."

The adults laughed, and Eliza reached over to tweak her nose. "Indeed, they are munchkins. And after last night, I think we can all agree that we've had enough sickness for one winter."

The twins nodded. "Yeah!"

Lizzie smiled and dabbed her mouth with a napkin. "I do have one idea, though. If you girls are up for it, I thought maybe we could go on a horse ride this afternoon. The fresh air should do you some good." She looked skeptically between the twins but was relieved when they exchanged surprised glances before bursting into cheers, not very much unlike the reaction she had the other day when Alexander suggested she'd be the one to take them sledding.

* * *

A few hours later, all three of them were on one of the roads Alexander had deemed one of the easier trails on the property. Their snow had melted significantly, and their horses all trotted easily along through the slush. The ice and patches of red holly and berries among the trees made for truly a magical image within the boundaries of the forest just on the outskirts of the property.

The girls were each on their own quarter ponies, and though Eliza wasn't surprised to find they were decent riders given their background, she had a lead rope tied to each of the horse's bridle, which she attached in the front of her saddle just in case. She, on the other hand, held onto the horn, and they meandered along at a leisurely pace.

"I've never been on a horse ride in the winter before," Effie confessed, turning to beam at Lizzie in the center of the little parade. "Mama always said it was too dangerous, but it's amazing!"

"It would've been too dangerous had we gone out a few days ago," Lizzie conceded. "But your uncle has been busy cleaning as much snow as he could. If he thought this path was unsafe, he never would've let anyone go on it."

"Yeah, especially not you." Effie giggled a little, then smirked and winked at her sister over Eliza's lap. "Oh? And just what makes you say that"

"Because he loves you!" Emma chimes in. "And so do we!"

The comment was so casual, so unexpected, that for a moment, Lizzie was truly at a loss for what to say. A lump rose in her throat, and she let herself take her time as she gazed at the little five-year-olds on either side of her. Though it had only been a week since they had met, Eliza had come to care for them as if they were her own. She knew from that very first day that they had taken a liking to her, but never had she experienced such an innocent expression of love given so freely before. They watched her expectantly, and she had to swallow back an unexpected tidal wave of emotions to reply, "I love you too, munchkins." She clamped her legs a little tighter around her horse's flanks to reach across and grab their hands at the same time.

Emma beamed and tried to lean over to hug her but couldn't do so without teetering. She had to sit up again before she lost her balance. She did, however, look at Eliza with bright expectant eyes as she asked, "Does this mean you'll stay?"

Eliza sucked in a breath, and her eyebrow rose near to her hairline. "St-stay?" She stammered out, already shaking her head. "What do you mean?"

This time, it was Effie's turn. She rolled her eyes and stuck out her tongue as if Eliza was missing the most obvious answer in the world. "She means that we think you should stay here with us instead of going back to your old home."

"Yeah," Emma added. "Everything is better since you've been here. Uncle Alex isn't so sad anymore, we get to do fun things all the time instead of being stuck inside, and even Grandma isn't so confused."

Eliza's heart nearly stopped, but no matter where she looked, she couldn't seem to escape their pleading eyes and sweet, heart-shaped faces. They were so young, so innocent. She didn't know if they even fully understood the tragedy they had undergone only a year ago. How could she possibly explain to them that it was so much more complicated than they thought?

But even then, finding the words wasn't the hardest part. The hardest part was knowing that the sweet innocent girls actually meant the words coming out of their mouths. Somehow they had fallen in love with her the same way he had fallen in love with them for exactly who she was; nothing more, nothing less. At that moment, she wasn't sure who she was going to miss more, them or Alexander and his brash, caring, soft, intelligent, puzzling ways she so desperately craved to uncover...

In her heart of hearts, she thought it would be just about equal.

"Girls... I wish I could. I truly do. Believe me when I say I want to stay more than anything. But, when your uncle takes me into town...well, no one knows what will happen." She paused, then shrugged. Effie pouted. "Aww! But do you have to go?"

She nodded sadly. "But no matter what, you must both always remember one thing."

"What's that?" Effie asked.

She eyed them both carefully, ensuring she had their rapt attention before she spoke. "No matter where I go and when we see each other again, I will always care about you."

She squeezed their little hands again, and they smiled.

At least that was the truth.

Chapter Nineteen

December 28, 1860

With the girls out on horseback with Lizzie and his mother taking a nap, Alexander went to the barn to feed the cattle. He had dumped the last of the food in their troughs and gone to check the back room in case he needed to secure more on his upcoming trip when sharp, fierce barking echoed through the air, inching closer and closer to the ranch.

He dropped the feed bag he had picked up to test its weight and sprinted out into the corral. "Anyone here?"

The barking grew louder. Alexander made his way outside and squinted into the sun, shielding his face with his hand. Slowly but surely, a trio of dogs pulled a wooden sled behind them. A familiar figure came into view, and Alexander smiled. Nathan stood at the head of the sled, yipping and gently pulling on the reins until the dogs stopped. Alexander met the farm hand halfway as Nate climbed off.

"Glad to see you finally made it back!" he shouted, grinning and holding up his hand as a greeting.

"Hey!" Nate waved back, and then they wrapped one another in a one-armed hug. When they parted, Nate took a long sniff of the crisp ranch air as a smile slid onto his lips. "Ah! It's good to be back!"

Alexander laughed and swung an arm around his friend's shoulder. "How's your Ma? Did you guys get by okay in that nasty storm?"

Nate snored and smirked. "You know her; always resourceful. I'm pretty sure she had gathered enough blankets and made enough extra food to feed half the neighborhood by the time the snow came.

Alexander shook his head but couldn't help a chuckle of his own. Yep, that sounded like Marie. "How she manages to keep this estate running and play godmother to half the town, I'll never know. I've barely been handling the upkeep for a week, and I'm about to drop." He ducked his head sheepishly. "Grateful for Lizzie. Honestly, I don't know what I would've done without her this week."

Nate's eyes grew wide, and he gasped. "You mean she's still here?"

Alexander gave him a dubious look. "Where else would she go in this weather?"

"No, you saddle stiffer! I meant I thought you were going to take her into town as soon as you could."

Groaning, Alexander gestured again to the snow-covered ground. "Believe me, I wanted to, but—" He shrugged. "Can't argue with Mother Nature." Then he paused and studied his friend. "Why are you so interested in her anyway?"

Nate rolled his eyes. "You really gotta get back into town. All anyone can talk about is this O'Connor girl who's gone missing. Part of the reason I came back here today, other than to get back to work, of course, was to check and see if Lizzie was still here. I wondered if maybe the missing girl in town could be her."

Alexander suddenly understood, and his eyes widened. "When did the girl in town go missing?"

"Just about a week ago," Nate replied. "So right about the same time you found Lizzie on your property."

Alexander scrubbed his beard. "Mmm, so the timing lines up too. I think she's on a ride with the girls right now, but we should definitely ask her about it when they get back."

Nathan raised a brow. "You left her alone with the twins? Are you trying to torture her for some reason?"

Alexander rolled his eyes and gently shoved him. "Ha-ha, very funny. They are not that bad. Actually, they've taken quite a liking to her, and she seems to have done the same." As he said it, he felt intense heat creep up his cheeks, and the knowing smirk on Nate's face as it grew hotter didn't help matters.

"Are you sure they're the only ones who have taken a liking to her? Sounds to me like you're a bit taken as well."

"Wha... What?" Alexander sputtered. He shook his head and held up his hand. "Of course not! That would be ridiculous! We just met!"

"So?" Nate challenged.

Alexander scoffed. "Shut your pan and come inside. You must be hungry."

***

Nate gladly agreed, and when he stepped into the sitting room, Alexander braced himself as his friend looked around at the leftover Christmas decorations and gave a little whistle. "Whoa, Swanson. Did you all get a new housekeeper or something while we were gone? I've never known you to be one to decorate."

"Don't look at me. This was all Lizzie's doing."

Nate smiled. "Well, when I see her again, I'll be sure to tell her I think it looks great. Feels different in here, too, somehow. Lighter, I guess."

Fireworks went off in Alexander's stomach as he smiled again. "That, too, can be credited to Lizzie. She's been so helpful and cheerful the whole time she's been here. Honestly, the whole house is happier now that she's around. It almost feels like... before Maggie died."

Nathan's knowing grin crept back onto his lips. "Are you sure you want her to leave?"

As quickly as they arrived, the fireworks were put out and replaced by a deepening pit in the depths of Alexander's stomach. If he were honest, he was beginning to wish anything but that was the case. But she had a home and a family that didn't include them, and sooner or later, she would need to get back to. And now that he knew there were people in town who were worried about her, Alexander was more than determined than ever to see her safely back where she belonged. He just had to convince himself that it wasn't here at the ranch.

Chapter Twenty

December 28, 1860

"I never went that fast on a horse before!" Effie squealed as they approached the house.

"See, I told ya it wasn't that scary," Emma replied. She had linked arms with her sister as they wandered up the path.

Effie stuck out her tongue and rolled her eyes. "I know you did, but you are braver than me."

Emma shrugged. "Only sometimes."

The three of them sighed as they entered the entryway. Eliza bent down and gave Effie a side hug. "I'm so proud of you! Just wait until we tell your uncle! I bet he'll want you to show off your new tricks to all of his ranch hands once the snow clears!"

Effie's blue eyes sparkled. "Really? You think he'll like it that much?"

"Think who will like what that much, Effie-Belle?"

Three heads jerked upward, and Eliza grinned when Alexander came into view. The twins, of course, rocketed away from her and straight toward their uncle.

"Uncle Alex, Uncle Alex, guess what?"

Chuckling, he bent down to scoop Effie into his arms. "What is it, munchkin? Did you three have fun on your ride?"

"So much fun!" she chirped. "Lizzie even taught me how to cantor!"

Alexander's eyes went wide and flicked between his niece and Eliza. For a moment, she was afraid she was about to get scolded because she couldn't tell if he looked impressed or terrified. Probably both. That's how she had felt when she had said she finally wanted to try the faster gait, but she was powerless to those pleading eyes, and finally agreed to let her do it only so long as she stayed within view and let Eliza cantor right beside her. The girls had only been riding quarter ponies, but she still wanted to be careful.

To her relief, though, Alexander smiled a wide, proud smile and hugged his niece. "You did? That's amazing! Was it scary?"

Effie shook her head, and Eliza felt a swell of pride in her chest when she said, "Nope! I thought it was going to be, but I had Emma and Lizzie there to help me, and it was easy. I love it so much I didn't wanna stop to come home for lunch!"

Alexander spun her around before he put her down. "That's wonderful! You'll have to show me next time we go out riding, okay?"

Effie nodded enthusiastically. "What if I show you right now?"

Alexander chuckled but shook his head. "We can't go now, Effie. We have a guest. Why don't you go into the kitchen and say hi to Nate, and then we can figure out what we are going to feed you rascals for lunch?"

"Nate's here?" Emma chirped. Alexander nodded, and the girls scampered off for the kitchen, yelling his name.

"Wipe your feet first!" Alexander called, but of course, he was completely ignored. He let out a long breath and ran a hand down his face. "I swear, sometimes, the way they act, I would think they were raised in a barn!" He winked.

Eliza couldn't help but giggle at their antics, but she gave Alexander a confused glance as she disentangled herself from her winter clothes. "They're just excited," she replied. "Who is Nate?"

Realization dawned on Alexander, and he facepalmed himself. "Oh, that's right! You haven't met him yet! He is my ranch hand. He's the one really responsible for keeping everything running around here when there's not a blizzard."

They laughed together, and Alexander gestured for her to follow him. "Come on, I'll introduce you."

They wandered into the kitchen, and Alexander made quick work of introductions. Nate dipped into a little half bow and held his hand. "Pleasure to meet you, Miss. Alexander here has been telling me all about you. It seems you've had quite an impact on his little family the days I've been gone."

Eliza blushed and didn't miss the sly wink he tossed in Alexander's direction. "The pleasure is mine. What brings you here today?" As the typical greeting tumbled from her mouth, a cold sweat broke out all over her body. If there were someone new at the ranch, that meant... Her smile faltered.

Nate smiled easily and brushed back his hair. "Now that the roads are finally safe enough to travel again, I thought I would come up and update Hermit Swanson on everything that's been going on in town."

Eliza tried to remain calm even as her hands shook. Was it really safe to travel? But that meant...

Alexander stepped up behind his friend and nodded. "Isn't it great? Now you can go into town and finally meet with the sheriff and be reunited with your family!"

"All anyone can talk about is a missing woman who was reported just short of a week ago." Nate chimed in. "Alexander and I think you may be her."

"M...me?" Black spots danced in front of Eliza's division. The floor tilted from underneath her, and she stumbled, catching herself on a nearby kitchen chair. She struggled to take a deep full breath. Instead, each one came out as hitching gasps. Someone was looking for her. Her haunting dreams came back to her in a crashing, bone-chilling way. It must be Bennie and Russel! But if they were looking for her, what options did she have left? Did she let them find her? She had made the decision days ago that when the time came, she wanted to face her fate bravely, but now that it was actually here, every fiber of her being was begging her to run the other way.

"Now you can finally get back to civilization." Eliza could tell Alexander was trying to joke, but his smile didn't reach his eyes, and his laugh was hollow and humorous. "Nathan says he can take you back right after lunch."

"I see." Her stomach churned, convulsing at a rapid pace as the room continued to spin. Left with nowhere to hide, she slapped her hand over her mouth and made a dash for the door. "If you'll excuse me, I'm not... feeling well."

Before anyone could protest, she was out the door and sprinting toward the privy.

Chapter Twenty-One

"Nathan says he can take you back right after lunch."

Alexander tried to interject some enthusiasm into his words, but the ever-present pit in his stomach seemed to be growing deeper and deeper every time he spoke of sending her away, and he could only muster mild enthusiasm at best.

When she paled and nearly stumbled in response, though, it was still surprising despite all of his suspicions. He knew the other night that she was afraid of something, but never in his wildest dreams would he have guessed it would be her own family. When Lizzie bolted out of there like a frightened stallion within the next second, well, there was no mistaking it.

"She's a wild one, ain't she?" Nathan quipped.

Alexander exhaled and turned to his friend. "Nate, I'm so sorry. She's been a little hesitant to go into town since she first arrived here, but I never thought she would react like that. I'll be back as soon as I get to the bottom of what's been going on."

Nate smiled and waved off the apology. "Take your time. I'll go keep an eye on the twins. I'm sure we can find some way to entertain ourselves." He smiled, and Alexander once again found himself overcome with gratitude. He may not have as many people in his life as he would've liked, but the people that he did were good as gold.

He started at the privy but, finding it empty, quickly headed up the stairs toward her bedroom – only to find her sitting on the edge of the bed, still struggling to get her breath.

"Lizzie?"

He rounded the doorframe and took a few slow steps inside. Her gaze flew up to meet his, and she turned away as more tears dripped down her cheeks. "Alex, please."

The quiver in her voice made his heart ache, but no matter what she wanted, he knew he couldn't leave her. Not now. Not at a time like this. He inched closer to the bed but didn't sit down, not wanting to completely invade her personal space.

"Lizzie, please. Just talk to me. I know you've been... afraid of something." His voice hitched on the word afraid. He had wanted to say she was hiding something, but without all the evidence, he knew better than to make assumptions. "Just, just tell me what it is, and we can fix it. Together."

Eliza whimpered and finally looked at him through red-rimmed eyes. "No, no, we can't."

Alexander frowned. "Why not?"

"Because... because after I tell you the truth, you'll hate me."

Alexander's heart lurched again, and it crawled into his throat. His palms were sweaty, and his vision swam. He sunk down onto the bed but made sure it wasn't close enough that they were touching. His pulse hammered in his ears as the room tilted. So, he was right all along. She was hiding something. The only question now was how bad it was.

"Lizzie... wh-what are you talking about?" She sobbed again as her name fell from his lips. It sent shivers down his spine.

"Th... that's not my name. It's never been my name. Not really. I'm... I know where Eliza O'Connor is. Or, I guess I should say I know *who* she is."

Eliza O'Connor. Hearing it again, he realized he did recognize that name. It was the family that owned a ranch about five miles away.

She met his eyes briefly, and his mouth hung open. A million thoughts swirled around in his mind at once, and he didn't know which one to start with first. One screamed louder than the other, though, so he plucked it. "Y... You? You're... you're Eliza O'Connor." Even though he had suspected for what seemed like a long time now that something in her past didn't line up, never in his most outlandish imagination had he imagined it would be something like this. He tried several times to speak, opening and closing his mouth like a gutted fish, but each time he couldn't find the words.

"I am." She had managed to dry at least some of her tears but still couldn't meet his eyes, focusing instead on the skirts of her dress. A hiccup escaped in the middle of her confession, and Alexander gritted his teeth.

"How... how long have you known?"

"A few days."

Betrayal curdled every emotion other than rage, and he practically vibrated from it. "Before Christmas?"

She whimpered, then nodded.

Alexander exhaled and tried to make out something outside of his confusion. "All this time. All this time, and you said nothing. Why? Your family was so close. Why not just ride back as soon as it was safe to do so? Why put on this charade?"

"I... I was afraid. My stepbrother got entangled with some bad people. I overheard something I shouldn't have about one of their schemes, he found me and... Well, I couldn't stay there anymore. I rode and rode and rode through the woods, but it was cold and dark, and my only concern was getting away from that... bandit. I would've told you as soon as I remembered, but I was afraid if I did, you wouldn't let me stay. I didn't know what else to do."

"Bandit?" Alexander spat, anger dripping from his words. "What kind of bandit?"

Eliza's lower lip trembled, but she forced herself to meet his gaze. The truth was already out. Alexander figured she found no use in keeping any more secrets. "Be... Bennie "Bullettooth" Boyle?"

"Boyle?! As in, *Bullettooth* Boyle?" he roared.

She nodded helplessly.

"Eliza! How could you do that?" A tiny pang of remorse pierced through his anger storm when he realized her whole body was trembling, but he had much more important things to worry about just then than her emotions: his family. His real, blood family whom she was now responsible for putting directly in the path of one of the most dangerous criminals in all of Wolfspell.

"Alex, I... I'm sorry. I only wanted..."

"Sorry is not going to keep my family safe, is it? Did you think about that when you decided to go through with this whole farce of yours? What if Bennie had found you here? You could've put the twins, me, and even my mother in mortal danger! Do you even care about that?"

Eliza, was crying openly now. "Of course I do! You know I do! I've come to love them like they're my own family."

Alexander snarled. "If you truly felt that way, you would have gone home as soon as you regained your memory. You wouldn't put any of us through any of this, and you wouldn't have let a criminal anywhere near my ranch or my family!"

"Bu...But Alex, I didn't!"

He scoffed. "Not yet! But one more day here, and you might as well have. You're going to go pack your things, march downstairs, and leave with Nathan this instant. Take any danger he may have brought here with you and leave everything that ever belonged to my sister behind."

Eliza nodded shakily. "Okay, I will. The last thing I would ever want to do is put any of you in danger. But Alex, please, if you would just let me—"

He had already begun stomping toward the door, but he turned around with his hand on the knob, sneering at her. "You know, I knew a long time ago that something about your story didn't match up. But you were so kind and so gracious and everything that we needed after this huge tragedy that I tried my hardest to push it away. I never really cared if I knew everything about you right away, but I never thought you would bring danger to my doorstep. I guess this is on me."

With that, he slammed the door behind him with a loud, hollow thud that resounded through the walls.

Chapter Twenty-Two

Guilt wound around Eliza's gut like a snake. She knew, of course, that she couldn't live in this blissful Christmas bubble forever. She knew one day it would have to burst. But not like this.

Maybe it was nothing more than a childhood fantasy. But she had hoped, really hoped, and almost made herself come to believe, that after everything she had done for Alexander and his family, when the truth finally did come out, he would find it in his heart to forgive her. Not right away, but with time. This holiday and her time with this family had been the best she could remember since her father died. She couldn't, wouldn't let it slip through her grasp so easily again.

When she got her breath back, her feet moved her toward the door of the bedroom, and her hand wrapped around the brass knob. She flung it open, only half feeling her bare feet slap against the hard wooden floor of the hallway as she followed Alexander down the stairs.

"Alexander, please, wait!"

Her heart hammered in her chest as he paused on the third step to the bottom before reaching the landing, and an agonizing beat of silence passed between them before he did anything. Finally, though, with an exhausted sigh, he turned around, one hand tracing the scruff of his beard. Only then did Eliza notice the bags under his eyes, the way his shoulders had slumped, and how haggard he suddenly appeared. A jolt of pain pinged through her. She had done that. The last thing she had ever intended to do to this family was hurt them, and now she had hurt the person she cared for most.

"Eliza, please. Not now."

Eliza's heart sprang into her throat. A part of her wanted to abandon the entire argument altogether, pretend that nothing had ever come out into the open, and rush into his arms if only to comfort him like she had a few nights prior. But she knew she couldn't. No matter how much she wanted it to, nothing could remain the way it used to be. But did that really mean he was willing to give up everything they had been through over one mistake?

Eliza exhaled but steadied their gazes and didn't let him break eye contact. "Yes, now. Listen, I know you don't trust me, and I don't blame you. The last thing I ever wanted to do was hurt any of you. I never meant for this ruse to go on as long as it did, but I was just so happy here. I wanted more than anything to become the girl you saw me as, and thought, well hoped really, that when the truth did come out... Well, I had hoped that after everything we'd been through it wouldn't matter."

Eliza's stomach dropped as Alexander gaped at her.

"You didn't think it would matter? You didn't think that pretending to be an entirely different person than who you were and putting my mother and my entire family in danger would matter?"

Eliza immediately heard the flaw in her logic, and she winced, reaching for him before realizing her error and pulling her hand back. "No, of course not. That's not what I meant! I only thought—"

"Relationships are built on more than what people do for one another. After I saved you from that snowstorm, you didn't owe me anything, and I didn't expect you to stay as some sort of payment. In fact, I tried to bring you back into town as soon as I could. You were the one who chose to refuse."

212

Eliza let her head sink to her chest and bit her lip as she clasped her forearms with her hands. He was right. She knew that. And when she thought about it, she didn't really have another defense for what she had done. She should have known that staying here any longer than she had to was dangerous. But Bennie and her brother were after her, not Alexander or his family. If it hadn't been for that dream, she would have had no reason to suspect they were in any danger until Nathan showed up at the door only a few minutes earlier.

"I'm sorry." It wasn't a good defense. Not even close. But it was all she had to offer.

Alexander nodded and ran a hand through his hair, but his somber expression didn't change. "I believe that you are, but I can't trust you anymore. You should have been open and honest with me from the start. If you had told me you were in danger, I would have helped find a way to keep you safe – keep everyone safe. You had the chance to come clean, and yet only now, when you don't have a choice, did you choose to take it."

Eliza sniffed and blinked back a few more tears but didn't bother wiping away the stray ones that slid down her cheeks. "Would you ever consider forgiving me? I promise I won't ever lie to you again." She took a desperate step closer to him but restrained herself from placing a hand on his shoulder.

Alexander said nothing.

Her throat tasted like sandpaper.

"Please. I know what I did was wrong, and I'm going to do everything in my power to make it up to you, but I can't... I can't leave Louise and the girls. I can't leave you."

Alexander's eyes softened, but only slightly. Eliza's heart fluttered a little faster against her chest, and she pushed

213

ahead. "I mean, I know it's only been a short time, but you all have been more of a family to me than I've ever had... I don't..." She choked on another quiet sob but did her best to push it back. No. Now was not the time to break down. She had made this mess herself, and Alexander was right to force her to face her choices and lie with them. No matter how much she regretted what she had done, she couldn't take it back. She could only hope and pray that he would allow them to move forward. Together.

Alexander reached around to scratch the back of his neck and gave her a slightly pitying look as he gently reached over and squeezed her hand. "I know you have your reasons for doing what you did, but it doesn't change the fact that you inadvertently put my family in danger. Besides," he paused but didn't move any closer. "No matter how hard you try to run from it, your past will always come back to haunt you unless you face it. You taught me that the night you found my mother in the east wing. Russel and Bennie are dangerous, and I need to put my family first."

Eliza's heart ached. And to think, not too long ago, she imagined that family included her. She nodded and swallowed the lump in her throat. Despite how much it hurt, she more than understood his reasoning. She imagined he would do anything to keep his nieces and his mother safe, and the last thing she wanted to do was put that in jeopardy.

"I... I understand." She cast a forlorn look over her shoulder toward her old room. "I suppose I should go pack."

Alexander pressed his lips together but released her hand and let her go.

As she made her way back inside the room and he moved down the stairs to the first floor, Eliza couldn't stop herself from following his silhouette until he was completely out of sight. After all, it might be one of the last views she ever had of him.

Chapter Twenty-Three

As Alexander made his way down the stairs and into the kitchen, his mind drifted to the twins. What was he going to tell them? Although he knew Eliza leaving was for the best, he didn't know how they could ever go back to life without her after everything she had given them.

He took his position at the kitchen counter, trying to distract himself by finishing the lunch preparations but proving unsuccessful. Every time he picked up a plate, or particularly the cups they had used that day, he was reminded of the tea party they had had in this very room not long after Eliza had first arrived. It had been one of the first times he had seen the twins getting along so well since their mother died; the first time he realized Eliza would be more than just a guest as long as she remained on the ranch. What would life be like without her seemingly boundless energy, kind demeanor, and the uncanny ability to always seem to find the right thing to say, no matter the situation?

He turned the question over and over in his head but couldn't seem to come up with a suitable answer. He finished cutting the twins' sandwiches into triangles the way they liked them and set everything out. Emma and Effie seemed to pick up on the sudden somber mood permeating the room the minute they wandered in with Nathan after he called them.

Nathan was the first to break the awkward silence. "So, what happened? Did you find out anything about—"

Alexander's eyes snapped from his friend and back between the twins as he mouthed *later*, but he wasn't quite fast enough to avoid piquing Emma's curiosity.

"Where is Lizzie? Isn't she hungry? I thought she was gonna eat lunch with us."

Effie, who had already dug in, looked up mid-bite and shared a confused glance with her sister. "Yeah, she's not sick, is she?"

Alexander sighed and put his own half of a sandwich down. "No, girls, she's not sick."

Emma smiled. "Good." Then her brow crinkled as she looked around again. "But where is she?"

Alexander only shook his head as he took another bite of his sandwich and chewed slowly. He knew he would have to tackle this sooner or later, but he had hoped he would have at least had one more meal to gather his thoughts. As he looked at the girls' earnest faces, he had half a mind to lie, or even worse, make a different decision. Eliza may have lied about her name, but from everything he'd seen, she hadn't lied about who she was. No matter what else she did, he couldn't deny what a good motherly figure she had been to the girls for as long as she had stayed at the ranch. Could he really deny them of that after everything they had been through?

But as quickly as the thought came, Alexander made it vanish. *No! That's impossible!*

No matter what, he had to do everything he could to keep his family safe. Even if that meant losing her.

"Uncle Alex?"

A small delicate hand touched his arm, and Alexander swiveled around to see Emma peering at him with big round blue eyes. "What's wrong with Lizzie?" she asked.

Alexander put his free hand over his niece's and offered a weary smile. "Nothing's wrong with her, munchkin. I promise. She just, well, she's packing."

"P-packing?" Effie asked. "Is she going on vacation?"

In spite of everything, that comment alone was enough to make Alexander smother a laugh. "No, Effie-Belle, I'm afraid not."

Her nose scrunched. "Oh. Well, then... are we all going on vacation?"

Alexander shook his head again. Perhaps it would be easier to just come out and say it, no matter how much he didn't want to. "Some other time, baby girl, but not today. Lizzie's upstairs packing because, well, because it's time for her to go home."

Emma frowned. "But–but she lives here with us! Effie and I just asked her to stay while we were riding horses."

Alexander sucked in a breath and sat back in his chair. He felt like someone had punched him in the gut. That he had not been prepared for. "You did?" he croaked out, doing his best to keep at least most of the rasp from his voice. The twins nodded, and Alexander looked at them, aghast. He had thought they had gone over this, how Eliza was only here temporarily. They had talked about her going home so many times before. He wanted to prepare them as much as possible. But it was apparent he hadn't done enough. "What did she say?"

Effie bit her lip and placed her hand under her chin, thinking hard. When the answer came to her, her expression changed immediately. It grew so sad that Alexander barely resisted the urge to scoop her up into his lap right then. "Oh..." She sniffed, and Alexander's heart cracked a bit. "She said she wasn't sure if that would happen. But, no matter what, she would always care about us." She wiped the back of her hand over her dripping nose, and Alexander didn't even bother correcting her to use a napkin. Instead, he simply reached over and squeezed her hand across the table.

"That's right," Alexander said. A short beat of silence passed, and he sent up a quick prayer of thanks. Maybe Eliza didn't know it at the time, but she was already making this difficult conversation so much easier.

Lord, what are we going to do when she is gone?

When Effie looked up at him, an iron-clad fist squeezed his chest. He hated seeing tears swim in her eyes, but when she spoke, her voice was surprisingly calm. "Uncle Alex, does that mean Lizzie has to go home now? To her... to her other family?"

Alexander nodded and reached over with his free hand to comb it through Emma's hair. "Yes. Yes, it does."

Emma and Effie nodded, then shared a look.

"Uncle Alex?" Emma turned to him, looking as serious as he had ever seen her.

"Yes, Em?"

"Can we go help her pack and say goodbye?"

Alexander's heart pounded in his chest as they waited expectantly. "That's a great idea, Emma, but for now, why don't we let her do that herself? I'm sure she'll say goodbye before she leaves. Okay?"

Emma nodded. "Okay. But promise you won't let her leave without saying goodbye?" She sounded so small and uncertain at that moment that Alexander couldn't stop his own eyes from welling up. He blinked away the burn. "I promise."

***

When Eliza came downstairs with a small bag of belongings twenty minutes later, Alexander stood between the twins at the bottom of the stairs. When her eyes met the twins' large, pleading ones, her chin trembled, and she bit down on her bottom lip until the skin around it turned white. Alexander winced when he saw her chest heave with uneven breaths the closer she drew to the three of them. Emma was the first to step forward, peering up at Eliza with those innocent, wide eyes of hers that never failed to undo him.

"Do you really have to go?"

Eliza sighed and exchanged a quick glance with Alexander – one last pleading attempt for him to let her stay. He opened his mouth. His heart ached to do just that, but when his gaze drifted back down to his nieces, his beautiful innocent, perfect nieces who had already experienced so much tragedy, he couldn't bear to put them through anymore. So, even though it hurt worse than losing a part of himself, he met her gaze just long enough to offer only a single imperceptible shake of his head.

With that, Eliza nodded, though he saw the moisture threaten to spill over her eyes. She pushed it back as best as she could and dropped to her knees in front of the twins. "I'm so sorry, Emma, but I really do."

"You have to get back to your real family, right?"

The rejection in Effie's small voice was nearly enough to unravel Alexander, and by the way, Eliza's balance wobbled at the question. He guessed it was doing the same to her. She gently cupped Effie's cheeks in her hands and leaned forward to place a gentle kiss on the girl's forehead. "I may be going away now, but no matter what, don't forget what I said, okay?

No matter where I go, no matter where you go, I will always, always care about you."

Even though the statement was directed at his niece, Alexander couldn't stop the way his heart skipped a beat when her eyes met his as she whispered the end of this sentiment. Did she mean she would always care for him, too?

"O-Okay." Effie nodded, and Emma sniffed before both girls threw their arms around Eliza's neck. Even as she wobbled, she hugged them back with equal ferocity.

"I'm gonna miss you both so much."

"Can we—" Emma hiccupped halfway through the question as she pulled away enough to look Eliza directly in the eyes. "Can we come and visit you? After you get home?"

Eliza swallowed so hard Alexander could see the lump in her throat. Her eyes met his again over the twins' shoulders, but he couldn't make himself react. He didn't know how to. As much as he didn't want to punish the girls by making Eliza disappear from their lives forever, he didn't know what would become of the situation with Bennie, and the last thing he wanted to do was make promises he couldn't keep.

"I'm afraid that's something you're going to have to ask your uncle, Emma."

He cringed when all at once, three pairs of irresistible blue eyes turned toward him. He should have seen that coming, but he was at a loss for words.

"Well?" Effie asked. "Can we visit her?"

Alexander cleared his throat and ran a hand over the back of his neck. Why did she have to put him in such an awkward position?

"Why don't we give her a few weeks to get settled, okay girls? Then we can all write her a letter together, and if she says it's alright—" he met her eyes very seriously with that amendment making it clear that alright meant safe. She nodded, and he gave her the faintest of smiles before pushing on. "Then we can go visit."

"Okay. But will you be ready soon?"

Eliza smiled, even though her sadness was still clear in her eyes as she disentangled Effie's arms from around her neck.

"I don't know how long it will take me," she said honestly, running a hand through their bouncing curls. "But I promise you that as soon as you can come, I will write to you."

That, at least, earned her the faintest of smiles.

As she pushed to her feet and hefted her suitcase once again, Alexander almost reached out to take it from her as she moved past him but stopped himself at the last second.

Just as her hand rested on the brass knob of the front door and she twisted it, only moments away from disappearing for their lives for the Lord only knew how long, she turned back one more time to face Alexander directly.

"Please tell Louise I said goodbye. It would be too hard..." she paused and dropped her voice. "I want you to know that I really am truly sorry. I never meant to deceive you as I did. I wanted to tell you so many times, but after I met your family," she shrugged and looked down, "It all felt so right that I didn't want it to end. I never meant for you to get tangled up in the rest of this."

She removed her hand from the door, and Alexander stepped up beside her to open it for her. As much as he could understand where she was coming from in wanting a place, even in wanting people to call home—after all, he would give nearly anything to have one more day with Maggie—he couldn't imagine what it must be like for her; knowing the life that awaited her back home, he found himself with little more energy to do anything except offer a hopeful smile and a regretful "Good Luck."

As she ventured out into the cool evening air, Alexander couldn't help himself from tracking her faded silhouette. At first, she headed toward Nathan's sleigh just as they had agreed. But then, she veered off at the last second, making a dash for the stables.

Alexander's brow furrowed. *What is she doing?*

He cast a glance back at the girls and nodded toward Emma. "Go sit with your grandmother in her room for a minute. I think Lizzie forgot something."

For a split second, Effie's eyes brightened. "Are you going to ask her to come back? Did you change your mind?"

Alexander let his eyes drift upward. *Lord, give me strength.*

Then he turned back to his curious niece and squatted. "You know why I can't do that, munchkin. She has to go home. It's where she belongs. I'm just gonna go say goodbye, and then I'll be right back, okay?"

Her lip trembled again, but she nodded. "Okay."

He smiled and kissed her forehead, then turned to Emma. "Look out for each other and tell your grandmother where I've gone. I'll be right back."

"We will," Emma assured him.

Alexander nodded. Then, without another word, he was out the door and down the steps. He ran past Nathan, waiting in his sleigh. His friend gave him a quizzical look as he passed. "Where are you two going? I thought we were leaving?"

Alexander shook his head. "I don't know. But that's what I'm about to find out."

He had to quicken his pace to catch up with Eliza, but eventually, he found her, saddling her gray mare in one of the stalls of his stable.

He stepped back and watched for a minute, at a loss for what to say or do and utterly bewildered. Finally, though, he decided he just had to come out with it. He approached her carefully and placed a hand on her shoulder so as not to spook her or the horse. Still, when she spun around, it was a little too fast for his liking, and her hand flew to her heart before she recognized him and relaxed again.

"Oh, it's you."

Alexander allowed the smallest of smiles to slip onto his lips as he raised an eyebrow. "Yeah, it's me." He gestured to her horse. "What are you doing?"

Eliza followed his gaze, and for a split second, a flicker of fear appeared in her eyes, as if she was afraid he wouldn't approve of whatever it was she was about to do. But just as quickly as it had come, she steeled her features and spun to face him. "I'm not going back into town."

Alexander blinked and did a double take. "What are you talking about? Of course, you are. Nathan's waiting right out—" She put her hand up.

"I'm not going with Nathan either. You said I had to leave, and I respect that. But I'm not going back to my old life. I can't. I almost got entangled with them once; I won't risk it again."

Alexander gaped at her and tilted his head. What in the world was she thinking? "I... I don't understand. What about your brother?"

Eliza pressed her lips into a thin line as she stepped backward toward her horse. "Stepbrother. And he can take care of himself. I won't always be around to protect him."

"But—"

"Goodbye, Alexander." She swung one leg into the stirrup and lifted herself onto the saddle, riding toward the barn doors with impressive grace. "I hope you know how much you've done for me these past few days. I'll never forget you or your family, even if you forget me."

Without another word, she rode into the snowy landscape, leaving Alexander with not even enough time to think of a suitable retort.

As he wandered back toward the house, feeling numb and helpless, a shadow figure crossing over the edge of the property line caught his eye. At first, only one emerged from the trees; a scrawny-looking man with an oddly protruding beer belly, an unkempt crop of brown hair, and a sour expression. He looked nothing like he was in the mood for pleasantries, and Alexander scowled as he marched across the property as if he owned it. Behind him stood another man, a full head taller than the first. Alexander was unsure why he hadn't noticed him until now.

Quickly, he crossed the fields to meet the men in front of the stable and just diagonal from the house. He couldn't say exactly what it was about him that made Alexander uncomfortable. Perhaps it was his hunched shoulders, and narrowed eyes or the overall jeering demeanor that seemed to follow him like a raincloud.

"Excuse me." He approached the man as civilly as he could and raised an eyebrow. "This is private property. Can I help you?"

The leering smirk that met this greeting made Alexander's hair stand up on the back of his neck and immediately sat every one of his senses on high alert. Whoever this man was, he wasn't going to take one step further toward the rest of Alexander's family. "We're so very sorry to disturb you," The man said in a gruff, gravelly tone. "My name is Russel Rivers. I'm simply trying to locate my missing sister." Out of his trouser pocket, he pulled out a missing person's flier that had been folded into eighths. As he unfolded it, Alexander leaned closer for a better look, and his eyes went wide when he recognized it as none other than Eliza. "I'm told she rode this way some time ago, but I've only just now been able to come and search for her on account of the storm. Have you seen her?"

Alexander's mouth went dry, and he pressed his lips together as the puzzle pieces slowly fell into place. If this was Eliza's brother, that meant... Horror rippled through him as he turned his attention to face the man standing behind Russel River.

The uncaring stare in his black eyes should have been a dead giveaway as to his identity, but just in case that wasn't enough, the rising moonlight glinted off the scar over his eye of the freshly polished pistol hanging at his hip. Alexander had seen the posters all over town.

Bennie "Bullettooth" Boyle.

Feral fear gripped his insides.

All at once, the realities of Eliza's home life crashed around him like an avalanche. Her brother truly was involved with one of the most heinous criminals in all of Wolfspell.

Russel cleared his throat. With his heart throbbing in his ears, Alexander turned his attention back to the matter at hand. He leaned over the picture again and scraped his beard between his pointer finger and thumb in fake contemplation. Bennie fixed him with a death glare that threatened to make his knees go weak, but he refused to show any vulnerability in front of such a backwater criminal. Finally, he met Russell's eyes and shook his head. "I'm sorry, I'm afraid I haven't seen her."

Russel crossed his arms. "You sure? I'd think *real hard* about that answer if I were you."

Bennie grunted, and his fingers twitched near the handle of the pistol at his waist. Sweat beaded down the back of Alexander's neck. He understood more than ever why Eliza felt the need to pretend for so long. Honestly, as much as it still hurt him to know how long she had hidden the truth, seeing with his own eyes what it was she was running from, he no longer knew if he could blame her.

Alexander steeled his features and held his hand up. "I really am very sorry, but I promise you I haven't seen her. Is there a way I may contact you gentlemen if I do?"

He moved one hand behind his back end and crossed his fingers, hoping that if they gave him some form of contact, he could pass it on to the sheriff, and it would be easier to track them down.

Instead, he was met with only a pair of sarcastic smiles and a menacing laugh that chilled the air. "Afraid not," said Bennie. His voice was much too calm and soothing for Alexander's liking. "I suppose we just have to keep looking. Unless of course–" He drew a sharp knife from out of his sleeve and carefully twirled it between his fingers. "There's anything else you think we ought to know?" The murderous gleam in his eye did not go unnoticed by Alexander, and he swallowed thickly.

They know I'm lying. Eliza won't be safe for much longer. I have to find her!

As those thoughts raced through his head at the speed of a freight train, Alexander set his jaw and gained enough courage to look the bandit directly in the eye. "I'm sorry, but that's all I know."

Bennie gnashed his teeth. "One moment I was promised her hand in marriage, and the next, she gets up and leaves, shirking all of her family's responsibilities. If you're lying..." He tightened his grip around the knife, and Alexander winced in spite of himself.

Alexander's ears perked up. Bennie had tried to propose? To Eliza? If there was any doubt left within him, it vanished the minute those words spilled from the bandit's mouth.

If I were a girl, I wouldn't want to marry swine like you, either. He seethed internally.

Out loud, though, he only murmured, "Understood."

"Hey!" Relief flowed over him like a river current as Nathan's familiar voice echoed through the fields, and he trotted up next to Alexander. "Is everything alright over here?"

Russel forced a smile, but Benny didn't say anything. He didn't need to.

"Yes," Russel announced, gently tugging on Bennie's arm. "We were just leaving."

Bennie resisted for a moment too long for Alexander's liking, but eventually, Russel pulled him away. They headed back to their horses grazing lazily beyond the outer fences and vanished from sight. When he was sure they were gone, he turned to Nathan, who was gaping at him expectantly with his hands turned up.

"What was that?"

Alexander shook his head and closed his eyes, silently cursing himself. Why or why did he have to get stuck in his stupid pride and let her ride away? He never should have let her go out into the snow alone!

"Alex?" Nathan waved a hand in front of his friend's face, and he sighed.

"No time to explain. I have to go. I have to go now. There's no telling how long it will take them to find her. I have to get to her first."

Nathan blinked. "Alex, slow down. What are you talking about? Was one of those men who I think it was?"

Alexander nodded grimly. "Bennie "Bullettooth" Boyle. He's after Eliza. I don't know why, I don't know how, but I have to find her and keep her safe." And without another word, he jogged off toward the stables.

The moment she had left his sight, he knew with every fiber of his being he had made the wrong decision. Given what had happened to her last time, who knew what kind of trouble she would get herself into it with that bandit and her brother pursuing her?

Assertive protectiveness rose within him again, and this time rather than ignoring it, he let it lead him.

Within a matter of minutes, he had settled his own horse, instructed Nathan to watch over his mother and the girls, and rode off into the woods. No matter what she has done in the past, Alexander knew for certain he couldn't go on in the present if he ran the risk of losing her.

SALLY M. ROSS

Chapter Twenty-Four

Eliza couldn't help but laugh bitterly at the irony in the situation as, once again, she rode and rode through unfamiliar woods with no sense of direction and even less of an idea of where she was going to go. She couldn't return to the O'Connell ranch, as surely that would be the first place they would look. A brief flickering thought of Perry – the friendly ranch hand who had always treated her like a daughter – flashed through her memory, but she dismissed that thought as quickly as it came. She had already put one family in danger, and she couldn't bear to do that again. Bennie had spies around every corner, and no matter how safe she felt, Nathan's arrival was just another cruel reminder that none of it was ever really true.

The towering pine trees shaded the snow trail until their tracks practically dissolved into darkness. Eliza kept an eye out for anything that looked remotely familiar. She passed several fallen tree branches and discarded foliage that had been downed from the storm but no real mile markers to indicate where she was.

Eventually, midday gave way to evening. Eliza's stomach began to growl, but she ignored it. She had only packed enough food for a couple of days' ride, and she didn't want to waste it. Within another hour, though, Natalie's once brisk trot had slowed to a barely walkable gait, and with each step, she snorted or painted.

Yet another wave of guilt washed over Eliza, and she groaned. How much more of this could she handle before she collapsed from the weight of it? She reached down and stroked the mare's neck, making soft clicking sounds with her tongue. "I know, girl. I know you're tired. I'm sorry for pushing you so hard." She tugged on the reins and veered the horse toward a safe-looking open clearing in a ring of pine trees. "Let's stop for a minute and take a rest, hmm?"

The horse whinnied in agreement, and Eliza dismounted. On wobbly legs, she rounded Natalie's left flank and fished some bread and cheese out of the saddle bag before popping down on a nearby log to eat. As she dug into her sandwich, she mulled over the fact that she was no closer to coming up with any suitable place to stay, but it was much easier to think with a full stomach.

She took a deep breath and allowed herself to relax in the early evening silence, doing her best to trust that, in the end, everything would work out. Eliza felt a strange sense of peace come over her, but it was almost immediately broken by the distinct sound of hoofbeats crunching against the falling snow.

Eliza's pulse pounded in her ears, and she scrambled to her feet. Natalie whinnied from where she had taken a break over by a nearby stream and obediently trotted over the moment Eliza put two fingers to her lips and let out a loud, piercing whistle. She winced upon doing that, though; whoever was following her would probably be more alerted to her presence by such an air-piercing sound.

A current of dread zipped through her as the trotting drew closer with each passing minute. Had Bennie and Russel really found her already? Was this really how it was going to end? These thoughts swirled around in her mind at once, and she sprinted through the trees to try to make out the features of the tall, looming silhouette as it grew closer and closer. She ran her foot into the stirrup to hoist herself up into the saddle once more. Just then, the horse came into view, though, and Eliza's eyes went wide. It was not Bennie or Russel, but a familiar cowboy with twinkling blue eyes and a long beard.

Alexander? A jolt of gratitude zipped through her, but she tried her hardest to squelch it. No. It couldn't be. Alexander had just kicked her out. Why would he be following her now? She blinked, rubbed her eyes, then blinked again just to make sure they weren't deceiving her.

It seemed not.

The closer he came, the more Eliza's heart leaped as she recognized his chiseled features and the relieved expression crossing his face. She urged Natalie into a gallop and rode out to meet him, disbelief radiating through her.

"Eliza!" he exclaimed, urging his own horse to a faster pace until he caught up with her. "Thank the Lord I found you. I thought I had waited too long."

"Al-Alexander?" She shook her head and reached out a hand, stopping just short of brushing the pads of her fingers against his cheek. She so badly wanted to touch him, to feel the warmth of his skin, to make sure none of this was indeed just a pleasant dream.

Although his face looked ghostly pale, he smiled and reached out to take her hand in his. "Thank God you're safe."

"Of course I'm safe. What are you talking about?"

He paused, and an unsettling silence simmered in the air between them. Bile crawled up her throat. "Alexander?" Her eyes started around the woods, and she took a breath. "What are you doing here?"

Alexander ran a hand through his hair and exhaled deeply. "You're right. Your brother came to the ranch. It was seconds after you left. Bennie was with him."

Eliza's ears rang, and her vision swam. *No, no, no, no, no!* This was exactly what she's been trying to avoid. The absolute last thing she wanted to happen; her nightmares came alive only to hunt someone else. She was the only person that deserved their torment. Alexander and his family had been nothing but kind to her, and somehow they were now even more entangled than she was.

"Is everyone all right? Your mother? The twins?" Her eyes welled with tears, and she covered her mouth with her free hand to stifle a sob.

Alexander nodded. "Everyone is fine. For now, at least. But neither Russel nor Bennie seemed too pleased to find out I didn't know where you were."

She tilted her head to the side. "You mean you didn't give up my location?"

Alexander shook his head. "Of course not. No matter what you've done to my family or me, I would never do something like that to you. Besides, the moment I met them, I knew why you did what you did. I still don't condone it, and I hope you never lie to me again—"

Eliza choked down but shook her head vigorously. "Never. I promise!" She crossed her heart for emphasis. Then her brow furrowed. "But wait. "What changed your mind?"

Alexander sighed. "I believe you. And I'm sorry for being so hard on you when you try to explain. If I had known..." He trailed off and looked away before turning back to her and holding out a hesitant hand.

"Come back to the ranch with me. I will talk to Nathan and figure out a plan. We need to go to the police as soon as possible."

Eliza smiled through the tears dotting her cheeks. "Alex, I... Thank you. Thank you for giving me another chance."

Alexander grinned grimly and leaned forward to brush a piece of hair away from her forehead. "Don't thank me until everyone is safe."

Eliza nodded, then kicked Natalie into a sprint, and together they rode off back to the ranch.

Chapter Twenty-Five

Alexander was adamant on the way back home that Eliza rode in front of him if only so he could keep an eye on her the entire journey back. Thankfully, she didn't seem to mind.

"So... what exactly did Bennie and Russel say about me?"

Alexander gritted his teeth. "A great many things I would rather not repeat," he replied honestly.

Eliza winced. "Sounds about right."

"Bennie did mention one interesting fact, though," he ventured. As the words resurfaced from his subconscious. They tasted like poison as he paraphrased them. "He told me that when you ran away, you also gave him the mitten." Raising an eyebrow suggestively, he asked the silent question.

Eliza snorted a laugh, and his heart glowed. Even in the direst of circumstances, it was good to hear her laugh. "Oh, is that what he told you? Russel tried to convince me three months ago to accept his hand in marriage, but there was nothing he could do to get me to agree. I rejected him long before any of this happened."

In spite of everything, Alexander felt every tense muscle in his body relax just the slightest bit at her answer. "I don't blame you. After seeing them with my own eyes?" He pursed his lips. "I can no longer say for certain I wouldn't have done exactly what you did if I had been in your place."

Eliza looked down. "Thank you," she whispered. "Still, though, I'm sorry I got you and your family mixed up in all of this."

Alexander cut a hand through the air. "Let's make a deal, okay? No more apologies. For either of us. What's done is done, and we can't change it. Now, we just need to figure out the next step. I think we should go into town as soon as we can and report this to the sheriff—"

Eliza bit her lip and shook her head regretfully. "I wish it was that simple, but I have my reservations about the sheriff. I remember now... I have seen him talking with Russel a few times. Who's to say he's not in cahoots with Bennie, getting a cut of the profits?"

Alexander sat back in his saddle and ran a hand down his face. Well, that at least explained why Eliza had never attempted to go to the sheriff about it before. Still, he couldn't believe the length that some people were willing to go to for a little bit of extra money. Setback aside, though, he wasn't going to give up.

"What if we involve a higher authority?"

Eliza looked at him curiously. "Like whom? There's no one of higher authority in Wolfspell."

"True," Alexander conceded. "But there is in Blue Creek. I could ride over there tomorrow and talk to the magistrate. Then, once Bennie and your brother are arrested, you'll be free to do whatever you wish." Secretly, now that everything was out in the open, Alexander wanted nothing more than for her to choose to remain at this mountain ranch with him and the girls, but that was a conversation for a later time. It was her life, and he had to let her make the best choice for her future.

Eliza smiled a thin but hopeful smile as they approached the edge of the property, which, thankfully, was free of unwanted guests.

"You would do this for me?" she asked.

Alexander reached over and squeezed her hand.

"I would do anything to keep you safe."

Truer words had never been spoken.

Chapter Twenty-Six

December 29, 1860

The next morning, Alexander left before the rooster crowed, and Eliza woke to a house that was much too quiet and much too empty. The thing she wanted today was to be alone with her thoughts. So once the girls were up and dressed — they had been relieved when Alexander had returned the previous day with Eliza and had barely left her side since then — she clapped her hands once all of the dishes were in the water basin and proudly announced, "Girls, I have another surprise for you."

"Yay!" Emma exclaimed.

"What is it?" Effie asked.

Eliza squatted down to meet their height and gently tweaked her nose. She didn't think she would ever tire of the twins' boundless love for life, and she hoped it was something they kept with them forever. "Well, since your uncle is away on..." She cleared her throat, "business, I thought we could do some more baking. How does that sound?"

She and Alexander had a long conversation late into the night about his upcoming journey. They both agreed at this point, it was better to keep the twins and Louise in the dark about what he was really doing. They were so young, so they simply told them that he was going to the next town to find more people to buy their produce when spring came. They told Louise the same story so as not to worry or confuse her.

"Yay! Baking!" Effie squealed. She scrambled for the cookbook, and Eliza didn't bother to stop her.

"Can we make thumbprint cookies like grandma used to make?" Emma asked.

Eliza nodded as she tied on her apron. "I think that's a great idea. Why don't you help your sister find the recipe, and I'll go outside and get some coal for the oven?"

The girls nodded enthusiastically, and Eliza smothered her laughter as Effie teetered under the weight of the large tome before tottering over to the counter and letting it fall from her grip with a loud *thwack.*

The twins' eyes met over the cover, and they both giggled before Emma raced around the opposite side of the counter, and they worked together to open the heavy cover.

"What about these?"

Eliza peered over to see Effie's hand resting on a simple cinnamon cookie recipe.

Emma scrunched her nose. "We always make those. I wanna do something different!" She flipped a few more pages, and her eyes widened at the picture of a puffy pastry. "Oooh! What are these?"

Effie winced. "I don't know, but they look hard. Let's try something easier?"

"Girls!" Louise shuffled into the kitchen, and both of her grandchildren immediately lit up.

"Grandma!" As one, they sprinted to her and wrapped each of their arms around one of her sides, and she didn't hesitate to bend down and give them both a hug.

"Hello, my loves!" She laughed and kissed each of their cheeks. "What's all the commotion in here?"

"Lizzie said she could help us make cookies!" Emma explained, pointing to the cookbook. "But we can't decide on which ones to make."

Louise smiled, and for a moment, it seemed to light up the room. "Oh, well then! Let's see what our options are, shall we?"

She paddled over to a chair with the twins trotting obediently after her. As she sunk down into the seat, she finally noticed Eliza.

"Are you going to join us, dear?"

Eliza smiled. "Of course. I'll be right back. I was just telling the girls that I had to go get some more coal for the stove. Seeing that they were now in capable hands, she opened the back door and stepped outside.

Halfway through gathering everything they needed, though, something caught her eye in the corner of her vision. The hair on Eliza's neck stood on end as she spun around. Was that... a man on the outskirts of the property?

She shivered. The silhouette didn't look at all like Alexander's. No, this one was slender and tall, with long arms.

Danny? The thought of Bennie's right hand watching her from the tree line entered her mind almost before she could stop it. It filled her with dread, unlike anything she had ever felt before, except perhaps for the night she ran. Her breath came in short gaps, and it took her a moment longer than she would've liked to steady it.

But when she squared her shoulders and braced herself long enough to turn around and fully face the impending threat, whoever or whatever had been lingering in the woods was gone.

Get ahold of yourself, she chided her inner voice angrily. *No one is watching you.* Alexander would never allow that. He would always find a way to protect his family. Her mind was probably only playing tricks on her because she was worried about Alexander and anxious to hear what the magistrate had to say. Or so she hoped. Still, rather than heading straight back inside, she veered off to the barn and went in search of Nathan. If anyone strange had been seen on the property, surely he would know about it.

She wandered inside and checked the tack room and several of the stalls before finally making her way to the stables, where she found him giving the horses their morning feed.

"Nathan?" She poked around one of the stalls. The ranch hand smiled and tipped his hat.

"Evening, Eliza."

She winced a bit. She liked it so much better when people called her Lizzie. Maybe after all this was over, she could go back to that.

"What can I do for you?"

Eliza rested her arms on the edge of the stall. "This may sound a bit strange, but... did you happen to see anything or anyone...strange on the ranch today?"

Nathan's brows furrowed, and he briefly paused his task. "Strange in what way, Miss?"

Eliza shrugged even as her pulse sped up slightly. "Just anyone you didn't recognize or anyone who looked like they might be associated with—" She swallowed the end of her comment, not wanting to jinx anything if her mind really was playing tricks. Nathan fixed her with a knowing look, and his eyes softened.

"You don't have to worry about Benny. Alexander told me that happened. I think he has a good plan. And I promise you I haven't seen anyone unfamiliar lurking around the land lately. If I do, you will be the first to know."

Eliza smiled a guilty but relieved smile as she combed her hair behind her ear. "Thank you. Honestly, I don't know how Alexander would run this place if it weren't for you. I can't thank you enough for staying around with us while he's gone."

"He wouldn't." Nathan offered her a dry chuckle, and she joined in. "No thanks needed, miss. Alexander has been my friend for a long time, and I would do anything to protect those he cares for."

"Well, I just want you to know that I appreciate it just as much as he does." Nathan blushed and pulled the brim of his hat a little further down.

A few minutes later, Eliza tried to calm her jangled nerves as she made her way back toward the house and ambled into the kitchen. Despite Nathan's reassurances, she knew what she had seen. And even more so, she knew how dangerous and conniving Bennie could be. It would be foolish to think they were completely out of danger. Still, without more evidence, there was nothing she could do, so she just had to hope that Alexander would reach the magistrate before anything dire happened. All at once, scents of sugar, flour, and homemade fruit compote tickled her senses.

She smiled as she found the girls had covered most of the open surface of the counter in flour and had set up an assembly line of sorts. Effie was using a cookie cutter to cut out round shapes with little crimped edges. Her sister had another pan of dough, using a smaller cookie cutter to edge out a hole in the middle. Louise stood in front of the last tray, which held both kinds of cookies. She delicately set a small teaspoon full of jam in the center of the plain sugar cookie before topping it with one that had a hole cut out of the center. By the time they were complete, they looked like little flowers with red pollen.

"It seems you finally agreed on something to bake."

Louise looked up and smiled broadly. "Oh! Maggie, you're back! Perfect. We were just about to put the first pan in the oven."

Eliza wandered to the stove and started stocking the fire with the new supply of coal. "I'm just glad to see you finally agreed on a recipe." She turned to Louise. "How did you get them to settle on something, anyway?"

Effie piped up with the answer, though she didn't look too pleased about it. "Grandma said since Emma picked first and we could make cinnamon cookies next time, but then we had to take turns." On the last two words, her face twisted up as though she had eaten something sour, and Eliza's lips puckered as she fought to keep herself from giggling.

"That sounds like the perfect compromise, Effie. And it looks like you're doing a wonderful job. Can I help?"

The little girl nodded and quickly slid over to make room for Eliza behind their workstation. "I think we're gonna need more jam. Grandma said to double the recipe, but I think we may have made too much."

Eliza glanced at the mixing bowl as her eyes widened. There was at least enough in there for two more pans. She chuckled a little as she ruffled Effie's hair. "I'd say so!"

Effie laughed, too, before playfully swatting her hand away. "Grandma can probably teach you how to make more of that fruit stuff. Go ask her!"

Eliza pressed her lips together in a grin. Oh, the joys of being a blunt young girl. "Okay, miss bossy pants. I will."

They spent the rest of the afternoon baking and laughing, and Eliza didn't even care that by the time they finished their five trays of cookies and got them all in the oven, the kitchen looked like a tornado had come through it. The girls had clearly had fun, as had Louise, and it was the most relaxed Eliza had felt since the truth came out.

By the time she finished cleaning everything and found some suitable leftovers to make for a nice dinner, it was growing dark, and there was still no sign of Alexander. But if she didn't want it to return, her anxiety about his whereabouts came back with a vengeance.

"I don't know if it would help," Nathan interjected. He stood at the wash bin, having insisted on doing the dinner dishes that night since Eliza had extended the last-minute invitation. She, on the other hand, stood on the third step of the stairs, hammering just about to head to the girls' bedroom and commence with their nightly bath. "But if it would make you feel better, I could stay the night. Just until Alexander comes back, of course."

Eliza's stiff posture immediately relaxed upon hearing that idea. "That would be wonderful, thank you."

Nathan chuckled and shook his head. "Like I said, miss, no thanks needed. If it helps keep you and the girls safe, you don't even have to ask."

Eliza's eyes grew a bit misty as she opened her mouth to reply but was interrupted by a shrill shriek, *"Lizzie!"*

They both laughed, and Nathan gestured up the stairs with his dish towel. "It seems someone really wants your attention. Go on. I'm okay to finish up here."

Eliza knit her brows together. "Alright, if you're sure."

Nathan smiled. "I'm positive. Get before they create another tornado."

Eliza obeyed, and as she climbed the stairs, she couldn't help but once again marvel at how much her life had changed in only a matter of days.

Chapter Twenty-Seven

December 29, 1860

Blue Creek Montana

It took Alexander much longer than he would have liked to cross over the hill into the nearest town. By the time he arrived, it was late afternoon. He supposed he could have gotten there faster if he were willing to push his horse a little farther, but the snow wasn't melting the way he thought it would, and it looked like another storm might be coming. He couldn't risk his only mode of transportation getting ruined. Not when he had something this important to bring to the magistrate's attention.

So despite his aching legs, Alexander bypassed the incredibly tempting sign at the town inn and moved straight toward City Hall. He tied his horse to a hitching post and marched up the stairs, heading straight through The large oak doors and up to the welcome desk.

Excuse me?"

A stout woman wearing round glasses and with her dark hair pulled back into a crowning braid looked up with glazed eyes from the stack of papers nearly tall enough to cover her head. She impatiently shoved them away and met his intense gaze with a bored one of her own.

"May I help you?" Her voice was raspy and monotone, but Alexander paid it little mind.

"Yes, My name is Alexander Swanson, and I must speak to your magistrate right away. There is a dangerous criminal who has been spotted on my property just one town over. I'm worried for the fate of my family and would like him apprehended right away."

"I'm sorry, sir, but the magistrate is away on business. He will be back in the office tomorrow morning. You may take up your claim with him then."

Alexander ran a hand down his face. "Tomorrow morning?" he repeated.

She nodded. "Yes, sir."

"And you're sure there's no way to see him sooner?

The secretary shook her head. "Come back tomorrow morning at nine."

Alexander held up a finger. "Really, ma'am, I don't intend to speak out of turn, but if you would just–"

"Have a good night, Mr. Swanson." And with that, she turned back to her paperwork and buried herself in it, giving Alexander no more chances. He exhaled sharply through his nose but reluctantly turned around and walked back out into the blustery streets and toward the saloon. As much as he hated knowing he had to be away from his family for a full night, this was too important to give up on.

***

The next morning, he returned to City Hall before the doors opened. When they did, he was the first one into the lobby and wasted no time marching straight back toward the magistrate's office.

"Magistrate Trevor?"

A balding man in an official-looking uniform looked up from behind his desk. He steepled his fingers in front of him and raised a bushy eyebrow. "Yes? May I help you?"

"I'm so sorry to disturb you, sir, but I think I have some information regarding a notorious criminal that you might want to know about."

The magistrate's eyes grew wide, and he gestured for Alexander to step inside. "Come on in, son. What's your name? Where are you from?

He obliged and held out a hand. "My name is Alexander Swanson, sir. I'm from Wolfspell, and if you let me, I believe I can help you catch the criminal bandit known as Benjamin "Bullettooth" Boyle."

The magistrate gasped, and his eyes nearly popped out of his head before he regained his composure. "Sit down, son." He gestured to a chair across from his desk, which Alexander gratefully sank into. "Now, tell me what you know about Boyle."

Alexander did his best to provide an accurate summary of all he knew, starting from the day he rescued Eliza and continuing forward until he learned about her brother's involvement with the bandits and the corrupted sheriff. The man appeared intrigued in all of the right places, and when he was finally finished, magistrate Trevor sat back in his chair and gently rubbed his chin. "You know, the rumor mill has had their tongues wagging about Bennie "Bullettooth" Boyle for quite some time and what dirty deals he may or may not have done with the sheriff of your town. This information may be exactly what we need to disband the whole operation."

Alexander beamed, and his chest swelled with relief as the magistrate leaned forward to shake his hand once again before pushing to his feet. "Thank you, sir, thank you so much."

"I should be the one thanking you, son. Now you just promise me that you can keep your family safe until New Year's Eve."

Alexander scowled, and his relief transformed into a mixture of confusion and anxiety as quickly as it had arrived. "No disrespect, sir, but why must we wait that long? My family needs help now."

"It's only another two days, Mr. Swanson. But that will give my office enough time to not organize a trap to catch those cattle thieves red-handed now that we know what they're up to. Finally, after so many years, we will apprehend Bennie Bluetooth Boyle."

Alexander's frown deepened. The magistrate's plan sounded more than reasonable. He knew that. He really did it, on the other hand...

"I understand you want to get this right, Magistrate Trevor. I really and truly do. But I'm afraid. I'm afraid that my family may be in danger now. Please, sir, there must be something you can do."

The magistrate gave him a steely look but eventually nodded and ran a hand over his bald head. "Very well. Would it be agreeable to you if I were to send two of my men back with you to your ranch to keep an eye on you?"

Alexander smiled, though it was a considerable effort to push down his shoulders as the fear hadn't fully dissipated." That would be greatly appreciated, sir. Thank you so much."

The magistrate grinned. "It's my pleasure, Mr. Swanson. And if this goes the way I'm hoping it might, you might be a town-wide hero by the time all of this is over."

As he walked out of the office that afternoon, Alexander couldn't deny that that thought sent a jolt of excitement through him. But if he were honest, he didn't really care whether he became a town hero or known by the entire state. As long as it kept Eliza and his family safe, whatever he had to do was worth all the trouble in the world.

Chapter Twenty-Eight

Despite Nathan's calming presence, Eliza barely slept that night and was up well before sunrise the next morning. No matter what she did, nothing was good enough to quiet her wandering mind. Alexander had said the trip into the next town would only take a matter of hours, but he had been gone nearly a full day. Had something gone wrong? What if the magistrate hadn't believed him? Or worse, what if Bennie and his crew had gotten wind of Alexander's plan and cut him off before he could execute it? That thought had kept her up most of the night, and by the time misty rays of sun filtered through her window curtains the next morning, she tried as hard as she could to shove it back into the deepest depths of her mind. Surely Alexander was fine. He was capable and knew how to keep himself safe. But had he ever gone up against anyone else as ruthless as Bennie "Bullettooth" Boyle? Eliza didn't know much about his past, but now wished she did more than ever.

Since she was up with time to spare, she got a jumpstart on doing everyone's laundry for the week, then proceeded to clean every inch of her bedchamber for the third time, only to look up at the grandfather clock in the hallway and discover not even three hours had passed. It was barely past eight in the morning.

She meandered down the hall and knocked lightly on their door?

"Lizzie, Lizzie!"

The twins, per usual, barreled into her at the speed of a racehorse and moved as though they were a singular being, nearly knocking Lizzie over in the process.

She teetered but managed to brace herself against the wall as she tossed bewildered looks between the twins. They were as energetic as lightning bugs, and they had been since the day she met them, but she had never seen them this excited this early. "Whoa, girls! What's the rush?"

"We want to see Uncle Alex. Is he back yet?" Effie asked.

Eliza's features dipped, and she shook her head. "Not yet, munchkin. But he will be soon." Or so she hoped.

"Ugh!" Effie groused and stamped her foot. "But he promised he'd be back yesterday! Why'd he break his promise?"

Eliza sighed. "Oh, Effie-Belle." She squatted and held the girl's shoulders while Effie tried to squirm away. "You know your uncle would never break a promise to you or your sister on purpose, right?"

Effie huffed and looked away, but after a beat, she mumbled, "Yeah, I guess he wouldn't," under her breath. Eliza leaned over to place a kiss on her cheek.

"Right. So even though he's not back yet, I guarantee you he'll be back as fast as he can. We just have to be patient."

That made Effie scowl. "But being patient is so hard!"

Eliza snickered. "I know, munchkin. But it's important for you to learn. The older you get, the more patient you're going to have to be."

"You mean I'm gonna have to wait even longer to get things I want sometimes?"

Eliza tweaked her nose playfully but nodded. "If it's something you really want, it'll be worth the wait. Just like with your uncle."

Her chest puffed up at that answer. She didn't know where it had come from, but judging by the pondering look on Effie's face, she knew it had been the right thing to say.

"Lizzie?"

"Hmm?" She turned to see Emma directly behind her.

"If Uncle Alex isn't home, then who did Effie and I and I hear outside this morning?"

Eliza cringed. "Oh, girls, I'm so sorry. That was just Nathan. He went out early this morning to take care of some of your uncle's chores so that the ranch is still spic and span by the time he gets back."

"But what are we gonna do until he gets here?"

Eliza pushed to her feet and frowned. That seemed to be the question of the morning. What were they going to do, indeed?

***

Throughout the rest of the day, Eliza did her best to distract the twins with anything she could, trying to teach them how to sew – which only lasted for about five minutes – reading books, or playing cards. But no matter what Eliza tried, every few minutes, one of them would ask about their uncle, and the entire activity would be derailed.

At her wit's end and just before lunch, Eliza managed to coax them into occupying themselves by straightening the earthquake of a mess that had hit their room. While they organized their toy box, Eliza took the opportunity to step outside and take a breath. The only thing that calmed her racing heart and spinning mind was knowing that Nathan was somewhere nearby. At least, if anything did happen, although she hoped and prayed that no such thing would come true, he would be able to protect them. Right?

He had to.

As they went about their activities, however, Eliza couldn't help but notice that each time her gaze drifted to the window, which remained disappointingly empty, the sky only seemed to grow darker overhead. And just as they sat down to eat, Nathan burst in through the back door, his hair disheveled from the wind and his cheeks frosted from the cold Eliza could feel sneaking it away below her petticoats.

"Seems there's another bout of storm coming," Nathan confirmed gravely. "Might want to start battering down the hatches. Don't know how bad this one is going to get."

With one of her worst fears confirmed, Eliza's stomach dipped, and she replaced her utensil on the table. "But... Alexander," she whispered, glancing at Nathan with wide eyes as her leg drummed a rhythm beneath the table.

"Alexander knows when to seek shelter when he needs it. Right now, I am more concerned about the three of you." He glanced outside again, and a flash of trepidation contorted his features. "Well, that and the ranch."

"Lizzie," Effie whispered. "What's Nathan talking about?"

Eliza looked at the little girl thoughtfully. "Remember that big storm we had before Christmas?"

She nodded. "You mean the one Uncle Alex had to rescue you from?"

Eliza grinned. "Yes. The one that kept us inside for a couple of days."

Emma's eyes went white next to her sister, and she glanced at Nathan. "Are we gonna have to do that again?"

"I don't know for sure, kiddo, but it looks like we might."

Effie scowled. "But being inside is so boring!"

Eliza deliberately chose to ignore that sentiment, no matter how much she agreed. At the moment, she was more concerned with the way Nathan's eyes kept darting toward the window. Everyone in Wolfspell had had nearly two weeks to prepare for the blizzard before, but by the stricken look on his face, it seemed as if they only had hours this time.

"How much time do you think we have? She asked, hating the nervous twinge that managed to make its way into her voice no matter how hard she tried to avoid it.

Nathan thought about that and ran a hand through his hair.

"I'd say until about nightfall."

Gooseflesh rose on Eliza's arm. She had suspected as much, but it didn't make the task at hand any easier.

She looked at Nathan. "What should we do first?"

"I'm going to put the cattle back in the barn. Luckily, a lot of supplies are still left over from the last time we did this, but I'm still going to check the stock to see how soon I need to venture back into town."

Eliza nodded. "What about the horses? Alexander hasn't had the chance to fetch the stronger lumber he wanted, so the stable is still not ready."

Nathan scratched his head. "I'm not sure I can get them all to fit in the barn, but I'll do my best."

Eliza hummed. "I'll check on the fences and see if there's any last-minute mending I can do and replace any of the lights on the path that need it. Then I will make sure we know where the medical supplies are."

Nathan's eyebrows rose. "You know how to mend fences?"

Eliza smiled. "There's a lot you don't know about me yet. If you need any help bringing in the cattle, I'm not bad with a lasso either."

Nathan laughed. "I'll keep that in mind."

"Lizzie, Lizzie!" Something tugged on her skirt, and she looked down to see Emma peering curiously up at her. "We want to help too!"

"Yeah!" Effie said. "What can we do?"

Eliza tapped her chin thoughtfully. "Why don't you go with your grandmother to gather some extra coal and kindling for the fire?"

Nathan hummed. "I want you to try to find every coat and jacket and blanket you have to stay warm."

Emma nodded. "We can do that. Right, Effie?"

The little girl flashed a grin. "Yep! Easy!"

Nathan walked over to ruffle her hair. "That's good, munchkin. And maybe if you all have time after you're done, you can help me feed the animals and give the cows one more milking before the storm hits."

With a plan in place, everyone scurried off to attend to their assigned tasks. Eliza tended to hers after she was sure the twins were safe in their grandmother's care for at least the next hour, and Nathan went straight to work corralling the animals. Though they didn't accomplish everything they set out to do by the time the storm hit, Eliza was proud of their progress, and she hoped Alexander would be too when he returned. By the time they called it a day, the snow had tumbled around them like blankets of white, and even as they huddled by the fire inside, Eliza couldn't make herself draw away from the window. With each heartbeat that passed, she hoped against hope to see Alexander's shadowy silhouette riding toward the safety of the house. But with each minute that passed, her hope dimmed a little more.

Chapter Twenty-Nine

Alexander and two of the magistrates' best men trotted through the snow at a steady, steady but brisk pace. On the way out of town, they had heard whispers of the oncoming storm, so Alexander kept one eye consciously fixed on the darkening storm clouds that seemed to follow them as they headed back down the trail that led toward Wolfspell.

A quarter of the way out of Blue Creek, large, fat snowflakes began tumbling around them with a vengeance. The wind picked up, and Alexander gritted his teeth as the chill snaked beneath his clothes. He tried not to think about it, though. Instead, he kept his eyes on the horizon and pushed forward.

Soon, the wind was whipping against his cheeks and the snow was coming down even harder. He could barely see five feet in front of him, but he was determined to keep going for as long as he could.

"Sh-Should we seek shelter?" asked one of the men between chattering teeth.

Out of the corner of his eye, Alexander saw the other official nod, but he hunkered down in his saddle. "Not. Yet," he wheezed between panted, icy breaths. "We only have a little further to go. If we can just make it back before things get any worse..." He trailed off. Hearing his words out loud, he knew his hopes were foolhardy and may even be dangerous, but what else was he to do?

A powerful current whipped through him upon picturing Eliza's face. His cheeks burned slightly. He wasn't sure when he had come to think of her as an integral part of his home. After all, he had sent her away, only to regret it almost immediately. But what did that mean? She had a home and a family to go back to, but after meeting her brother, he wasn't sure Russel counted as much of either. Bennie "Bullettooth" Boyle certainly didn't.

"Sir?" piped up the other official. "I know apprehending Bennie is important to you, but I really think—"

"It's only a few more miles," Alexander reasoned again. "Please, just... hold out a little longer."

His desperation must've been obvious because they didn't say a word for the next hour. Soon enough, though, the snow was nearly thick enough to blind them, and Alexander had no choice but to concede to their well-deserved requests for shelter and rest. By the time he came to that conclusion, though, they were so far off course, and they had lost track of the road so long ago that they had little other option than to change trajectories. Alexander managed to make out a sign for a nearby ranch through the cascade of snow and guided the other two men in that direction.

"Do either of you know who this ranch belongs to?" he asked uncertainly.

One of the magistrate's men shook his head, but the other one squinted at the appearance of the house. "I think this is old Davis' place. But," the official looked around for any sign of life, "It doesn't seem like anyone is home."

Alexander hummed and stroked his beard. "You think he would mind if we took shelter in his barn?" He pointed to the other side of the ranch, and the two men followed his line of sight to a red double-door barn off in the distance.

The magistrate's associate shook his head. "Davis has always been a pretty hospitable man. Besides, if we're gone by morning, he won't even know we were here."

Alexander nodded, and when he kicked his horse into gear, all three of them eagerly rode toward the barn.

***

Once the animals were sufficiently watered and warmed with some blankets they found in the tack room, the three men settled down onto their makeshift beds put together by bales of hay. The magistrate's men fell asleep almost as soon as their heads hit the straw, but as hard as he tried, Alexander couldn't seem to let slumber take him. Every time he closed his eyes, all he could see was a vision of his mother, Eliza, or the twins, being put in some kind of horrible danger because he wasn't able to hold up his end of the bargain and capture Bennie before he could get to them.

The fear nearly paralyzed him, yet somehow only got worse; the victim haunting his dreams was Eliza. A part of him was acutely aware of how odd this seemed, especially given how he had felt about her only a few days before. True, she had said all the right things, but it was her eyes that had really convinced him. And after everything she had done for his family, he never truly believed she would ever willingly put any of them in danger. But at that moment, knowing such a ruthless bandit was so close to his ranch? Alexander let every rational thought go away with the wind. Once he had met Russel and Bennie in person, it was much easier now to see why she had done what she did. All he knew now was that he wanted to return to her just as much as he wanted to return to his mother and the twins.

Eventually, his utter exhaustion won out over the endless thoughts turning over and over in his brain, and he fell into a restless sleep. He dreamed once again of Eliza, but this time the two of them were playing in the snow, lobbing snowball fights at the twins and his mother. It put a playful, relaxed smile onto Alexander's lips, and it was a moment he never wanted to leave.

***

To everyone's relief, when they awoke and emerged from the barn the next morning, the sky was clear, which made the ride the rest of the way to Wolfspell easy and without incident. Within mere hours, Alexander would be back where he belonged, and soon, all of this chaos would be behind them. It was that thought, along with countless memories of Eliza spurred Alexander along as he led the way home.

Chapter Thirty

December 30, 1860

Like the previous morning, Eliza woke to misty rays of sun filtering through her sunshine yellow curtains but, to her relief, a birdsong also echoed in her ears. Eliza yawned and raised her aching arms above her head in a cat stretch. Every muscle seemed sore, and she felt as though she had only fallen asleep a mere hour ago.

The ranch just wasn't the same without Alexander, and knowing that the twins were now her responsibility until his return, well, that was more than enough to keep her from a peaceful night's sleep. She realized that she had become oddly accustomed to their morning routine. She would rise shortly after the rooster crowed and get started on early breakfast. Alexander would come in from his morning rounds, milking the cows and feeding the animals, and they would sit with the twins and discuss their plans for the day. No matter what they were doing, Alexander had a way of making every task seem like a new adventure. Even the most mundane things he would liven up for the sake of the twins, and Eliza didn't think she would grow tired of hearing his stories. Without them, the ranch seemed unnaturally quiet and lonely.

Nonetheless, though, she wasted no time getting herself ready and prepared a simple breakfast of oatmeal and dried fruit for the twins. Emma simply stirred her spoon listlessly in the porridge and Effie all but turned her nose up at her bowl and pushed it halfway across the table before Eliza noticed. At the sound of the China sliding across the wooden table, however, her eyes widened, and she delicately wiped her mouth with her cloth napkin.

"Girls, what's wrong? Don't you like your food?"

"Not hungry," Emma muttered.

Eliza frowned. "Why not, Em? Are you sick?"

She shook her head, but Eliza stood up and rounded the table anyway to feel her forehead.

"Hmm." Her frown deepened. "You're not warm."

Emma rolled her eyes.

"Wanna wait for Uncle Alex!" Effie finally huffed by way of an explanation.

Eliza sighed and blew some hair out of her face. "Effie-Belle, I know you miss your uncle, but we don't know when he'll be back. Don't you think you'll get awfully hungry if you wait that long?"

Effie pursed her lips and crossed her arms. "Don't care! Gonna wait!"

Eliza stood up and placed a hand on her hip. On the one hand, she had half a mind to make the girl sit here until she finished every spoonful of her breakfast, but on the other, she wondered if that was even a battle worth fighting. In the end, she decided that if the little girl didn't want to eat, she wasn't going to make her. Instead, she walked over and scooped up Effie's nearly full bowl of oatmeal.

"All right. That's your choice. But if you change your mind, no snacks until lunch, understand?"

Effie scowled but nodded just as a solid *knock, knock, knock!* echoed through the house. All three of them swiveled in the direction of the front door, but no one answered it.

"Uncle Alex?" Emma wondered aloud. Eliza's heart leaped in her chest at the thought. Oh, how she wanted that to be true. But then... Why would Alexander knock before entering his own house?

He wouldn't, her inner voice warned before she could stop it. Dread seized her. Her shoulders and her jaw clenched. She turned to the girls and hoped against hope that her face still appeared calm even if her pulse was racing.

"Stay here," she whispered, leaving no room for argument with a bite in her tone. "I'm going to go and see who it is." She spun on her heel and walked as slowly as possible toward the front door with a million thoughts racing through her mind at once. No matter what, she would die before she ever let Bennie or Russel lay a single finger on the twins. But she also hoped and prayed that whoever this was, nothing would happen for it to come to that.

Lord protect us, she prayed. Then, mustering every ounce of courage she possessed, she reached out and grasped the doorknob. Eliza gently twisted it open and gasped when she saw who it was.

***

"P-Perry?" She blinked twice, rubbed her eyes, and shook her head. The well-built ranch hand was the last person she had expected to see standing on her porch at a time like this, but relief seeped from her like a waterfall when she recognized his familiar form. "Thank God it's only you!"

She lunged forward to hug him, only realizing as he returned the gesture that his grip was not nearly as firm or reassuring as she remembered. Beads of sweat formed on the back of her neck as she pulled away and took in his somber features. "Wait, what are you doing here?"

Perry sighed and removed his hat. "Eliza, listen. You have no idea how much I wish I were here to simply exchange pleasantries. You and I have a lot to talk about." His serious gaze turned stern and fatherly, and Eliza dipped her head as a blush colored her cheeks. She opened her mouth, a profuse apology on the edge of her tongue.

"Perry, listen, I'm so–"

"There's no time for that now." He held up a hand to stop her, and a chill ran down Eliza's spine.

A lump formed in her throat, and her chin quivered as she asked, "What, what are you talking about?"

"Eliza, Russel sent me here to warn you."

The room spun. "W-warn me? Warn me about what? What do you mean Russel sent you?" But even as the question left her mouth, every one of her senses was on high alert. She already knew, but she needed him to say it. Her worst fears were coming true right before her eyes.

Lord, please let me be wrong.

But when she fixed her big, pleading eyes on Perry's kind but clearly worried ones, her stomach dropped to the floor.

He sighed and ran a hand through its hair. "Eliza, it's... it's only Bennie. Someone told him they saw you hiding here."

"But... but Russel?" She shook her head. "I thought he was working with Benny. What changed?"

Perry shrugged. "I guess he finally grew a heart. Said he was tired of seeing others get hurt because of Bennie's schemes, and he didn't want to add you to that list."

She shivered as her blood turned to ice in her veins. So she had been right to fear someone was staking out the ranch the other day. Bile churned in her stomach. If only the sheriff would do something. If only she had had enough courage to tell the truth, earlier... Perhaps all of this could've been avoided.

"How did they find me?"

"I think it might've been that lackey of his. What was his name?" Perry's brows scrunched together. "Daniel?"

"Danny," Eliza choked out. It tasted like lead on her tongue. "You... you really think he ratted me out?" She had never liked Bennie's right-hand man; in fact, after the night he exposed her eavesdropping, she was downright terrified of him. But still... She never expected Bennie would be smart enough to turn the tables on her like this.

Perry nodded gravely. "If you value your life, then I highly suggest you leave now, before it's too late. I don't care where you go. Don't tell me, don't tell anyone, just get out of here and stay out of sight until it's safe."

Hearing the threat on her life laid out so bluntly, Eliza reeled as a brief flash from one of her nightmares overtook her. Suddenly she felt as though she really were staring down the barrel of Bennie Bullettooth Boyle's gun. The vision was utterly bone-chilling but not nearly so much as the idea that she might have inadvertently put the girls in harm's way.

She felt the color drain from her face as the reality of all that he had just said sank in. *Oh no, the girls. Not to mention Alexander's mother!* How in the world was she going to explain any of this to them without horrifying them out of their wits?

"Eliza?"

Perry laid a gentle hand on her shoulder and jolted her back to the present. "Do you...do you have somewhere safe to go?"

Immediately, she thought of Nathan. His place was close enough that she could justify their abrupt change of plans by saying Nathan and Marie had invited them there, so they didn't have to continue awaiting Alexander's return alone. As reasonable as it sounded, though, the plan still made her uneasy. She hated the idea of putting people in any more danger. She was the one Bennie was after. She should be the only one to face the consequences of her actions. And now more than ever, she wished she had done things differently, but everyone was in too deep, and this was their best option. She only hoped Nathan wouldn't take too unkindly to the plan.

"I... I think so," she stammered.

Perry nodded. "Good. Then I would gather whatever is necessary and leave as soon as you can. I have to get back to the ranch. If anyone finds out I was here, it could be my neck on the lynching post as well."

Eliza winced. "I won't tell a soul."

She stepped in for another hug, and this time he held on just as tightly. "Be safe," he whispered affectionately.

Tears welled in Eliza's eyes, and the lump in her throat grew. "You too."

She shut the door a moment later and braced her back against it, taking as long as she dared to gather her bearings and catch her breath before going off in search of Nathan.

She found him occupying the girls by playing sheriff to two of their dolls.

"Who was that?" he asked, voice light and casual.

Eliza didn't say anything for a long moment. Even though she knew she had to explain, her head was still swimming, and she barely knew where to begin. Nathan diverted his attention from the game and looked up at her. When he caught sight of her stricken expression, he immediately pushed to his feet.

"I... I think you and I need to talk," she rasped out.

"Of course." He strode to the edge of the room and turned to face the girls. "Keep playing, okay?" Lizzie and I will be right back."

Once they were in the kitchen and safely out of earshot, Lizzie explained the encounter and the plan in a rush. When she was done, she dipped her head and blinked back her tears. "I'm so sorry to have put you in the middle of all this." She sniffed and shivered a bit when he reached out to place a hand on her shoulder.

"Hey, no. You listen to me, all right? None of this is your fault. The only one responsible for this chaos is Bennie. He's the one who should pay the price. Not you. Of course, you can stay with me until Alexander gets back. Hopefully, he'll bring the sheriff with him, and all of this will be over in a matter of days. "

She wiped her eyes with the back of her hand and caught his gaze. "Are you... are you sure your mother won't mind?"

Nathan barked a laugh. "Are you kidding? She's been begging to see the twins ever since I came back to the ranch. She would have come herself, but I told her the snow was still too deep, especially after yesterday. I'm sure she'll love the extra company. But maybe," he looked around and licked his dry lips. "Maybe we should give her the same story we're going to give the twins and Louise, eh? No need to scare anyone."

Eliza nodded. "Of course. Anything we can do to keep you all safe. I don't know how we're ever going to repay you."

He smiled, and the lines around his eyes crinkled. "How many times do I have to tell you no thanks are needed? Family helps family, and as far as I'm concerned, you're a part of ours now."

Eliza couldn't help but smile at that thought, though it quivered. "That's going to take a bit of getting used to."

He winked. "Believe me, once all of this is over, you'll have nothing but time. For now, though, shouldn't we get packing? "

Eliza agreed with Nathan's assessment, and immediately they each went off in search of the twins and Louise. When the packing was done and they were ready to go, Eliza scribbled a quick note to Alexander, letting him know what had really happened and where to find them when he did arrive back home. She placed it on the table in the hall and then closed the door behind her with a final, hollow thud. She hoped and prayed that this would not be the last time she stepped foot in the Swanson estate.

Chapter Thirty-One

The journey home took much longer than Alexander had anticipated; The horses were exhausted, and the newly fallen snow certainly didn't help. But finally, mercifully, the familiar picture of his home came into view. The magistrate's men waited patiently outside as he unpacked his horse, before leading them up the steps toward the front porch. He turned the knob, only to find it locked.

Odd, he thought.

It wasn't even sundown yet. Why would Eliza lock up already?

Perhaps one of the girls tried to make a run for it to play in the snow, and that was easier than trying to keep track of both of them and my mother at once. But even as that thought crossed his mind, he knew it was almost impossible. Eliza had never blocked the door until everyone had gone to bed. What could have possibly changed between yesterday and now? A barrage of possible answers that wanted him, and none of them were pleasant. As much as he feared finding out the truth, he deplored being left in the dark even more. Fishing his spare house key from the pocket of his trousers, he unlocked the door and gestured for the magistrate officials to enter first. The rusty hinges creaked like they always did, but somehow today, they was uncharacteristically loud in such a quiet surrounding.

He stepped through the threshold and cupped his hands over his mouth. "Eliza! Mother! I'm home."

He paused and listened for a beat, but none of the familiar sounds greeted his ears. No high-pitched laughter, no high-spirited arguing. Not even the pitter-patter of two pairs of tiny feet against the hardwood floor. That was even stranger, as his niece was always the first one to greet him when he came in from a long day of work. He could only imagine it would be the same when he came back from a trip.

One of the magistrate's men frowned and gave him a curious look. "Are you sure they're home, Mr. Swanson?"

Alexander looked around uncertainly, disturbed down to his core by the unnatural silence. "I... I'm not sure. They should be."

His brow furrowed as he stepped into the sitting room only to find that it, too, was empty. He turned back to the men with a grim expression and pressed his lips together. "Spread out and help me search. Something isn't right. I'm afraid the worst has happened."

The men exchanged grim glances but immediately leaped into action. They searched the kitchen, the dining room, and every bedroom only to come up empty-handed. But just because the house was clear didn't mean Alexander was ready to give up. He helped each of the men resettle their horses before tending to his own, and they spread out across the ranch. It took them another hour, but when they returned to meet up at the house, they still knew nothing more than they had before.

"I'm terribly sorry, Mr. Swanson, but it appears there's no sign of them."

Alexander's stomach flipped, but he nodded and hummed, glancing outward toward the expansive field. *Oh, Eliza. Where are you?* A small part of him wondered if she had run away again, but even if that were the case, that wouldn't explain his mother's sudden absence, nor what happened to the twins.

"Search again," he ordered them gruffly.

"But sir..." the second man spoke up, but Alexander silenced him with a single glare.

"I *said* search again."

This time, both of them nodded, but just before they were about to take off, the steady sound of hoofbeats caught Alexander's attention. He turned only for his heart to crawl up into his throat.

It was not Eliza and the girls returning from a long ride down the trails, but Bennie Bullettooth himself.

Chapter Thirty-Two

When they first arrived at Nathan's house, Eliza was relieved. As much as she had come to hate hiding, she was overjoyed that, for now, at least, all of them were out of Bennie "Bullettooth" Boyle's reach. Nathan's mother had spoiled them by greeting them with a homemade meal just hours after their arrival that both Eliza and the girls gobbled down with surprising vigor. Upon glimpsing how quickly their plates had been emptied, Marie simply laughed and whacked her son on the back of the head. "Have you even been feeding these girls while looking after them?"

Nathan rolled his eyes but smirked good-naturedly.

"Can I have more, please, Mrs. Lane?" Effie barely stood tall enough to peer over the top of the stove as she held out her bowl, and Marie happily filled it with another ladle of soup and another rather large piece of skillet cornbread. "Eat as much as you wish, Effie," she said kindly. "There's plenty for everyone."

Effie beamed and carefully waddled back to the table. A few droplets sloshed onto the floor, and Eliza winced, but Marie just wiped it up behind her and offered Eliza a reassuring smile as though she was used to it. Come to think of it, she probably was after being their housemaid for so long. Having finally reached the table, Effie set down the steaming bowl of soup and climbed back into her seat.

"Don't forget to blow on it," Eliza warned as the little girl scooped up her first large spoonful. Effie did as she was told, and Eliza smiled around her own mouthful. She was just glad to see the little girl eating after refusing breakfast that morning.

Thankfully, Nathan had been right about his mother not minding the extra company. The second she saw the twins, Marie practically smothered them in affection to the point where they were both eventually squirming to get down from her embrace. Eliza had been shocked to discover that Marie even kept some of their old toys in the house, which was hopeful for entertaining them in the restless hours that followed the delicious meal.

It was late afternoon now, and once again, Eliza couldn't keep her gaze from drifting to the window. Where was Alexander? Surely he had returned to the ranch by now. Had he not found the note? Had something happened?

"You know, if you keep pacing like that, you're going to wear a hole in the floor." She blushed and looked up at Nathan.

"I'm sorry. I know I probably seem ridiculous, but..."

Nathan shook his head and held up a hand. "You don't have to say it. I'm worried too. But I'm sure he'll be here soon. Have a little faith."

Eliza bit her lip. "I know it's probably rude of me to even think of asking for another favor after everything you've done for us these past few days, but—"

"Hey." Nathan gently shook her shoulder, and she blinked. "This is difficult for everyone, so anything I can do to make it easier, I will. Now, what do you need?"

Eliza looked down and twisted the hem of her skirt in her hands. "I can't really explain it," she said. "But I just, I have a really bad feeling. If Alexander was safe, I know he would be here by now."

Nathan nodded and offered a resigned smile. "Do you want to ride back to the ranch and check? Make sure he got your note."

A rush of gratitude overcame Eliza, and she hugged him. Would you? I can't begin to explain how much it would mean to me."

"Of course."

After reassuring everyone that they would be fine, Eliza reluctantly decided to leave the twins and Louie in Marie's capable hands. Nathan led her down the back road toward a sort of secret entrance to the ranch that she had never seen before.

"Remember," he hissed quietly as they marched through the underbrush and drew closer and closer to the edge of the property line. "We have to be quiet. We don't want to be spotted just in case your hunch is right."

In lieu of responding, Eliza nodded and mimed zipping her lips. Nathan smirked. "All right, now, if we round the barn then–"

BANG!

The blood-curdling pop of a gunshot rang out through the trees. Eliza yelped out loud before slapping a hand over her mouth even as her heart thudded in her ears. She glanced at Nathan as if to say, *Was that what I think it was?*

He nodded. His eyes were wide, and some of the color had disappeared from his face.

They crept a few paces closer, despite the terror racing through every nerve ending of Eliza's body and urging her to run. Suddenly, a blistering rush of heat burst through the air. It was followed in quick succession by a whooshing sound, as an explosion of flames engulfed the barn.

Sheer panic tore through Eliza's body, and this time she couldn't quell her scream. Any doubt of what was occurring had been swiftly vanquished by the terrifying blaze.

He had found them.

Bennie "Bullettooth" Boyle was here.

And he was out for blood.

Chapter Thirty-Three

As soon as they had spotted him, Alexander and the magistrate's men had made a dash in the house. They had barricaded the door with every movable piece of furniture they could find, and we're now locked inside, though Alexander kept vigil watch from the window.

Bang!

His heart hammered against his ribcage as he threw himself against the barricade when a bullet shattered the glass, sending shards scattering in every direction and rendering the very spot where he had been standing a guaranteed death trap.

The magistrate's men rushed to his side, each of them inspecting his body for potential wounds.

"Sir!" One of them was panting with white eyes, but somehow he still managed to put Alexander's needs before his own. "Are you all right?"

Alexander fought to catch his breath as he patted himself down, but as far as he could tell, he had miraculously escaped unscathed. "I... I think so."

"What... What do you suppose he wants?" the second man whispered.

"I don't know," Alexander said. "He already sought me out, and I insisted I had no idea where Eliza was.

The first man frowned. "Is it possible he found out you were lying."

Alexander ran a hand through his hair and shrugged.

The second man mustered enough courage to walk over to the remains of the bullet casing and inspect it. "Well, if this is any indication, I don't think he intends on giving up until he gets what he wants."

"Never." Alexander groaned and puffed out his chest. "If he wants to get to her or any member of my family, he'll have to pry them out of my cold dead hands."

The moment the words left his mouth, though, Bennie's malicious laughter echoed through the fields. "Come out, you yellow-bellied cowards," he yelled. "I know you're in there. You have exactly three minutes to surrender the girl to me, or else your barn will be nothing but a useless pile of kindling."

Alexander gritted his teeth but managed to crane his neck far enough to peer out the one window in the front of the house that still remained intact. To his horror, the barn was already more than halfway engulfed in flames. He hated to think of all of the helpless animals stuck within the blaze, but he wouldn't dare to mount a last-minute rescue attempt. If he valued his life, and more importantly, if you value the lives of his family, then the safest option right then was to say exactly where he was. As much as it pained him to think it, he knew animals could be replaced while Eliza, the twins, and his mother could most certainly not be. Still, the mere thought of leaving them to suffer made him sick to his stomach.

"What... what do you want us to do, sir?"

"Nothing," he informed them regretfully. "As much as I wish it weren't the case, he followed through on his threat long before he even made it. The safest thing for all of us right now is to stay right here. Though, perhaps we should move further inside the house in case he decides to use that pistol again."

The men agreed, and everyone ventured into the hallway. As Alexander surveyed his still ghostly empty surroundings, an overturned piece of paper near the hall table caught his eye. He strode over and picked it up. His heart leaped when he recognized Eliza's elegant handwriting.

Dear Alex,

Please know that I had no intention of leaving you in the dark, and I hope you find this as soon as you return. The girls and I, along with your mother, had to leave the ranch. My ranch hand from back home came to the door this morning. He said my stepbrother Russel sent him to come and warn me. I'm so afraid Benny's going to come after us. The last thing I would ever want to do is put more people in danger. Nathan has agreed to host us at his house for the time being. Please meet us there as soon as you return. I promise to do everything I can to keep your mother and the twins safe. If that wretched bandit wants them, he'll have to kill me first.

Ever Yours,

Eliza

Alexander's mouth dropped open, but his heart soared as he reached the end of the letter. Although he couldn't quite believe Russel had decided to warn Eliza, as he hadn't seemed like anything more than a spineless lackey when Alexander laid eyes on him, at least, if nothing else, Eliza and the girls were safe.

Chapter Thirty-Four

Elisa and Nathan took shelter behind a barricade of foliage. When they were safely out of sight, Nathan looked at Eliza and whispered, "What are we going to do?"

Eliza bit her lip and surveyed the scene. She had an idea but didn't know if it was worth the risk. From what Perry had said, she wanted so badly to hope that Russel really had had a change of heart and was now on their side. But for as long as she had known him, she didn't know if she really believed that. If she wanted to escape with her life, though, and maybe more importantly, with Alexander's, she was afraid they didn't have a choice.

"I didn't see Alexander's horse by the barn, and judging by the trajectory of that bullet hole..." She cut her gaze toward the house and crossed her fingers behind her back. "I'm guessing – I mean, I hope that Alexander is still inside. I'll distract Bennie; you go in and rescue him. Then, we should be almost equally matched enough to overpower Bennie."

Nathan gaped at her. "You cannot be serious. You mean you want me to let you go after a lunatic by yourself? Eliza, think with your head! He has a gun! What are you going to do against that?"

She didn't have a suitable answer, but she was desperate. She couldn't let Alexander die for her mistake.

"I don't know!" she burst out. "I'll figure something out. First, we have to get them out of there."

He placed a hand on her arm and gave her a desperately pleading look. "Eliza, listen to me. I know you care for him, truly I do, but he would skin my hide if I let you—"

But Eliza ignored him. As Bennie's taunting, nasal voice echoed over the ranch, she scurried into position.

"Come out, you yellow-bellied cowards!" He yelled from his horse. "I know you're in there. You have exactly three minutes to surrender the girl to me, or else your barn will be nothing but a useless pile of kindling."

She waited. *Don't come out,* she prayed. *He's taunting you.* The barn had been all but incinerated right in front of her eyes, but she had no idea if Alexander could see that from his vantage point inside the house. At this point, she didn't even know if he was inside the house; although the way Bennie was sneering at it provided evidence enough.

One beat passed.

Then two.

Still, Alexander didn't emerge from the house.

Bennie's sneer morphed into outright rage, but that didn't stop Eliza from releasing a relieved exhale, nor did it diminish the sudden surge of courage that rose up in her. If anything, it gave her more. If she was going to go down, it wasn't going to be without a fight.

"Took you long enough to find me." She pushed to her feet and stepped boldly out of hiding in full view of the bandit. "I would have thought someone who had pulled off as many successful heists as you have would have been smarter about tracking their prey." Eliza winced at the brazen words. She had no idea where they had come from, but it was too late to take them back. Bennie's spine stiffened for the slightest of seconds before slowly, painfully slowly, he swiveled around with a wicked glint in his eyes.

"There you are, you little tongue-wagger," he growled. He wasted no time reloading his pistol and, nearly in the blink of an eye, had the barrel aimed straight at Eliza's forehead.

"You don't have to do this," she pleaded. "We don't want anything to do with you."

"Oh, but I do," Benny barked. "You see, you've heard too much. And I'm pretty sure you've told all about my plans to your charming friend while you played house out here."

Eliza opened her mouth to protest, but Benny shook his head, eyeing her warningly. "This time I'm not taking any chances."

Her heart thudded in her chest as she realized Benny was going to kill her.

"Now, any last words before we finally put this foolish chase to an end?" he asked.

Eliza felt that time slowed down as her entire life flashed before her eyes. Most of it was actually of the last few weeks. Playing hide and seek with the girls, trying sledding for the first time with Alexander's firm grip holding her safely to the otherwise unstable plank of wood. Every time she had made him laugh or smile over the last two weeks. Somewhere in the back of her mind, she also thought of her father and Russel, but if this was how it was going to end, she wanted to spend her last moments thinking of the people she truly considered family.

At the same time, her throat was dry, and her forehead beaded with sweat. Her eyes darted toward the house, but still, she saw little movement. Did Alexander know what was happening? She hoped and prayed that he didn't. The last thing she wanted was for him to see this. He'd already been through enough tragedy in his life. If she truly was about to face her end, she wanted to spare him that agony.

She didn't know what she expected to feel in these last moments. Whenever she was presented with a similar scenario in her dreams, and even if she thought back to the last time she was in this position, everything had been clouded by a blanket of sheer panic. But now, as she stared at the barrel, she felt at peace. If she had to die to keep the rest of the people she loved safe, then it would be worth it.

She took a deep breath and made sure to look Bennie squarely in the eye, but just as she opened her mouth and tried to think of some sort of triumphant last speech, Russel charged in out of her peripheral vision. His horse reared with a powerful whinny and then galloped forward. Russel, in a feat like nothing she had ever seen before, dove sideways, clawed into the other side of the bandit's shoulders and knocked him off of his horse.

Eliza could do nothing more than watch the scene unfold in front of her, filled with a mixture of shock, awe, and a strange twinge of pride for her stepbrother. Perhaps Perry was right, and he really had grown a heart after all.

They wrestled on the ground until the pistol flew free of Benny's hand, and as it landed on the snow-covered grass, another splitting bang echoed through the property.

Without warning, two unfamiliar men in uniform burst through the front door of the Swanson estate, followed quickly, mercifully by....

"Alexander!"

His appearance was the only thing that shook Eliza free of her awestruck stupor, and she took off at a Roaring Springs toward him. His eyes widened, and a face-splitting smile immediately appeared on his face. He opened his arms, and Eliza flung herself into them. She wrapped her arms as tightly around his neck as she could without choking him.

"You're safe!" She choked on a sob as she cupped his face between her hands. He smiled softly and gently brushed the sides of her cheeks with the pads on his thumbs. Only then did Eliza realize she was crying. "I was so afraid he'd..." She trailed off and buried her face in his chest. He rewarded her by holding her tighter and entangling a hand in her hair.

"I don't care about me," he said, but there was a warm note in his voice that made Eliza's heart glow. "You were the one I was worried about. I was so afraid I wouldn't make it in time. He stepped back and held her at arm's length just long enough to look her directly in the eye. "Thank you. Thank you for everything you've done to keep my mother and the twins safe."

She smiled as a passionate heat crept up her cheeks. "I hope you know that I meant every word I said in that letter. I would do anything for you all. Including laying down my life."

Alexander leaned forward and kissed her forehead as he brushed some hair out of her face, and she hummed contentedly as she took a moment to let herself relish in his touch. "After what you just did, I have no doubt that you would. I'm just grateful that you didn't have to."

"All right, sir. Up you go."

Eliza and Alexander turned back toward the scene and watched, transfixed, as the two uniformed men hauled Bennie to his feet. "You have a lot to answer for. I have a feeling you're going to be spending a lot of time in the hoosegow. *If* you survive your trial."

The men smirked over Bennie's head, and Eliza couldn't help the jolt of pride that ran through her at the idea of finally seeing justice done.

Finally, it was over.

Only then did she remember she still had to deal with her stepbrother.

She glanced uncertainly at Alexander, but he gently spun her around to face him and nudged her forward a step.

She took in his form. It seemed he was finally beginning to lose that beer belly of his, though if she had to guess, she would venture to say it probably wasn't from better nutrition. His once lovely eyes were sunken and hollow, and his skin was paler than usual. His clothes were tattered from the earlier struggle, and, standing there, shuffling from foot to foot and fiddling with his hands, Russel looked every part the scolded schoolboy.

He cleared his throat and opened and closed his mouth a few times before he finally succeeded in producing words. "I know it probably doesn't mean much," he began, "but I just want to say I'm awfully sorry for everything. I knew Bennie was a no-good bandit when I met him, but I never thought..." For an instant, he got a faraway look in his eye before returning to the conversation. "I never thought it would get that bad. I don't know if I can ever do anything to make it up to you, but..." He looked wearily at Alexander before focusing on Eliza again.

"If... If you let me, I'd like to try."

He looked so tired, so strung out – like a shell of his former self. Eliza wasn't sure if she should pity him or focus on how grateful she was that he had saved her life. She chose both. "We may never be the closest siblings," she began, and his head drooped. "*But,*" his gaze darted up, and an unexpected twinge of hope flickered there as he waited with bated breath for Eliza to continue. "But saving my life was a pretty good start." She held out her hand as a smirk danced on his lips.

"It was nothing."

Eliza shook her head. "Actually, it was everything." Her eyes darted down to her extended hand again. "Why don't we start over? Put the past behind us and try to get to know each other again?"

He smiled and finally returned the handshake. "I'd like that."

And as much as it surprised her, Eliza found herself thinking that maybe, just maybe, she would too.

Chapter Thirty-Five

Alexander watched adoringly as Eliza, and her stepbrother finally clasped hands. They may not always have the best or the smoothest relationship, but if Maggie's tragedy had taught him anything, it was that family should always be high on his list of priorities, and he was glad Eliza was finally coming to see that.

When the moment between them passed, Russel separated from his stepsister and boldly approached Alexander. "I'll understand if you won't accept it, but if you let me, I'd like to pay to repair any damage Bennie may have caused."

Alexander's brows rose, and he exchanged surprised glances with Eliza over Russel's shoulder. "That's... very generous but..." His eyes flickered uncertainly to the incinerated barn, and he thought once again of all of the animals he had lost. "I'm afraid my animals would be very expensive–"

Russel held up a hand to stop him. "I don't care how much it costs. After everything Bennie and I put your family through, it's the least I can do." He turned to face Eliza again. "Even if you have to sell the ranch to do it."

Eliza blinked and looked at him in disbelief. "Me?" she sputtered. "But... But the ranch is yours. Papa gave it to you."

Russel chuckled and shook his head. "Not anymore. You and I both know you've always been more invested in that old place than I ever was. So, it's yours. Whatever you want to do with it, whether you want to come back and live there or stay here with the Swansons, it's yours to do with what you will."

Eliza gaped, then frowned. Alexander could practically see the wheels turning in her head, so he decided to step in before she made a decision they might both regret forever. Stepping around her brother, he once again stood in front of Eliza and gently touched her hand. "I know you have a lot to consider," he said quietly, "but while you're thinking about what you want, I want you to at least consider staying here with us. You were right before. Everyone has been so much happier since you've been here. None of us want to lose that. Especially me."

Eliza beamed but seemed to restrain herself moments before leaping at the offer. "I... Alexander, please know that I'd love that more than anything, but are you sure?"

Alexander nodded. "I know it might be a lot, but Eliza, I'm more sure about this, about you, than I have been about anything in a long time. I... I love you, Eliza. And, if you'll let me, I'd like to help you make this your true home."

Eliza practically leaped at him. Their lips met in a chaste but lingering kiss, and it took every ounce of control Alexander had not to deepen it. Instead, he relished in the soft, honeyed taste of her. When she pulled away, Alexander swore he was floating.

"I love you too, Alexander Swanson." She whispered it against his lips, and it felt like taking his first breath of oxygen after spending far too long underwater. Refreshing. Exhilarating. Life altering. When she turned to face her stepbrother again, Alexander didn't think he'd ever seen anyone more radiant.

"I appreciate the offer, Russel, but you can keep the ranch." She flashed Alexander a giddy smile, and he swore he was ten feet tall. "I've found a new home. One I highly doubt I'll ever want to leave."

And as she stepped back into his embrace, Alexander didn't think he had ever agreed with a sentiment more.

***

Russel got back on his horse, and when they were finally blissfully alone, Alexander swiveled Eliza around from where she nestled in his arms and stared into her green eyes. Everything faded away the longer he looked into them, and soon nothing else in the world mattered.

The longer he stared at her, the deeper she blushed. "What?" She let out a breathy giggle, and he returned it with a lazy smile.

"I just... I can't believe you would do that for us."

Eliza inclined her head and smiled bashfully. A lock of her copper hair drooped into her face, and Alexander leaned forward to brush it away. As the pads of his calloused fingers grazed her smooth cheek, she leaned into his touch and closed her eyes.

"Of course, I would," she replied breathily. she brought her own hand up to entangle it in his here, and he stepped forward so they were centimeters away from touching. "Like I said, I love you."

Alexander's heart threatened to beat out of his chest as he took in every beautiful inch of her adoring expression. A heated moment of pure bliss passed between them like a lightning bolt. He tipped her chin up, so they were making direct eye contact, and his pulse skipped a beat when he noticed the excitement sparkling in her courageous gaze.

"Eliza..."

The sparkle in her eyes grew brighter, and when their lips finally met, he made sure to take his time. When they pulled apart, Eliza's eyes were wide with admiration, and Alexander's chest swelled in satisfaction.

He smiled and brushed her hair back again. "If it wasn't clear before, I hope you know now just how much you mean to me."

"I never doubted it," she replied with one of those dazzling smiles that never failed to make his knees go weak. "Because I love you just as much."

Epilogue

December 25, 1861

"Girls!" Eliza gently cupped her protruding belly as she waddled into the kitchen. "How are those cookies coming? Are they almost done?"

She stopped short in the doorway when she took in the sight before her. Much like last year, the now six-year-old twins each stood on a step stool as they prepped the frosting for the gingerbread cookies. Eliza was more than happy to continue keeping their mother's memory alive with that long-standing tradition. But instead of mixing the frosting and leaving it aside as Eliza had left their grandmother to supervise, it appeared they had decided it would be a much more fun idea to smear it on each other instead. The moment she walked in, Effie, who had had a real growth spurt over the last twelve months and was now a few inches taller than her sister, stood on the edge of her wobbly seat and hovered an icing-covered hand over Emma's cheeks.

"Effie! Be careful!" Eliza raced over much faster than her swollen legs usually carried her to swoop her petulant niece off of the precarious seat and place her firmly on the seat. Once she was safely settled, Eliza was careful to avoid the stains as she wedged herself between the counter and stove and wagged a disapproving finger at her niece. "Just what did you think you were doing, young lady?" she asked. "You know better than to stand on the chairs. You could've fallen and cracked your head open."

Effie stuck her tongue out. "But Auntie Lizzie! We were having an icing war!"

"Yeah!" Emma squeezed in on Eliza's other side and showed off her appropriately chubby cheeks, which were also covered in icing. "See?"

Eliza shook her head but left, moving to the sink to wet a rag and wipe both of her nieces' faces. "You are real troublemakers, you know that? Am I going to have to watch you two when your little cousin is born?" She rubbed her pregnant belly again and smiled. It had been three months since she and Alexander found out they were expecting, and nearly a year since they were married. But Eliza couldn't think of a time in her life when she had ever been happier, and she couldn't imagine the level of joy she was about to experience when she finally had a child of her own. She loved Emma and Effie as if they were her own daughters, but the feeling of carrying her own child inside her was something beyond happiness.

"Yeahhh." Emma shared a smirk with her sister, and then they giggled. "We're going to teach him all the best places to hide when he wants to play hide-and-seek and show him the sledding hill and–"

Effie cleared her throat and placed a hand on her hip. The gesture alone made Eliza's cheeks puff out as she swallowed her own laughter. Clearly, her influence had been rubbing off on them. "Excuse me, but don't ya mean her?"

Eliza shrugged. "Actually, munchkin, we won't know until he or she is born. But whatever we're having, I know you two will go up to be the best older cousins!"

She wrapped her arms around them, no longer caring about the icing blanketing their clothes. At least she had been smart enough to put each of them in some old outfits this time rather than getting their new dresses dirty. They giggled and gently tried to wiggle out of her grip as she peppered each of their cheeks with kisses. Eventually, she let them go and turned back to the mess on the kitchen counter. "Now, let's see what is going on with these cookies. And we've got to get this counter clean! Your uncle is going to be appalled if he comes back from fetching Uncle Russel to find all the work we did has been covered in cookie frosting."

Emma wrinkled her nose. "Auntie Lizzie, what's *apaulaed* mean?"

Eliza's eyes creased, and she gently tweaked the little girl's nose. "It means we've got to get all of this cleaned up before your uncle gets home, or he's not going to be not so happy with me."

Effie's eyes widened. "You mean he might put you in the corner?"

This time Eliza laughed outright as she winked. "He just might, minx. Unless you two can be the best little elves ever and help me clean all of this up before he gets back. Deal?" She glanced back and forth between the two of them, delighting at the mischievous twinkle in their eyes.

"Deal!" They chorused.

As they set to work at straightening the mess, Eliza couldn't help but marvel at how different this year's holidays were turning out compared to the previous one. Unlike last time when everything had been thrown together at the last minute, this year, they had spent the last week covering every available surface in greenery, cranberries, and candles to bring in the Christmas season. Alexander had even sprung for chopping down one of the pine near the edge of the forest and bringing it inside as their Christmas tree. It still wasn't that common among families in Wolfspell, but the twins adored the way the candles nestled in the garland on the fireplace twinkled when they lit them at night, and they loved stringing and branches with the colorful popcorn and berry-filled string decorations Eliza had helped them make. The kitchen, though not decorated, had been pristinely clean only moments ago, and Eliza was seriously beginning to wonder where her common sense had gone when she left the twins alone to wait while the cookies baked. Except... she hadn't actually left them alone.

Eliza looked around the kitchen, only then realizing that Louise was nowhere to be seen. "Girls, what happened to your grandmother?"

Emma scanned the room. "She said she was going to change her clothes, and then she'd be right back. I think she was tired of wearing flour on her apron. Maybe she just forgot again?"

Eliza nodded. "Okay, I'll go check on her in a minute. First, let's get these cookies out of the oven so they don't burn."

Louise's condition had not changed. She had good days and bad days, but lately, there have been more good ones. Today was somewhere in the middle. She was calling Eliza by her real name, but she often forgot what she was doing halfway through completing a task.

Eliza slipped on their oven mitts and pulled both pans of gingerbread people in the oven. She set them on the counter that was just a little bit too high for the twins to reach while they cooled. "There, now let's go check on your grandmother."

"I'll do it."

At once, all three of their gazes shot up. "Alex!"

"Uncle Alex!" the twins echoed.

They rounded the counter at the same time, and Alexander smiled behind his thick beard as he wrapped the three of them in his arms. "How are my favorite girls?" He sniffed the air, and his grin grew wider. "Something smells awfully good in here!'

"We made gingerbread men!" Emma piped up excitedly.

"Oh? And where are they?" He glanced around the kitchen, and Eliza had to laugh at the hungry glint in his eyes.

"They're cooling," she explained. "And the girls still have to decorate them, so no sneaking bites."

Alexander laughed and kissed her gently. "Me? Never!"

They all laughed together, and then he pinched Effie's arm. "Are you going to decorate them like you did last year, munchkin?"

She nodded, "Uh-huh. 'cept this year you're just going to have a big smiley on it, Uncle Alex. Emma and I love that you're not sad anymore!"

He kissed her cheek and smiled affectionately at Lizzie. "You know what, Effie-Belle? So am I."

"We're going to make one for Uncle Russel," Emma added. "Right, Aunt Lizzie?"

"Of course, we are, Em. Everyone deserves a cookie on Christmas. But speaking of Russel, where is he?"

Alexander shrugged. "Probably still finishing up with the horses in the barn. He should be in in a few minutes."

"Did anything interesting happen on your trip to town?"

Alexander shook his head. "Nothing to speak of. Though somehow, even after so long, tongues are still wagging about Bennie and the deal he managed to cut with the sheriff." Bennie had traded in the crooked law officer in exchange for a lifetime in prison rather than a lynching.

296

"At least we know that this year nothing will disturb our anniversary."

Eliza's heart skipped a beat when she noticed that adorable gleam in his eye that told her he was planning something. "Are we doing something special?"

Alexander wrapped his arm around her. "If I told you that, it wouldn't be much of a surprise, would it?"

Her eyes gleamed. "So *we are* doing something special!"

"Every day with you is special, Eliza Swanson."

He dipped her lightly and kissed her.

She giggled. "If I agree. Does that mean you'll finally stop trying to spoil me?"

"Never! You'll always be worth going the extra mile for, Eliza, especially on Christmas."

"I'd go to the ends of the earth for you, Alexander. On Christmas Day, and every other."

Because now, for the first time in her life, Eliza Swanson could truly say she knew what it meant to have a family who loved her. And she couldn't imagine a better Christmas present.

THE END

Also by Sally M. Ross

Thank you for reading **"The Cowboy's Unexpected Christmas Miracle"**!

I hope you enjoyed it! If you did, here are some of my other books!

Also, if you liked this book, you can also check out **my full Amazon Book Catalogue at:**
https://go.sallymross.com/bc-authorpage

Thank you for allowing me to keep doing what I love! ❤

Printed in Great Britain
by Amazon

27281368R00165